Just This Once

Stone Family Series
Book 2

Sophie Andrews

Just This Once

I'm a single mom trying to keep my head above water. He's the one night stand I was never supposed to see again.

As a divorced parent of two teenagers and the manager of a bed and breakfast about to undergo a major renovation, I don't have time for a relationship.

But when a charming, younger guy approaches me during a night out, I give in to the desire to relieve some stress and invite him home. After he agrees to this being a one time thing, he makes me see stars, and then I send him packing. The end.

Until he walks into my B&B as the project manager for the renovation.

And now I have no escape from his constant grin and annoying optimism. That capable, work-of-art body and those jeans he wears to perfection make it impossible to forget our incredible night together.

So I'm faced with an impossible choice: maintain my boundaries around work and my family, or give in to the way he makes me feel when no one's looking. And that wink he gives me across the room? Let's just say my walls aren't the only thing in danger of coming down.

Content Note

Just This Once is a fluffy and spicy reverse age gap romance with a MMC who's got two reading disabilities, which are discussed on the page, as well as the verbal abuse he experiences from his father. Our grumpy FMC has an emotionally manipulative and abusive ex-husband, which is shown on the page. But our greenest of green flags more than makes up for it.

Stay healthy, my friends, and enjoy!

To all of the women who have a Craig—you are so much stronger than he is, ever has been, and could hope to be.

Wishing all of the Craigs in the world limp dicks and constant constipation for the rest of their miserable fucking lives.

Chapter 1
Dante

I hate it here.

Well, not *here*, but here with my family. Celebrating my brother's new engagement. Listening to my father toast his precious baby boy. Pretending I'm interested in seeing more pictures of my nieces. Sure, they're cute, but there's only so much a person can hear about a toddler's pooping habits without a shot of whiskey or two.

Yet I make *one* innuendo about sex, and I'm the "jackass" ruining dinner. Not my older brother and sister-in-law practically drawing a diagram of their kid's shit. And definitely not my younger brother feeling up his fiancée under the table. Like we all can't tell what he's doing with his hand.

"To Johnny and Emily. Salute," my father finally says, finishing up his long-winded speech. He lifts his glass of wine, and we all follow. "Salute."

The quiet little blonde has no idea what she's getting into with my family. Like the Corleones but with less murder.

Supposedly.

My grandfather told me stories. As the personal handyman

for one of the five families, working late nights, being picked up in the custom Rolls-Royce and taken to houses to spackle holes and unclog fingers from toilets. You know…the usual.

I set my still nearly full glass of Pinot on the table and sling my arm on the back of my mother's chair. She smiles at me, patting my knee as if I'm a fifth grader in need of a pep talk. "Your time'll come. Don't worry."

"Not worried, Ma," I reply, and she winks at me like we're sharing some sarcastic joke. "I'm not."

She merely winks again and sips from her drink. I roll my head back on my shoulders, sighing up at the ceiling, tiled with beveled tin, the color of a penny. It's nice. Well-done.

The Tabby Cat is a bistro and wine bar with warm lighting, comfy seating, exposed brick walls, and a few plants placed around to make it feel almost like somebody's living room. I knew a couple of the guys who worked on the crew, and they said the owners were great people, so I'm happy to support a new business. Especially one that treats its workers with respect.

As our server comes around to take our plates away, offering us the dessert menu, the ladies excuse themselves to use the bathroom, which of course gives Dad the opportunity to pull out his phone.

"How's next week looking?"

Being Friday, our work week just ended, and I'd prefer not to have to think about the next job for at least twenty-four hours, but I'm the odd man out.

"Good. Got the final inspection for the medical center scheduled for Tuesday, and I've got meetings with three equipment vendors about the clean room specs," Robbie says.

Johnny goes on about shaving off eight percent from the bottom line. None of them ever looks to me or asks my opinion.

My family—my father and brothers—think I don't care

about the business. They assume I'm not as driven as Robbie or as dutiful as Johnny, but I'm the one who has Moretti Construction in my blood. Literally. I've got the calluses and scars to prove it.

While my brothers went off to college, I started working right out of high school. No fancy finance or business degrees for me. I learned everything I know out on the jobsite, like my old man and his old man before him. And I'm damn good at what I do.

But try telling that to my father. Or Robbie. Or Johnny, the golden child who can do no wrong. To them, I'll always be the screwup. The middle son who barely graduated high school, parties too much, and doesn't take life seriously enough.

They're not completely wrong. I like to have a good time, but when it comes to work, I'm as dedicated as they come. I'm the one up at six a.m., on-site by seven, and coordinating work with dozens of employees and subcontractors. I'm the one with a scar on my forearm from a circular saw kickback. I've got a permanent groove across my right knuckles from a slipped hammer. And let's not forget the chunk taken out of my calf from a falling pipe.

But none of that means anything because I'm the idiot who can't read. I'm merely the grunt.

Though I'd rather be a grunt than an asswipe, like Johnny with his wandering gaze. When he shoots a smile at a group of girls at the bar, I kick him under the table. "What the fuck, man?"

"*What?*" he asks. As if he doesn't know.

"Are we or are we not here because you put a ring on your girl's finger?"

He shrugs. "Yeah, but I'm not blind."

"Also not husband material either."

"Hey." Dad sets down his phone to protect his favorite. "Leave the kid alone."

I roll my eyes, ready to leave it alone until Johnny comes back with, "More husband material than you are. Least I'm engaged and not living at home."

I pitch forward in my chair. "Listen, you little—"

"Enough," Dad cuts in. "We're here for a nice family dinner. Everyone settle down. Johnny, you might not be blind, but neither is your future wife. Treat her with some respect."

Which is ironic because he's cheated on my mother several times and clearly doesn't care about respecting much besides money.

Johnny smirks at me. He's been getting away with this shit since we were kids.

I try not to be bitter. I try not to let it get to me, but there are times when I can't slap on a smile and pretend. Not when my douchebag brother wants to rub it in my face about how my girlfriend broke up with me. Since then, I've had to move back in with Mom and Dad until I find a place of my own.

It's not a big deal. People do it all the time. But according to my father, I'm the only one.

By the time the ladies make their way back to the table, I'm ready to head out, yet Mom insists on ordering dessert. Dad orders another bottle of wine, and I blow out a breath as I sip on my still-full red, ignoring the side conversations that I'm not privy to—my mother and Robbie and my father and Johnny.

There's a *thing* in Italian families. Firstborn sons.

They're saints. Living deities. Robert Jr. can absolutely do no wrong. He wouldn't either. Would never dream of it.

He's perfect. My mother still has a lock of his hair from when he was a baby and refers to him as *my* Robbie. I mean...I guess in some cases, she does need to specify because when we get together with the extended family, there are approximately fifteen Roberts and twenty-three Michaels.

So, we've got the firstborn that mothers worship. And we've got the baby. The spoiled one. The one who will always win because by the time parents get to them, they're tired. That last kid doesn't have rules. They're given whatever they want to be kept quiet.

And that's Johnny to a T.

Except with the backing of our dad. If my mother claimed Robbie, my father wanted to claim his too. And it certainly wasn't going to be me. So I'm left out of the loop and any whispered conversations.

Sure, my mother loves me and insists on doing my laundry and tells me I'm not eating enough and makes me a lasagna to put in the freezer "just in case." And yeah, I *think* my dad loves me. He's not told me otherwise, but he's also never made it clear either. My parents have given me everything I've ever needed, a roof over my head and food in my belly. But I've never been *chosen*.

The only times my parents ever pulled me aside for solo conversations were to tell me I needed to "smarten the fuck up" or to "make sure you don't make me a grandmother before you walk down the aisle." Naturally, I'm not super into these family dinners, where I'm mostly on my own.

To keep myself busy, I like to play a game. I make up lives and stories for the people I see. Like, the couple in the corner who are both on their cell phones, not having spoken a word to each other since I started watching them. I imagine they've been together so long they're bored with each other. They think there is nothing new to learn and instead scroll social media. He's probably looking at sports scores while she double-taps photos of girls she went to high school with who now have three kids and drive minivans.

I slide my wineglass from one hand to the other, twirling the stem between my fingers as I skirt my gaze around to the open kitchen window that shows the chefs working. They fry and chop, passing one another in their black coats. I imagine the guy laughing has the hots for the server who stands in front of him and waits for her plates. He's still vying for her attention as she walks away with an eye roll that is more flirtatious than serious. I imagine she'll give in sooner rather than later.

Then I shift and spot three women at the bar, including one who looks awfully familiar. I sit forward, studying her, the perfectly styled golden hair and waving hand as she talks. A real-life Barbie, if Barbie were five foot nothing with a penchant for talking nonstop.

Just as I'm about to get up from the table to say hi, the crème brûlée arrives along with the dark chocolate mousse, and I'm waylaid. So, I accept the mousse and fake interest in my sister-in-law's story about how my nieces learned to count...or something.

I watch my old friend Clara chat, laughing and smiling exactly like I remember. She moved here to West Chester, Pennsylvania, in our junior year of high school. She was the new kid and helped me pass math, while I—the popular jock—helped convince her parents she was straight by taking her to all the dances and prom so she could make out with her girlfriend while we were there.

It wasn't a hardship. She was cool and sweet, and it was too bad we lost contact.

I smile to myself remembering the dumb shit we did back then and absently dip my spoon into the mousse, sticking it into my mouth as I let my attention drift to Clara's side, where a Black woman sits with her back to me, but clearly listening intently, her hand on Clara's thigh. On the other side of Clara, facing me, is a third woman. She's white with narrowed eyes, pursed lips, and one long leg crossed over the other.

Bittersweet dark chocolate overwhelms my taste buds as I mentally trace her curves, the side of her thigh and hip revealed from her position on the stool. Her white button-up is both incredibly alluring and modest in how it shows nothing and still everything, the top few buttons open, revealing her collarbone, the shadow of her cleavage, and the nip at her waist, where it's tucked into her jeans. Her feet are capped off with plain black shoes, her left one barely clinging on as she swings her foot back and forth.

With her oval-shaped face, smooth skin, and a tan like mine, I briefly wonder if she's Italian. My mother would love if she's Italian. Her dark brows are slightly angled down, like she's in a perpetual state of judgment, even though her lips tick up in amusement at whatever Clara's saying.

I have another bite of my dessert, admiring her long fingers as she wraps them around her glass and takes a sip, tilting her head back. Her hair is short, cut above her shoulders and curled in that way women do that probably takes hours but appears like she just got out of bed. It's dark brown at the top, transitioning down to light blond, with every color of brown mixed in. I'd like to run my fingers through it, find and name every single hue. Honey. Gold. Walnut. Cedar. Coffee.

Dark Chocolate.

I take another bite and try to rip my gaze away, but it's impossible.

In fact, I don't know why everyone isn't staring. How can you ignore royalty?

She sits so primly, her chin pointed and lips sharp when she speaks, as if what she says is final.

Lord, I wish I could hear what she's saying.

Off with her head!

But Clara is laughing, so my lady is clearly funny.

Finishing up my dessert, I lick my lips, the intense taste lingering on my tongue, and the check can't come fast enough. I need to talk to her.

I offer hugs and handshakes, saying goodnight to my family when we all stand, and I head off to the bathroom while they exit. I use the facilities and check my reflection, swiping my palm over my face, my five-o'clock shadow grainy on my jaw, then up to comb my fingers through my hair. *Good enough.*

Stepping back out onto the floor, I take a breath, slap on my best smile, then amble over to the bar. To get a taste of this bittersweet duchess.

Chapter 2
Taryn

I take a long sip of my Aperol Spritz, savoring the bubbles and citrus flavor. Marianne wanted to order a whole bottle of Prosecco to celebrate, but more than two drinks in one night sends me right to bed. Not to mention, this once-a-month sip and chat is more than enough for me. I don't like testing the genes that run in my family.

I trace the condensation on my glass with the tip of my finger as Clara chatters on about some funny interaction she had with a customer at Lux & Lace, the lingerie boutique she and Marianne own. While I love the girl, have known her for a few years now, with her being married to my best friend, I still haven't gotten used to how she can *talk*.

She well and truly could hold an entire conversation with herself. As she goes on about lace getting caught on hair in *delicate* places, my mind drifts back to the renovations starting next week.

The Nest is my baby. I don't own the bed-and-breakfast, but the place has meant so much to me, I want everything to be perfect. It's where I took my first steps toward independence after my divorce, and I want to show it off. Give it the facelift it desperately needs.

"Hey." Clara elbows my side with a laugh. "You still with us?"

I blink and take another sip. "Sorry, just thinking."

"The renovations?" Marianne guesses, and I nod.

"It's so exciting. You should be proud of yourself," Clara says. "Taking that place from nothing to everything."

"Not nothing," I correct, and Marianne raises her brow in disagreement.

"Kinda."

The Nest was a bit run-down when I took it over. But the former manager hadn't been able to market it correctly. Didn't know how to reach a new audience. West Chester is picturesque, Instagrammable, and The Nest merely needed someone to know how to showcase it within the location. In the age of digital media and online influencers, a person had to know how to highlight its uniqueness. How the backdrop would be perfect for pictures. Add in a little folklore about a certain celebrity who was born in the area staying there, and voilà. Back in business.

Clara lifts her drink. "To Taryn, for being forty-two and a boss-ass bitch."

Marianne raises her glass. "To all of us being boss-ass bitches."

"Hear! Hear!" I agree and take a long drink.

"Sounds like a party."

Clara whips her head around to the man suddenly standing behind her. "Oh my god!" She throws herself at him. "Oh my god, Dante! I can't believe it!"

I scoot my stool back, giving Clara room to jump around, arms flailing as she goes a mile a minute, her hands bouncing from his shoulders to his face back to his shoulders. "I haven't seen you in a hundred years. How are you? You look exactly the same."

"I'm good." He grins. "And you look exactly the same too. I saw you earlier and wanted to say hi, but I was having dinner with my family."

"Oh, well, come here. Come here. Come sit." She takes his hand, pulling him in to our group, depositing him on the seat between Marianne and me. "This is my wife, Marianne, and our best friend, Taryn."

He turns to each of us, nodding his greeting, though his attention stays on me longer than it did on Marianne. As his dark eyes coast over me, his lips twist up in a ridiculous smile— one-part mischief, one-part sex, and a whole lot of *not* working on me. "Nice to meet you, Taryn."

"Hi," I say, ignoring how he brightens when he says my name. How he takes in my body like a dehydrated man getting his first taste of water, his tongue wetting his lips.

I mean... *Come on.*

It might have been a while since I had sex, but not *that* long.

He only smiles bigger at my disinterest then slants his focus back to Clara. I angle away so my legs aren't in his manspreading vicinity. Though I don't know how his thighs can even move that much with the fit of those pants.

"Dante and I graduated high school together," Clara explains, and it all makes sense now.

He's a baby. A generation that loves tight pants and showing a lot of ankle.

I let my gaze wander down, and, yep, his pants are cuffed, and he's got a bare ankle above his Adidas. I don't understand why the fashion industry insisted on prying my skinny jeans away, just to let men have them.

"We were basically best friends back then," Clara goes on,

stealing my focus away from Dante and his legs, only for it to stick on his mouth when he clucks his tongue.

"Clara Shaw, I can't believe you're here."

"Actually, it's Clara Wilkenson-Shaw now." She wraps her arm around Marianne's waist. "But, yeah. I can't believe you're here. You said you were having dinner with your family?"

He glances my way, lazily rubbing his hands up and down his thighs, and I don't let my eyes or mind linger on his thick fingers or the well-defined forearms, shown off by shirt sleeves rolled up to his elbows. "Yeah, my brother got engaged."

"Which one?"

"Johnny. Robbie's married with kids now."

Clara coos. "Amazing. Good for them. What about you? You have anyone?" When he shakes his head, she pushes his shoulder, "Now, *that* is unbelievable."

He chuckles good-naturedly, and I don't like how the sound reaches my ears even over the din of the restaurant. He's tall and clearly muscular beneath his clothes. With shoulders that seem sturdy enough to, like, haul a tree trunk across them. I clear my throat with a long drag of my drink, forcing myself to stop admiring him. If he graduated with Clara, that means he's thirty years old. Much too young for me. And from all his laughing and smiling, much too peppy.

I don't trust peppy people.

No one can be that naturally optimistic all the time.

But unfortunately for me, he angles his head my way again, and my traitorous eyes find his strong jaw with scruff, a long, wide nose that speaks to some Mediterranean heritage, and up to find his brown eyes studying me.

I flash hot. Not unusual in my perimenopausal state, but I don't normally get the sweats from men. That's saved for the two a.m. wake-up, drenched and tangled in my bedsheets. And suddenly, my brain assaults me with images of being drenched and tangled in bedsheets for whole other reasons that begin and end with Dante's lips.

I zip my gaze away, fiddling with the napkin on the bar top as he leans toward me, speaking to no one in particular. "Seemed like I interrupted a celebration."

"We're celebrating Taryn's birthday," Clara says, and if I could reach her, I'd punch her in the tit because Dante goes positively neon.

"Really?" He brushes my thigh with his—seriously, how big are his legs?—as he shifts for the bartender's attention. "We need to order another round on me."

"No. No, thank you."

He glances at me over his shoulder, brows drawn down. "It's a big day. You only turn..."

"Forty-two," Clara supplies, and I shoot her a death glare. She shrugs in innocence, and Marianne laughs into her shoulder.

My birthday was actually last week, and I had a small cake with my kids, but I couldn't get away until now to celebrate with my friends. Not that it matters. I don't have friends anymore.

"You only turn forty-two once." Dante helps himself to a sip of my drink before I can stop him, and my jaw hangs open as he orders me another spritz. Once he faces me again, he shakes his head, like he doesn't understand why I'm glowering at him. As if what he did wasn't totally inappropriate.

"You can't have a sip of a random stranger's drink."

He tips his head to the side. He might think he's adorable, but I do not. "You're not a random stranger. You're Clara's best friend, which kind of makes you mine, by association."

"That's not how friendship works."

He ignores me, simply nodding at the bartender when she

delivers my drink and smiles at me. "Plus, I crashed your party, so I have to gift you something."

I have a feeling I won't win this argument—or any with how he exudes confidence and charm, ugh—but I try anyway. "I don't want anything."

He lifts his shoulder. "Maybe not, but you deserve it. If you don't like it, I'll get you something else. Did you eat? Want a special dessert? They have a dark chocolate mousse I think you'd like."

I huff. "You are..."

He grins, waiting.

"Ridiculous."

"Thank you."

"It wasn't a compliment."

"Don't be mean," Marianne says, but Dante waves his hand.

"I like her kinda mean."

"I'm not mean." I scowl at my so-called best friends, who are watching this...spectacle with interest. Then I arch my brow at Dante in a challenge. He's practically a child, obviously still working on his frontal lobe if he thinks he can swoop in here and take over. He has a lot to learn.

He crosses his arms, and I absolutely do not drop my gaze to his chest, where his collar is open, revealing the hint of a tattoo. "Maybe, maybe not. But you are beautiful."

I cough a laugh. I'm not beautiful. I've never been called beautiful. By now, I'm confident in myself and who I am and what I look like, but I've never been the pretty girl. I'm too tall or too thick or too muscular. My face is too long, my lips too thin, and my personality too harsh.

The funny thing about being too much is that it doesn't extend to time or fucks. And I'm almost out of mine for the night.

I roll my finger around in a circle. "Can we skip to the end of whatever it is you're here to do? Because if it's to reconnect with your old pal, you're facing in the wrong direction."

He smiles, sucking air through his teeth. Pure male satisfaction. And I squeeze my legs tighter together. I will not give in to the tingle rushing over my skin or the way my blood responds when he whispers, "What if I came over here to make new friends?"

"No."

He chuckles. "No?"

"No," I repeat. "I have enough friends."

He glances at Clara and Marianne as if to say *Is she for real?*

And, yes. Yes, I am for real. Who the fuck does this child think he is?

When he lazily props his arm up on the back of my stool, I straighten my spine, moving away from him to concentrate on ripping my napkin into strips, balling each one up, readying them to throw at Clara and Marianne once this guy leaves. Because I know he will eventually, and when he does, I will be ready to bring the hammer down on them for continuing this farce.

I keep quiet as Dante and Clara catch up. He asks what she's up to now, and she explains how she and Marianne own Lux & Lace, and how they met shortly after she graduated from Drexel with a degree in fashion design. Apparently, Dante didn't go to college, went right to work instead with only a few community college credits under his belt. Not that it matters. I don't care.

Couldn't care less when he talks about how proud he is of Clara and how happy he is to hear she's doing so well. Especially because he was there for her when she began to explore her sexuality. Of course I know her history. Even though she gets along great with her parents now, they're heavily involved with their church, and she'd been afraid of what her parents would say when she came out as gay and hid it through most of college. And the stories about how Dante was there for her in those early years in high school don't warm my heart.

At all.

I finish my drink and start in on the one he bought me, which is probably why I don't feel it when my stomach rolls because of his fingertips skating across my back. Nope. It only makes me realize I've gotten too comfortable, and I have to adjust my position on the stool. Away from him.

"And how do you fit in, Taryn?" he asks, and I really wish he'd stop using my name.

In that voice.

Like sandpaper and honey. Rough with a hint of sweet.

When I don't answer, Marianne does. "We've been best friends since we were kids."

He nods knowingly. "Third-wheeling it."

"No," I snap because he's really starting to get under my skin. "Actually, Mari was my third wheel way before I became theirs."

"I didn't know you're married," he says, eyes on my bare left ring finger, his hand finally falling away from me.

And I don't regret losing the heat.

It's not as if I enjoyed the curve of his arm behind me. Or his crisp, woodsy scent. Like he chopped down a few trees before coming to dinner.

And despite myself, I tell him, "I'm not married. Not anymore."

He hums next to me, his heat and smell and presence close to me once again. Taking over. He lowers his voice so I'm the only one who can hear him. "I should probably say I'm sorry. But I'm not."

That has me meeting his eyes, honesty tripping off my tongue in more ways than one. "Me either."

His gaze coasts over my face, and I can't deny the way he makes me feel. As if he does actually believe that I'm beautiful. Then he parks his attention on my lips, and the warmth in my chest shifts to a fire in my belly.

It's been so long since I've felt this way—have *wanted* to feel this way. I don't know what to do—I don't understand it. Or him.

So I ask, "Why?"

Chapter 3
Dante

The one word from Taryn's lips is both a demand and a plea. I'm not sure if she's questioning why I'm here, why I'm talking to her, or why I'm so fucking desperate.

I don't know why, but I answer all of the above.

"Why? Because as I was sitting there at the table—" I tilt my head back in the direction behind me "—I saw you. I couldn't take my eyes off you. The way you hold yourself back from laughing. I want to hear it. See how your face changes when you let go. And I saw your foot wiggling, like you were impatient, your shoe dangling from your toes at one point. I wondered if you didn't notice or just didn't care. I had to know."

She swallows, the line of her throat lifting and then relaxing, her jaw working like she wants to speak but can't. I chance a touch of her shoulder, sweeping my hand under her hair, the soft strands settling over my skin when I wrap my fingers around her neck. "And it's your birthday. I couldn't miss out on that."

Her dark-chocolate eyes narrow. I'm sure she doesn't want to believe me, but it's the truth. Now that I know it's her birthday, I have to see this through. Make sure she enjoys it.

Since she's not moving away or aiming her sharp words at me, I like my odds. Especially when she licks her lips. They're bare. Like her. No nonsense. Very little makeup and nothing that screams high-maintenance about her clothes, but it suits her.

Classic.

Elegant.

Fit for a duchess.

"What do you want?" she asks, and I take a deep breath.

What do I want? Fucking everything. But I'll start small. "Time."

"Time?"

"More time with you." Because I know she'd have fun with me, but also, maybe, very possibly, she might be something special.

She purses her lips, considering me. "I'm a mom. I have two kids."

If she's trying to scare me away, it's not working. "Okay."

"I don't date. I don't have time."

I shrug. "Understood."

"I'm not having sex with you," she says loud enough for everyone in a six-foot radius to hear, earning snickers. Clara bursts out with a big laugh behind me. I ignore it all.

"I didn't ask."

She heaves a sigh like I'm boring her. Like she can see right through me. Although I've never been one to hide what I want. I've always been transparent. This is no different.

"But you will," I amend, and she shakes her head, still not pushing my hand away from her neck, so I let my thumb rub along the base of her skull.

"I'm not fucking a guy named Dante."

I grin, leaning in close enough to brush the tip of her nose with mine. "Famous last words."

When I move away from her, she huffs, all haughty and tough shit, but she immediately sticks her drink straw in her mouth and sucks half of it down. No matter how hard she's fighting, she wants me as much as I want her. So, I'll play it cool for a little while and get to know Marianne more.

I learn she's the daughter of a math professor at the local university and a nurse. With a head for numbers and a desire to stay close to her family, she agreed to help a plucky young upstart with her lingerie business. And the rest was history.

The Wilkenson-Shaws seem really happy, and it's nice to be around people who aren't in constant competition. Because that's what it feels like being with my family—constant competition—but it's clear this little group of women supports and lifts one another up. And me. Since Clara and Marianne are both on my side when I try Taryn again.

"So, you about ready to get out of here?" When she ignores me, I lightly elbow her side, shooting my thumb over my shoulder. "Can I give you a ride?"

"Are you always this persistent?"

Out of the corner of my eye, I see Clara nodding, but I shrug. "You've had two drinks. I'm simply being a gentleman by making sure you arrive home safe."

"Two drinks in three hours. I'll be fine."

"But didn't you walk here from work?" Marianne says, and, *yes*, Marianne!

"You walked?" I shake my head. "You can't walk home. I'll take you."

"No," Taryn tells me then reiterates it to her friends. "No. You two said you could drop me off."

Clara was always a terrible liar, but she tries for me. "We have so much work to do at the store."

Taryn glares at her. "Since when?"

"Since my old friend came to talk to us and seems to really be into you, and he's one of the best people I know."

I grin at my grumpy lady. So deliciously grumpy.

"No," she says again, pressing the tip of her index finger against my chin to turn my head away from her. Even if she can't completely squash the tremor of her mouth.

I sweep my gaze right back to her. "It's only a ride home. Come on."

"Go on," Clara says.

Marianne doesn't say anything, but when I look between her and Taryn, they're having some silent conversation. Taryn glaring. Marianne seeming unfazed. It's Clara who asks the bartender to close out their tab. "It's getting late."

"It's only nine," Taryn says, holding her cell phone with the time then gesturing my way. "And before this guy showed up, you were ready to order another drink."

Clara's eyes go round. "I don't recall that at all." She slips her credit card back into her purse and takes Marianne's hand. "Come on, babe."

I hide my laugh behind my palm and the couple says goodbye to Taryn, who whispers what I can only guess are a lot of four-letter words before Clara wraps her arms around my neck. "You take care of our girl."

"Of course," I promise.

"You still have my phone number?"

I dig my cell phone out of my pocket and bring up my contacts, scrolling until I find her name and then double-check it's still correct. I text her a couple of emojis. "It was great seeing you."

She nods. "Now that I've found you again, I'm not letting you go."

"Counting on it." I kiss her cheek then shake Marianne's hand. "Nice meeting you."

"I'm sure we'll be hanging out again."

Meanwhile, Taryn has her arms folded, and I hope these two have their wills written. I'm not sure they'll survive the next time she gets them alone.

As for me, I'm looking forward to it.

Once it's only the two of us, I move my stool so I'm facing her and wrap my hand around the leg of hers, dragging it closer. Taryn squeaks out a surprised gasp, her eyes widening for a second before narrowing at me once again. But she doesn't refuse me when I place my knees outside of hers.

"Did you have a good day?" I ask, and she slants her attention toward the kitchen, offering me her profile. And what a nice profile it is. Her slender neck, where she slowly drags her fingertips under her chin. Her skin looks so soft, and I envision burying my face there. Kissing that delicate place, over the flutter of her pulse. She purses her lips, making that Cupid's bow even more pronounced. With her high cheekbones and severe, dark eyebrows, I wouldn't call her pretty. She has a kind of unapproachable beauty, and I bet she put on part of her armor because the boys she grew up with never talked to her. I'd wager my next paycheck she was self-conscious growing up and started deflecting with this whole nose-in-the-air thing. But, really, boys are idiots, and she needs a man.

Especially one who won't back down from her.

"You really want to talk about my day?" she asks with the exact right amount of venom to send adrenaline flowing through my veins. I presume this is how snake handlers feel. But snakes only strike when they feel sense danger, and there is nothing more I want than to prove she's safe with me.

I sweep my index finger along the back of her hand and wrist she dangles off the bar top. "I'm trying here. Throw me a bone."

She runs the tip of her tongue over her top teeth, her head shaking in suspicious amusement. Like she can't believe her bad luck that she's found herself here with me.

I do love a good challenge.

"That's what you want?" She meets my gaze, brows arched. "To be treated like a dog?"

"Well, I *can* be a very good boy."

That wins me a reluctant twitch of her lips. "I don't deal with boys."

I try and fail to bite back a grin. "Of course not. Only the manliest of men for you."

She rattles the ice left in her glass then sips the dregs of the liquid. "Exactly."

"And what qualities make up the manliest of men for you?"

"Catching a fly with chopsticks, punching a kangaroo, killing a fish with your bare hands."

I cough a laugh. "I'm not sure if that's a list of qualities for men or to show you're a sociopath. What do you have against animals?"

She shrugs. "It's caveman stuff. If modern-day men ever had to actually take care of anyone in their home, I very much doubt they'd be able to. So, maybe in order for a man to prove his worth, he should be forced to go hunt and gather some food before being allowed in a bed."

"Not actually a bad idea."

It might make me a dick for admitting it, but I love when women rely on me. I love being their protector and provider. It makes me feel strong and supportive. Not in the "I have to make more money" kind of way, but in the "I want to make sure they are completely cared for" kind of way. I don't want them to be subservient or dependent on me, but I want to be their stability.

And obviously, Taryn wants that too.

I suspect if I ever learned who this ex-husband of hers is, I'd hate him on sight.

"Let me take you home," I say, and she considers me seriously, her eyes roaming over my face. I hold very still until she decides.

"Just a ride home."

"Just a ride home," I affirm with a smile I know she doesn't trust.

I back up, giving her room, and she loops her purse across her body. With her standing next to me, I finally get to see how tall she is—probably only a few inches under six foot—but she carries herself like she's eight feet tall, not waiting for me to guide her out the door. Although, once we hit the sidewalk, she pauses so I can catch up. I motion to the right, and we stroll to the next block slowly, hands brushing.

"Did you enjoy yourself tonight?" I ask, and she shoots me a look.

"Until you showed up."

"Can't scare me off that easy," I say because I like her attitude. Then I offer her my phone to plug her address into my Maps app and direct her to where I parked my Indian Scout.

She stops short. "You ride a motorcycle?"

"Yeah."

"You didn't say anything about a motorcycle."

From the way her skin goes ashen, I can tell she's scared, and I recalculate my plans. "Hey, it's all right. If you don't want to ride, I'll call us a car. I'll—"

"No. It's fine." She tosses her arms out, sighing, and I get the impression this woman doesn't like being fussed over. She's one of those independent ladies. And, hey, love that.

But, also, there's nothing wrong with a bit of chivalry.

I step up close to her. "Are you sure? If you're afraid, I don't want to make you uncomfortable."

"I'm not afraid."

I smother my smile. "Right."

"I'm not."

"Okay." I hand over my leather jacket. Besides safety, it's also a few degrees cooler than it was a couple hours ago. But, again, she rolls her eyes.

Still, I hold it out so she can put her arms through then zip it up to her chin and help slip my helmet over her head. I slide the visor down into place and knock my knuckles on the side. "How's it feel?"

"Fine," she says, then stops me when I start to get on the bike. "What about you?"

"What about me?"

"Don't you need...?" She gestures to the helmet and jacket, and I wave her off. I don't plan on hitting the pavement, but if we do, I'd rather her be covered up than me.

"Don't worry about it. Just grab a seat. You're in good hands. I promise."

It takes her a long moment to stretch her leg over the bike, settling behind me, though she's reluctant to sit up against me. She needs to for comfort *and* safety. "Move up."

She doesn't, so I wrap my hand around the outside of her thigh and tug her toward me. She resists. "You don't have to hold on to me, but you'll need to put your hands on the tank in front of me."

Still, she doesn't, and I shake my head at her stubbornness, pointing to the pegs on either side. "Put your feet there and try to relax. If you fight the turns, it'll make it harder for both of us. Think you can handle that?"

"I can handle it," she snips, barely audible from under my helmet, and I smile to myself.

"I'm sure you can." Then I rev the engine and carefully pull out onto the street with her still not holding on, her hands on her thighs as if she can keep herself on the bike by sheer force of will.

I don't doubt her will. But she won't win a fight against gravity.

I check traffic at the stop sign then hit the gas, jerking forward, forcing Taryn against me with a frightened screech. Her arms wrap around my torso, her thighs snug against mine.

"Oops," I say, glancing at her over my shoulder, and she pinches my side.

"You did that on purpose."

Ignoring her accusation, I squeeze her thigh before taking off down Aster Street. Taryn shrieks, burying her head against my back, her hands curled in tight balls against my stomach. Her entire body is tense, and even though I'm not going very fast, she's hanging on to me as if we're going one hundred. But I did ask for it, so I can't be that upset.

I like that Taryn was afraid yet got on the bike anyway. I'm happy she trusts me enough to give her this ride home, and I relish the feeling of her arms squeezing the shit out of me because she knows I won't break.

And I certainly won't break her.

Even though she only lives about five minutes away, I navigate us out of downtown, winding around the university campus to longer stretches of road without lights or stop signs, and Taryn starts to relax into the ride. Eventually, she lifts her head, looking over my shoulder. I'm not sure if she can hear me with the combination of the wind and her helmet, but I ask anyway, "You all right?"

She doesn't answer, so I wrap my hand around her knee,

keeping it there as I carefully maneuver us back toward her house, to a neighborhood full of twin brick townhomes. Being a suburb of Philly, West Chester is close enough to the city, while still having the small-town feel with historic buildings and architecture in almost every direction. She indicates which street I should make a left on, and I slow down so she can point out her house. After parking, I hop off and hold out my hand to make sure she's steady as she swings her leg over and stands.

She wobbles slightly, falling into my side, and I wrap my arm around her waist as she pulls off my helmet, messing up her hair. I tuck the strands behind her ear, taking in her flushed cheeks. "What do you think of your first motorcycle ride?"

"If I wanted to feel like I was punched in the crotch, I would've just taken a spin class."

I stifle my laugh. "Sorry."

"No, you're not."

"You're funny," I say, taking note of the staircase on the side of the house, leading up to a third floor. It wasn't uncommon for houses built around the turn of the century to be multifamily. "This is nice."

She leads the way up the walk to the set of three steps to her small porch, finding her keys in her purse. "Thanks."

"You got an apartment on the top floor?"

"One of the few still left with it. Most people renovated to combine."

I place my hand on the brick. On the sturdy foundation that so many new builds lack anymore. That's why renos are my favorite. Keeping those old structures alive and well maintained, that's what I enjoy most. "It's smart to keep it for the extra cash flow. But I hope you vet your renters."

She snorts at me. Because of course she does. "I have kids. I would *never* not."

"How's your roof situation?"

"Replaced right before I bought it," she tells me, unlocking her door.

"And how long have you been here? Because the ductwork in homes like this sometimes—"

"Did you come here to talk about my house or to fuck?"

Chapter 4
Taryn

Dante stares at me wide-eyed. As if he's shocked I don't want to beat around the bush when he'd been clear with his intentions all night.

At some point, maybe around the time he took genuine interest in getting to know Marianne and reacquainting himself with Clara, talking about how she helped him out with school, making sure he passed all his classes, and he apologized for not staying in touch, I realized he was a good guy. In my experience, it wasn't often a man apologized. Full stop. No excuse, just a simple, "I'm sorry for not doing better."

Between that and his flirty smiles and wandering hands, he wore me down. As much as I wanted to convince myself I didn't like the attention, I couldn't. It felt too good to have a young and hot guy want me.

He is a dozen years younger than me, for God's sake. I couldn't ignore that if I tried.

But I did just get my hair and brows touched up yesterday, so I am feeling myself today. And it's my birthday celebration. Don't I deserve this? To have a few hours of fun. That's high hopes, but I'm assuming his age and stamina will play in my favor.

Plus, the ride on the back of his motorcycle might have helped seal the deal. As terrifying as it was, the adrenaline rushing through my veins made sure I wouldn't be able to go to sleep anytime soon.

And if he's willing, so am I.

"Say it again," he tells me, and I step inside my house, hearing the familiar prance of my dog's paws upstairs.

"Did you come here to talk about my house or to fuck?"

He smiles, the same big grin that's been growing on me all night. "I really would like to talk more about your house. *After* I fuck you."

I'm not at all interested in giving him any more information about my house, but I let him inside anyway as Frankie happily plods down the steps and across the hardwood floor, skidding to a stop in front of me.

"Hey, baby," I coo, kneeling down to scratch his ears.

Next to me, Dante bends and sticks his hand out. "Heya, buddy. What's your name?"

"Frankie," I answer, watching as my dog greets my guest with a lot less suspicion than I'd hope for. I adopted the black-and-white boxer with the idea of his being my alarm system, but if anyone ever tried to break in, he'd show them around the house, permitting them to steal whatever they wanted before he ever alerted me to their presence.

"Frankie. I like that." Dante leans in to accept a few kisses on his jaw and cheek from my dog. "Yeah, you're so sweet. Nice to meet you too."

I stand and remove his leather jacket, setting it on the couch, next to my purse, as Frankie and Dante continue their lovefest. That is until I cross through the living room and dining room to the kitchen at the back of the house. Then

Frankie races to the door so I can let him out. Dante is not far behind, resting a hip on the counter next to me.

"I like him," Dante says with a tip of his chin to the windows, where we watch Frankie sniff the grass of my small backyard.

"Yeah, he's a good boy."

I feel more than hear Dante's hum when he dips down, closing the few inches of height difference between us, his chest against my back. "I like the way that sounds coming from you."

I lean back, relaxing into him when he curls his hands around my waist. "You don't really want to be referred to in the same way I refer to my dog." I tilt my head, catching his gaze. "Do you?"

He squeezes my sides, fingers working to lift the hem of my shirt to find my bare skin. "I like hearing your voice go all soft. Like you love him. I like seeing that side of you because I'm sure not many people do."

I haven't had a man in my house in a long time, and I don't really like the implication that this man can *see* something in me. Since my divorce, I haven't had the desire to be in a relationship, to ever give up that power again, and while I'm willing to strip naked physically for this man, I'm not willing to strip naked metaphorically.

Stepping out of his hold, I open the back door and whistle. "Come on, buddy. Inside."

Frankie finishes up and trots over to get his treat, which he immediately takes under the dining room table. So, I reach for Dante's hand and lead him upstairs, where I close the door to my room behind us, allowing him no time to look around.

Although with the way he cages me in against my wall, he's clearly only interested in one thing, and my previous confidence takes a nose dive. I'm 5'8", and while I'd grown up athletic and have never been especially self-conscious, I've birthed two kids and that rude bitch perimenopause has been screaming at me since I turned forty. So, I'm dealing with *a lot*.

Meanwhile, this Greek sculpture come to life is tugging at my shirt. With the lights *on*.

I smack my hand on the wall, searching for the switch, and flip it off.

This motherfucker flips it right back on.

"What are you doing?" I flip it off again.

"You usually have sex with the lights off?" He flips the switch *again*. "How do you see anything?"

"That's the point," I say, and he catches my hand, pinning it above my head when I go to turn them off one last time. I start to argue, but he grabs my other hand, holding them both against the wall, his mouth taking mine, stealing my breath, along with any words I had in my head.

His lips are demanding, directing mine to open to him with soft pulls until he slips his tongue inside, sliding against mine, then teasing me with a curl against my upper lip that sends goose bumps across my skin. When I chase him for more, he laughs into a kiss, because he evidently likes to torture me.

With his thigh between mine, he tightens his grip on my wrist, pulling slightly, stretching me until I'm almost on my toes, and gazes down at me like some maniacal villain who's got me strung up on a rack.

Then again, it might not be too far off from the truth with how his eyes roam slowly over me from head to toe, his gaze hot and hard. If it weren't for the pinch of his fingers at my wrist, I might think they were on my cheeks and throat and breasts and legs with how my skin warms and feels heavy like his palms are on me. Everywhere. All at once.

When I can't take it anymore, I squirm, absently rubbing

myself on his thigh, and he nods in this self-satisfied way that I shouldn't find so attractive and yet...

Here the fuck I am.

Like a pig on a spit for the taking.

"Kiss me," he says, and I don't hesitate, inclining my head forward, but he doesn't do the same. I can't reach.

"What are you doing?"

"Seeing how bad you want it."

I hate his stupid smile. "You're not cute."

"Really? I would've guessed otherwise from your little needy sounds."

I mash my lips closed. He won't win.

But then he bends, his mouth ghosting over the shell of my ear. "From how you're grinding your pussy on my leg."

I freeze immediately, my head against the wall. "I can't stand you."

"We'll see how you feel in another few hours."

"Few hours? That's a bit cocky."

"The fact that you even believe that makes me sad for you."

"Oh, shut up," I say, attempting to push him off me, but he kicks my feet apart with his own and presses his body against mine, completely immobilizing me.

His mouth quirks up. So arrogant. "Yeah? You think you're in charge? I bet you do, huh? All day, you're the boss. You're the one making decisions, telling people what to do. What would happen if you stopped? Just for the night? Let me be in charge."

I don't answer because I don't want to tell him he's correct. That's exactly what I am. I like being the one in power. I want to be the one making decisions, partly because I know what it feels like to be powerless, but also, I know I won't fuck it up.

Except spread out and pinned against the wall under a man bigger than me, I understand he is the one in charge. And I'm okay with it. Especially because I know I could say no, and he would stop immediately.

He kisses me, sucking my bottom lip between his, letting it go with a nip. "Can you do that, beautiful? Let me take care of you for the night?"

I inhale sharply when he leans in to suck on the sensitive skin below my ear, and my nipples harden to tight, almost painful peaks. I nod, needing relief.

The jackass lifts his head, smirking. "Did you say something? I missed it."

I grit my teeth. "I said yes."

"Yes, what?"

I squint, contemplating if it's worth it, but then he takes both of my wrists in his right hand and skates his left hand under my shirt, roughly squeezing my breast over my bra cup before gently rubbing his thumb back and forth across my hard nipple. Even through the layers of cotton, I feel it. Feel how it would be if I gave myself to him.

I moan. "Yes, you can be in charge tonight." I feel him smile against my throat and add, "Just this once."

"Mm? So you're saying there's a chance for more than once?"

"No." I close my eyes when he bites the tender flesh at the slope of my neck.

"We'll see."

"No."

His responding chuckle is soft, barely a puff of air, as he backs away, releasing my wrists to sit on the edge of my bed, appearing wholly out of place on my threadbare quilt and the lacy curtains billowing in the breeze from my open windows behind him. With his messy hair, richly tanned skin, and dark clothes, he has a roguish vibe about him. I can't put my finger on it—if it's the smarmy, I'm-gonna-fuck-you-raw smile or the overall arrogance that makes him seem too big for his britches—but whatever it is, I'm a fucking sucker for it.

And I hate myself for it. Especially when he says, "Take your shirt off for me."

"Not with the lights on."

He heaves a sigh then reaches over for the small night-light and turns it on. I then flip the switch to turn off the overhead lights.

"Better?" he asks, and I nod. "Strip."

I don't even hesitate. I work each button apart, letting the shirt fall from my arms. I hadn't planned on coming home with anyone tonight, and I wore my favorite but trusty beige bra with a wire that has perfectly formed to my shape. My tits are nothing special, a little worn like socks full of nickels from breastfeeding two babies, but in this bra, they at least have some oomph under them.

"Bra off too," Dante orders, and I pause, which earns me a playful raise of his brows.

"I don't want to."

He shrugs. "Doesn't matter. You said I get to be in charge tonight, and how am I going to lick your pretty little nipples with your bra on?"

"How do you know my nipples are pretty?"

"I have a feeling," he says, lounging back on his elbows as if he's paid for a private room at a strip club, and while I don't feel confident about myself in front of a man who is a little too good-looking to be real, I remind myself this is what he wanted. If he weren't attracted to me, he wouldn't be here, so...

I unsnap the clasp at the back and let it hit the floor too.

Dante's eyes are dark to begin with, but in this low light, they seem to go black the longer he gazes at me. I resist the urge to fidget or cover up, hiding my imperfections, hoping he doesn't notice how they're different sizes, how my left nipple sort of lazily stares off to the side, while my right will look him in the eye. And to say nothing of how low they hang.

But I don't think he notices. Or if he does, he doesn't care, because he licks his lips and juts out his chin. "Come here. Get on top of me."

I set my shoes aside and scoot onto the bed, my knees on either side of his hips. Like this, I'm taller than him, and he tilts his head back, cheeks ruddy, face boyish when he commands, "Feed them to me."

I'm not sure if it's the crude request or my own lack of sexual experience, but I huff. "What?"

"Feed me your tits." Like a king, he doesn't move. Simply waits, completely placid, as if it's totally normal to request someone to feed him their tits.

I don't have an argument, so I bend forward, feeling the hard, thick ridge of him between my legs, and wrap my hands around the bottom of my breasts, lifting them up, offering them to him.

"Closer," he murmurs, attention locked on the hard tips, and I swallow thickly at the heated request, as if he's dying to taste.

I'm suddenly dying for him to have a taste too.

I arch my back so my right nipple brushes his lips, and he captures it, sucking hard. I gasp, surprised at the pleasant sting as he hums a satisfied sound, circling his tongue, and I feel the echo of pleasure deep in my core, a line connected between my nipple and clit. One he plucks by scraping his teeth over the glistening wet tip.

I barely have enough time to breathe before his mouth is on my left one, giving it the same treatment, and my hips roll reflexively, searching for friction. Still, he stays on his elbows, his hands loosely balled in fists next to him, forcing me to work, find where it feels good, grind down harder on him.

Though I suspect that's what he wants from the way his eyes find mine, silently imploring me to keep going as he continues to lavish my breasts with his mouth, alternating side to side until I'm completely gone. I throw my head back, moaning up at the ceiling as I rock myself on him, hitting my clit, reaching for the precipice, but never quite making it.

"Please," I beg, breathing hard, skin warm and prickly.

Dante releases my nipple and flips us so he's on top, hands on either side of my head, lips quirked to the side. "Whatever you want, duchess."

"Duchess?"

"You're the ruler, aren't you?" He dips his head to kiss a trail down my breastbone.

"I thought you were in charge."

He reaches the button on my jeans, flicking it open as his eyes meet mine. "Only because you're allowing me."

When I don't stop him, he pulls them off, raking his gaze over the length of me, then takes his wallet from his back pocket to retrieve a condom. He tosses it onto the pillow above me and proceeds to strip naked. Truly, he's like a sculpture. Tall and well-built with a line of dark hair extending from his navel down to the trimmed patch above the erection he fists, sliding his hand up and down the length as he continues to look his fill of me.

And I have the sudden fear that I'll disappoint him. That I already do.

I'm soft and squishy all over, with stretch marks and cellulite covering my belly, hips, and thighs. My C-section scar is prominent, clearly visibly above the line of my panties, and I'm afraid to even look down at how badly I need to do my own trimming.

And yet, he is not at all turned off by the bush that appears when he yanks off my underwear, tossing them over his shoulder and kneeling on the floor. I try to cover up, close my legs, but he stops me, shoving my thighs wide, and not even Moses, Jesus, and Muhammad put together could save me from the mortification that makes me go hot all over. The only other person to be this close to my vagina in the last few years is my OB-GYN, and she's always gentle.

Dante is not.

He's demanding and rough and doesn't give me any warning before diving down, kissing my pussy like he kissed my mouth, licking up the length of me, holding me open with his fingers to tease my clit with the tip of his tongue, then pressing inside.

It's an onslaught of sensation, and I automatically dig my fingers into his hair, forgetting all about my insecurities. Too tormented to think of anything other than his tongue and what he's doing with it.

His groan is one of self-satisfaction as he slides one of his hands over my lower abdomen, right on top of my scar, his fingers extending wide, almost possessively, like he's claiming as much territory as possible. I can't make sense of it, of how I want him to possess me, because he lifts his head and thrusts his fingers inside me, ridding me of all logical thoughts.

With gentle pressure inside, he tenderly presses down at the same time, and my eyes roll to the back of my head. A clever little trick that he knows works from the quiet, "That's it. Almost there."

He's right. I am.

After only another minute, I shout my pleasure to the ceiling, my hands flying to Dante's shoulders, gripping him tightly as I come hard against his mouth. He doesn't let up, continuing to lick and suck until I'm a trembling mess, oversensitive and pushing him away with a smack to his shoulder. He sits back, grinning, his face glistening with my arousal. I should probably be embarrassed, but I'm too sated to care.

He wipes his mouth with the back of his hand, his eyes never leaving mine as he moves up my body, his lips soft and still tasting like me when he kisses me. I forget about all the reasons why I thought this was a bad idea.

Because this is exactly what I deserve for my birthday.

And I apparently do fuck guys named Dante.

He grabs the condom and opens it, carefully rolling it down his hard length, cupping his balls as he straddles me, his dark eyes bright, mouth slightly quirked up in the corner. "You don't know how good you look right now."

I seriously doubt that, with how I know I flush an unappealing red when I'm hot, but I play along anyway. "Yeah? How good?"

He places his hands on my thighs as he shifts backward, and it's funny how in only half an hour, he's taken me from afraid to take my clothes off to teasing him about my nakedness. Maybe it's because he so obviously doesn't mind how my breasts point east and west when I'm lying down like this or how I'm not offering to go down on him in return for his efforts.

Nope. He's completely content. Happy, even.

"Hours wouldn't be enough. I'd need days to do all the things I want to do to you. I need more than tonight."

I hope my face doesn't give away how surprised I am. While this is an indulgence for me, that's *all* it is.

He's practically a kid.

And I have responsibilities. A life. Children.

He may want to do a lot of things, and he can. Being barely out of his twenties, he doesn't have half of the number of obligations I do. So, while I'm truly flattered, I also live in reality. "I told you. Just this once."

His frown is fleeting, his *dare me* smile taking over almost as quickly, but even that millisecond of disappointment settles behind my rib cage, and it takes Dante palming my breast, my nipple caught between his index and middle fingers, to bring me back to the moment. "We'll see," he says, then lightly bites a fleshy bit of my stomach. I shriek in amusement, and he shoots me a grin. "You can't resist me."

It's true.

As hard as I tried earlier, I gave in, and I continue to let him have free rein now.

He bends down to press a kiss between my legs once more before leaning up and spitting.

My intake of breath is sharp as he rubs his saliva over my pussy. I've never... I wouldn't...

I exhale in hiccups, shocked and turned on that I like it. And as if he can read my mind, he smirks and spits again, using it as lube, gliding the head of his cock through my soaking-wet flesh.

I never thought I'd like something so obscene, so dirty, but it's strangely thrilling. Even better when he finally slides into me in one long, slow thrust, the muscles in his chest and abdomen tight, his biceps and shoulders tense as he holds himself above me, watching as he enters me.

He's thick and deep, and it feels incredible, each drive sending waves of electricity into me, lighting up every nerve ending until I feel like a firework shooting into the sky. I wrap my arms and legs around him, keeping myself tethered to earth, digging my fingernails into his back, and he moans, his face buried in my neck.

In all my previous experience, I'd been complacent. Accepted that not-great was good enough, and now, at forty-two years old, I finally know I should never have settled. *This* is what I deserved.

A man who grunts his pleasure, who speaks soft words

against my collarbone, who gazes down at me with admiration, and who wants me to find my pleasure. Even more than his own.

"You feel so good. Fuck, I can't stand it," he murmurs, reaching between us to finger my clit, pausing his thrusts to stroke the already oversensitized bud. All it takes is a pinch, and I'm gone again, another orgasm ripping through me, leaving me boneless and breathless. He follows soon after, his body rigid, his cock pulsing inside me, his breath hot on my neck, his chest damp against mine.

We lie together, our bodies entwined, until we come down from the high, my heart rate slowing to its regular pace, sensation eventually flowing back into my extremities from where it had coiled and exploded at the single point of contact between us.

Dante rolls off me, collapsing onto the bed, throwing his arm over his head with his eyes closed. He appears in no hurry to leave, and I watch him for a moment, his chest rising and falling in an easy rhythm, his dark hair a mess from my fingers. He's at ease in himself, exhausted from what we just did, and maybe...blissed out? Because of me? Because of this extraordinary moment we shared.

And yet, I can't think too hard about how it makes me feel. How *he* makes me feel. That rabbit hole is too narrow and winding, much too unsafe to tread.

The sooner I get rid of him, the sooner I can move on.

I sit up, swinging my legs over the side of the bed and dig through my pajama drawer for one of my sleep shirts, long enough to cover all the important bits. When I turn around, I find him focused on me, a curious gleam in his eyes.

"Whose shirt is that? The ex-husband's?"

I absently tug on the black cotton with the white logo for

Stone Ink in the middle. "It's a hundred years old. My brother's."

He doesn't reply, except to purse his lips. Before he can ask another question, I snatch his clothes from the floor and toss them at him. "Get dressed."

"We literally just finished." He waves at his now-limp dick. "Don't even have the condom off yet."

I circle my hands, wordlessly telling him to get moving, and he shakes his head at me, laughing. "You're serious."

"Yes."

"What if I want to stay? Give you another couple of orgasms?"

I help myself to a dig through his wallet. There is no other condom in it, and I throw it so it lands on his taut belly. "All out of luck."

He presses up to his hands. "I don't need condoms for what I have planned."

I wave my hand, dismissing any of his ideas. "I plan on sleeping."

He slants his gaze to the bed meaningfully. "I don't take up much room. I could curl up right here on the end."

I bite back the laugh threatening to erupt. I can't stand that he can be so irritating and charming at the same time. "No. Up. Dress. Out."

"All right. All right." He heaves a sigh but pulls on his clothes, while I stand by the bedroom door with my arms crossed, making sure he leaves nothing behind. When he's fully dressed, I lead him downstairs, and Frankie pads out of his hiding spot, following us to the door, where Dante bends to kiss him. "You know, I think your dog is sadder to see me leave than you are."

I don't disagree, and Frankie sits at Dante's feet, looking up at him with pleading eyes, his tail thumping softly against the floor.

Traitor.

Dante grins, sliding his arms into the leather jacket he let me borrow. "How about you give me your number?"

"No. Absolutely not."

He isn't deterred. "You know you had fun."

"I did, and now you can go. Thank you."

"Harsh," he says with a laugh, casually holding on to my hand, his fingers twining with mine, pulling me closer. I go willingly, putting my other hand on his chest. This close and in this light, without the haze of sex between us, I appreciate exactly how young he looks. No wrinkles or crow's-feet to be found as his eyes drift between mine.

It feels intimate. Familiar. He exudes a kind of safety I'm not sure I've ever felt from a man before, and it's difficult to find words to form an argument against him.

"Your eyes have streaks of amber in them," he tells me right before he cradles my cheek in his hand, his thumb ghosting under my eye. "Let me see you again."

It's difficult, but I force the answer out, offering more of an explanation than I would any other person. "I can't. I have kids and... My life is complicated."

He studies me for a moment, then nods. "All right, duchess. If you say so." He leans in, pressing a soft kiss to my cheek. "But I have a feeling we'll see each other again."

I don't dare respond, my head and heart at odds with each other, and I step back, putting space between us.

With a tip of his chin, he opens the door. "Goodnight, Taryn."

"G'night." I shut and lock the door behind him, leaning against it, letting my smile loose as his voice carries through to me.

Sophie Andrews

"I told you...famous last words."
And I cover my laugh with my hand.

Chapter 5
Dante

I pull up to The Nest Bed & Breakfast in one of the company's trucks, polishing off the last of my protein bar and the coffee my mother had poured into a travel mug for me this morning. While I don't enjoy living back in my childhood home again, there are some perks. Like my mom cooking all my meals and writing little notes in my lunch box like she used to do when I was a kid.

As I step out of the truck, the crisp October air bites at my skin, and I grab my zip-up from the passenger side, coasting my gaze around the area. It's a picturesque plot of land with pumpkins and hay bales dotting the property. Too bad all the construction vehicles will block the views soon enough.

As a project manager for Moretti Construction, I oversee renovations and new builds from start to finish. It's demanding but rewarding work, and I take pride in delivering quality jobs on time and on budget. I might not be the numbers guy or the one signing contracts, but I know my shit when it comes to managing construction sites. My crews respect me, and I treat them right in return. Moretti Construction is a family business, but it's the men and women I work with on a daily basis whom I consider the real heart of the company.

Heading up the stone walkway to The Nest, I take in the charming exterior of the stately Victorian mansion turned B&B, painted a soft yellow with white trim that could use a bit of a touch-up. Despite the age, it's warm and welcoming, with a wide wraparound porch that spans the front, complete with antique rocking chairs and potted mums along the railing.

I climb the few steps up to the door, my work boots heavy on the weathered wood, and I make a note that if we're redoing the paint, we might as well refinish the porch as well. Iron sconces flank the forest-green front door with an old-fashioned handle that needs to be pushed down to open. Inside, I note the small artificial tree with Halloween decorations all over it. Little Jack Skellington and glitter bat ornaments.

I'm impressed by how the cozy antique feel of the exterior has been brought to life inside as well. The foyer has original hardwood floors and a worn rug runner leading down the center hallway. Framed black-and-white photos of what I assume to be West Chester from the late 1800s line the walls. A slender table sits against the wall, displaying brochures and flyers for upcoming local events.

To my right is a sitting room furnished with floral couches and chairs, their faded fabric adding to the vintage vibe. In front of me is the staircase that I assume leads to the guest rooms upstairs. It's nice but old, and I can see why the owners wanted to update it.

After finishing my quick assessment, I turn to the dining room, where two men and a woman stand, her back to me.

"Hey, I'm looking for a..." I double-check my clipboard with my brother's notes on it. "Miss Stone. I'm Dante Moretti, the contractor for the reno job."

When the woman spins around, I'm momentarily stunned.

No way.

It can't be her.

But those chocolate eyes and lips open in surprise, similar to the shape they made when she orgasmed, and leave no doubt it's her.

Taryn.

She seems as shocked as me, frozen in place. The gray-haired bearded guy next to her elbows her forward.

"Yeah, you've found her," he says wryly.

Taryn moves toward me as if in a trance, muttering a quiet greeting. I stick my hand out for an awkward handshake, unable to look away from her face. From her mouth and that single freckle by her left eye, to the wrinkle between her brows as she strains to put the puzzle pieces together.

After all her bullshit about me not being able to see her again, my guardian angel went and set her down right in my path. Amen and hallelujah!

She reaches for my hand but ends up knocking over the little cardboard coffee cup in her hand, spilling it on the floor. She mutters a curse, and I spring into action, using the bandanna I'd tucked in my back pocket to mop it up.

"I got it. I got it," I assure her, nudging her away from the puddle. She drags a hand over her face, looking utterly bewildered. As do the two men with her.

I try to ignore the mix of curiosity and jealousy that pinches my side like a cramp after a long run. Because, who are they? Why are they here? And why is she okay with them touching her? Like the one on the left does, shouldering her as if they're old buddies.

Fuck buddies?

After I have it cleaned up, I stand, flicking my gaze between the two men. Neither seems inclined to introduce himself to me, so I don't either. Instead, I focus on the woman I haven't been able to stop thinking about for the last forty-eight hours.

And do you know how uncomfortable it is to be a thirty-year-old man living at home and yanking it in his childhood bedroom while imagining the taste of the sweetest pussy he's ever had as his mother sings along to Billy Joel downstairs?

Pretty goddamn uncomfortable.

But here she is in front of me, exhaling audibly, gaping up at me with wide eyes.

One of the men clears his throat, and in the thick silence, that jolts her into action. She nods at my soaking bandanna. "Uh, thanks."

"Yeah. No problem. I'm gonna toss this back in my truck," I say, tipping my head toward the door. "And then you wanna walk me around the property? I have the list, but I'd like to make sure we're on the same page."

She nods, her voice uneven and unlike herself. "Mm-hmm. Yep. Sure."

I only hope it bodes well for me that she's off-center. Won't take more than a slight push to have my face between her legs again.

With a burst of hope and appreciation swimming through my veins, I jog outside, throwing my wet bandanna and my zip-up into the truck. I know she liked my muscles on Friday. Might as well remind her of them.

Gotta use what the good Lord gave me to convince that goddess to take advantage once again.

By the time I make my way back inside, the two men are gone, and Taryn appears to be more in control of herself, her shoulders back, chin up, pursed lips, and hard stare in place.

There she is.

My duchess.

I grin.

She arches her brow in return.

As if she doesn't know that turns me on.

"You're looking good," I say, to which she merely shakes her head. "Taryn Stone, huh?"

"Come on. I'll show you around, Dante Moretti of Moretti Construction."

"Who were those two guys?" I ask before I can think better of it.

And for a moment, I assume she won't answer, but she surprises me on multiple fronts by saying, "My brothers."

I probably shouldn't feel so relieved to know they're related to her, but I'm hung up on this woman, and while I don't mind some competition, I want her for myself.

"I had no idea who you were when we met," I say and follow her through the arched doorway into the dining room, my eyes drawn to the sway of her hips. She's wearing these tight black pants that hug her curves just right and a silky blouse that drapes over her shoulders, revealing a hint of her collarbone. I can't help but imagine tracing my tongue along that delicate line, feeling her tremble beneath me.

She tosses me a skeptical look over her shoulder. "And if you did, would you have approached me?"

"I would have approached you the instant I met you, no matter if it was at a bar or a business meeting."

She huffs. "That's a lawsuit waiting to happen. This is the dining room. We serve breakfast here every morning, and sometimes we host small events, like bridal showers or baby showers."

I nod, scanning the room and making mental notes of the changes we'll need to make. "Got it. And what about the kitchen? We'll need to bring that up to code if you want to expand your catering options."

Taryn leans back, clearly impressed. "You've done your homework."

I shrug, trying to play it cool. "I'm not just a pretty face."

We move on to the kitchen, and I'm immediately struck by how outdated everything is. The appliances are ancient, the countertops are chipped, and the floor tiles are cracked and stained. It's a far cry from the sleek, modern kitchens we usually install.

"I'm assuming you spoke to my brother Johnny about quotes and time frames and then signed the contract with Robbie, but I can't promise that will all remain the same. I didn't realize you'd need...the works in here."

Taryn sighs, running a hand through her hair. "I know. It's been on my list for a while, but we just haven't had the budget for it until recently."

I glance up from where I jot down a few notes, catching the worried look in her eyes. "Hey, I've got you. I'll make it work."

"Dante, don't—"

"You ready to go upstairs?"

I can tell she wants to fight me, but I won't have her working herself up over this job. I'm the one in charge, and I'll see to it that she gets what she wants in a timely manner and for a price she can afford.

We continue the tour, moving upstairs to the guest rooms. Each one is unique, with its own color scheme and decor, but they all share the same outdated aesthetic. Even so, I can see why people love staying here. It's like stepping back in time. If a bit on the kitschy side. She wants to keep the feel while opening up the space as much as possible to live in this century.

"So, how long have you been working here?" I ask as we walk down the hall.

Taryn hesitates for a moment before answering. "About ten

years. I started out as the assistant manager, but I'm the general manager now."

"And you enjoy it?"

She nods, her eyes scanning the walls as if taking in every detail. "I do. It's not just a job for me. It's my home away from home. I want to make sure it's the best it can be."

I can see the pride in her eyes, the dedication in her voice. It's sexy as hell, and I have a surge of desire. To find out what the pride on her tongue tastes like.

To make her feel proud of me.

After she comes on my mouth and dick eighteen times in a row.

We reach the end of the hall, and Taryn turns to face me, her expression serious. "Listen. I need to make something clear."

At the sharp sting in her voice, I put my hands behind my back like a good little boy. "Okay?"

"What happened between us the other night... It can't happen again. I mean it. We need to keep things strictly professional."

I can't help the grin, even as I nod in agreement. "Understood."

She narrows her eyes at me, clearly not convinced. "I'm serious, Dante. No flirting, no innuendos, no...anything. We have to work together, and I can't have any distractions."

I hold up my hands in surrender. "Hey, I get it. You're the boss. Whatever you say goes."

She scrutinizes me for a moment, as if trying to gauge my sincerity. Then she nods, satisfied. "Good. Now, let's get back to work."

As we head downstairs, I bite back a smile. I know she thinks we have to pretend I didn't fuck her good and raw, but she won't be able to. I'll make sure of it. So that when she does eventually give in, she'll know I'm serious when I say I got her.

For now, though, I'll play by her rules. I'll be the perfect gentleman, the consummate professional. But that doesn't mean I can't enjoy the view or the occasional stolen glance.

Because even if she won't admit it, I know she feels the same spark I do. And I'm not one to back down from a challenge.

As we reach the bottom of the stairs, Taryn's back to business. "All right, so what's the next step? What do you need from me?"

I flip through my notes, scanning the list of tasks ahead of us. "First things first, I'll get a crew in here to start demo on the kitchen. That's gonna be the biggest job, so we might as well tackle it head on. In the meantime, I'll start sourcing materials and getting quotes from suppliers."

Taryn nods, taking it all in. "Sounds good. And what about the guest rooms? When can we start on those?"

I shrug. "Depends on how quickly we can get the materials in. But don't worry, I'll make sure we have everything completed by your date. December third, right?"

She nods. "I want to do a relaunch for Christmas. I already have the rooms booked. I can't mess this up."

"I'll get it done for you. Eight weeks," I say, extending my hand.

"Eight weeks," she reiterates, placing her palm against mine, her long fingers wrapping around my hand, shaking it. The boss.

Except she doesn't release my hold immediately. In fact, she lets me tug her a few centimeters closer to me. "Happy to be working with you."

"Mm-hmm. Yep." She drops my hand and takes a big step back.

I don't bother hiding my amusement at her babbling. "Mm-hmm. Yep." Then I show myself out, stopping with the door open. "Guess those are your new famous last words."

She rolls her eyes. "You are exasperating."

"And I know you wouldn't want it any other way." I wink and pivot around to Taryn's mumbled, "I hate you."

Because I know she doesn't hate me at all.

Not one bit.

Chapter 6
Taryn

I've been meeting my brothers for coffee every other week for the last...ten years or so. Ever since that one random afternoon when I dissolved into a puddle of tears at Griffin's feet. He stopped at my house back when I was married and miserable and needed help. He asked me "What's up?" and I completely broke down. Ian took it upon himself then to make sure nothing like that ever happened again, so here we are.

Ian's already seated when I enter Cuppa Jo. He nods at me from our regular booth with my regular order of full caf, lots of sugar and milk. When I sit opposite him, he tilts his head, and I cut off the question before he can speak. "No. Let's wait. I'm not going to explain it twice."

"Fair." He retrieves his cell phone from his back pocket to check the time. "Don't know where Cap is."

"Yes, you do," I say after a sip of my coffee. Ever since Griffin and Andi—the former nanny to his twins—got together, he's almost always late. Griffin is ten months older than me, and I've only ever known him to be stringent, from the way he folds his clothes to his daily schedule planned out to the second. Until Andi came roaring into his life.

Now, he's more relaxed. And for that, I'm grateful to the woman. He deserved to have some of the weight of responsibility taken off his shoulders. He's had enough of it from his previous career as a SEAL and now a firefighter.

Ian, on the other hand, has built up his tattoo business from nothing and lives a life of flexibility. I think because he's always had to be the one taking care of everyone else, he requires an adaptable lifestyle. He's used to the curve balls of life, excellent at swinging away.

Ian's got a big heart, much more forgiving than me, and everything a girl could ask for in a big brother and father figure. Almost ten years older than me, he helped to take care of us—Griffin, me, and Roman—after Dad split when we were little kids. Ian would give someone the shirt off his back if needed. But he also lives to give us—his siblings—lots of shit.

"Probably fucking his girl."

I splutter on a gulp of my drink. "Can you not? I'd prefer not to think about my brother's sex life."

He blinks in innocence. "You were the one who told us you fucked your construction guy."

I grab a napkin from the holder, ignoring his curious stare. "I told you, I'm not explaining it twice."

"Well, you're in luck," Ian says a moment before I hear, "Sorry I'm late."

Griffin scoots into the booth next to me, gently elbowing me in greeting before taking his coffee from the middle of the table.

"Right on time, actually." Ian motions to me. "Tar was about to explain what's up with the young buck."

Griffin takes a swallow of his coffee then settles his attention on my face, his words biting. "You're *really* going to work with him?"

Since my brothers were there to meet Dante, I gave them the barest of information, that we had slept together, not knowing who the other was. And now it's time to face the music. But I won't go down without a fight. I scowl in Griffin's direction. "Funny you ask since you were sleeping with your nanny."

Ian nods, wagging his finger. "Facts."

Griffin rolls his eyes and chooses to quietly sip his drink instead of continuing with me, and I blow out a breath, mentally sorting out the information they need to know. "We met when I went out for drinks with Marianne and Clara. He was apparently really good friends with Clara in high school, and... It was only one night. One time, that's it."

My brothers both nod in understanding. For as close as we are, I don't know much about their personal lives in terms of who, what, where, when, or why. Sure, we help and support one another, but my brothers are my brothers. Not my gossiping girlfriends.

Really, this was all Clara's fault.

"So, what? You never spoke with him when you made arrangements with the construction company?" Griffin asks, and I shake my head.

"Apparently, it's a family business, and Dante is the project manager. I never spoke to him before."

"And now you're his boss for all intents and purposes," Ian fills in like a smug bastard. "Yikes."

"Yikes," I agree, sighing.

"What are you going to do?"

"Nothing. I handled it."

"You handled it?" Ian and Griffin both say at the same time.

I divide my attention between them. "I told him that it's never happening again and he needs to remain completely professional."

Ian runs his hand over his beard. "*He* needs to remain professional?"

"Yes. *He.*"

Griffin lifts his cup to his mouth. "What about you? Never seen you act like that before when he walked in."

"Because I was surprised."

"You dropped your coffee all over the floor," Ian says, as if I don't know. As if my brain hadn't come to a complete and total stop when Dante sauntered into The Nest. As if I hadn't been thinking about his callused hands on my thighs and his wicked smirk when he told me to feed him my breasts. As if I didn't remember him *spitting* on me.

Good god.

I couldn't stop thinking about him the whole weekend, and then he appeared as if by black magic. All charming smiles and muscles on display.

What an asshole.

"It's fine," I tell my brothers. "I'll be fine."

I know they don't believe me with their dubious stares, but I change the subject. "Andi's going back to California soon?"

Griffin's shoulders rise on a deep breath. "Yeah, she leaves the first week of November, but it's only for two weeks."

Andi is a songwriter and worked on her best friend's album this past spring. I don't know much about the business, but after living in Los Angeles for a long time, she's finally made some good connections and is getting her work out there. "Let me know if you need help with the kids."

Griffin's twins, Logan and Grace, are in sixth grade and are good friends with my daughter, Maddie, since she's only a year older. My son, Jake, is in high school, and while he'll always choose his friends over spending time with the twins and his sister, they all get along. And I'm happy to help Griffin out since his schedule is irregular.

"Thanks," Griffin says with a nod then looks to Ian. "We were actually thinking of coming in to get something done."

"You and Andi and matching tattoos? You sure? Ink is more permanent than a wedding ring."

Don't I know it. Ian, too. Both of us divorced.

"That's why I want it."

Ian sets his elbows on the table, wiping his teasing smile away. "I knew it was serious. But *that* serious?"

Griffin doesn't hesitate. "Yes."

Honestly, I'm jealous. Of my brother for finding love like that. Of Andi being so lucky to have a man who would answer so immediately and securely. I thought I had that, but I was confused at the time. It took me a long while to realize genuine love didn't come with expectations or conditions. I assumed Craig's control of me was love. I hoped it meant he wanted to take care of me.

Naively, I thought if I was perfect enough, if I pleased him enough, then it would get better. It never did.

And I'd rather be single and struggle than married and unhappily kept.

"You going to get down on one knee soon?" I ask, leaning my elbow on the table, angling my body to face Griffin.

"Eventually," he says confidently, "but not right now. We need to see how her career's going to play out. We're in no rush."

"As long as she has your name tattooed on her skin," Ian adds, and Griffin doesn't disagree.

"Such cavemen," I mumble with a shake of my head. I have one tattoo, for my mother. My brothers have many more.

"So you're not going to be asking me to put a construction

hat on your shoulder anytime soon?" Ian asks after a sip of coffee, and I toss a sugar packet at him.

"I told you. It. Was. One. Time."

He nods sarcastically, and when I turn to my formerly favorite brother, he shrugs. "Kind of hard to believe, that's all."

I let out a frustrated growl and comb my fingers through my hair, tugging slightly, earning a snicker from Ian. I aim a glare at him. "You were the one giving me shit about it the other day. How he's so young. Now suddenly, you want me to jump him?"

"No. Not saying that. But if you're thinking about it...seems like you don't need much pushing."

"No. Not happening, and you can shut your fucking mouth about it."

"Touchy," he murmurs like it's all a big joke, but he relents and updates us on his daughter, Juniper, who has started dating someone. Ian has three kids with his ex-wife—Jasper, Jaybird, and Juniper—but there're also a few stragglers he's collected along the way too. They all work in his tattoo shop and are practically part of the family now. Exactly how Ian wants it.

I suspect the need to keep everyone together comes from our childhood and his divorce. How he couldn't make our father or his wife stay, so he'll do it now. A hero in his own right, in how fiercely he protects his family.

Though, I doubt he'd see it that way since he calls Griffin Captain America. With Griffin's traditional good looks and his chosen career paths, he's a poster boy superhero.

Then there's Roman. The baby. The one who couldn't give a shit about anything or anyone. The one I don't have the time or patience to deal with. While Griffin and I are close, so are Ian and Roman. Or, were.

Since the guy hasn't been around in years, too busy doing whatever-the-hell, he hasn't responded much to anyone, including Ian, who argues that we should give him another chance. That he'll be back. That he's simply sorting himself out.

Okay.

Sure.

I've got enough on my plate without holding my breath for my baby brother to stop acting like such a baby.

Griffin receives a call and tells us he has to get to the fire-house for an emergency. He's off after a quick goodbye, so Ian and I decide to take our time strolling around downtown. Ian's shop is right in the middle of Aster Street, sandwiched between a bakery with *the best* cinnamon buns and a bookstore, run by a woman who cuts us off before we reach Stone Ink.

She smiles at both of us, holding up a pile of mail in her hands. "Special delivery."

"Hey, Nic," Ian says quietly, accepting the envelopes from her. My brother, all six foot three inches and two hundred and some pounds of him, practically melts. He's pure muscle, covered in tattoos, with shoulder-length hair and beard, but the quiet bookshop girl never fails to bring him from bear to cub. And I don't think she has any idea.

She smiles at me. "Hi, Taryn. How're you doing?"

"Good. You?"

"Fine, thanks." She motions to the mail, her attention back on my brother. "I was just dropping these off on my way to grab lunch."

"It's two o'clock," Ian says, checking the time on his phone. "Why didn't you eat yet?"

"Got busy stocking and..."

Ian grunts like the animal he is, but Nicole merely lifts a shoulder. "Anyway. I'll see you later."

I watch my brother watch her cross the street toward the sushi place, and I'm not sure how these two have worked next to each other all these years without ever realizing what's going on between them.

But what do I know? I accidentally slept with my thirty-year-old project manager.

And I don't want to meddle, especially when Nicole is married.

"So," I start, stealing Ian's focus, "I'm going to get back to work."

He squeezes my shoulder affectionately. "See you later, boss."

I head toward The Nest with a wave, taking my time, enjoying the fifteen-minute walk. Being a working single mom of two teenagers doesn't leave me a lot of time to myself, but my therapist makes sure I always schedule daily walks and weekly pottery sessions to release the stress.

Which ratchets up when I step inside the B&B, noticing Dante in the back, talking with one of the contractors. It's his third day on the job, and fortunately for the bottom line, he is impressively efficient and knowledgeable.

Unfortunately for me, I can't stop instinctively finding his lips. They're wide and constantly curled up into a smile. I don't know how he is always *always* smiling.

But suddenly, I'm thinking about how he made me smile last weekend.

How he pressed those lips to the soft and tender flesh between my legs and ate me up like I was his favorite flavor.

As if he can see inside my head and the memories scrolling like a movie, he flashes me his grin, licking those torturous lips of his.

I can't deal with this right now.

And I power walk in the opposite direction.

Chapter 7
Dante

There's something weird about opening the front door of your childhood home as an adult. Like coming home and yet...not. Even weirder to open the door as an adult *living* back at home. Because it's not really. Not anymore. I mean, it always will be, with the scent of my mother's lasagna and the familiar strains of "She's Got a Way" filtering out from the kitchen, but I don't feel like I belong anymore. Even as Mom pokes her head out into the hall, smiling like she hasn't seen me in years when she kissed me goodbye on the cheek this morning, reminding me not to forget my lunch like I'm in sixth grade.

"Hey, Ma."

"Right on time." She wipes her hands on a towel before gesturing me to the kitchen. I drop my gym bag in the corner and let myself be tugged into a chair opposite Dad.

He's glued to his phone and barely acknowledges me with a "Good day?"

I scoot my chair closer to the table. "Yeah. Making good progress on the B&B project."

He nods and then quiets, attention on his screen as he picks up his fork to cut into the lasagna.

Mom brings me a plate, along with a bowl of salad. She knows I hate when my food touches. And, yeah, I'm absolutely spoiled. The whole having home-cooked meals and my laundry done is great. That part about her being all up in my business again is not so much.

"So, how was the gym?" she asks, taking a seat next to me with her own serving.

"Fine."

"You've been going there a lot lately."

I shrug, stabbing a forkful of tomato and lettuce. "Every day. No more than usual."

"Yeah, but you're going for a long time, huh?"

I lift my eyes, considering her observation. I haven't purposely been extending my workouts, but I guess I have. Needing to expend some of this restless energy and keep myself busy so I'm not here.

"Staying in shape for Kim?" she guesses, and I huff a sarcastic laugh.

"No."

"No?" She frowns. She loved my ex-girlfriend. "You don't think you'll get back together?"

Dad actually sets his phone down for this, listening. I'm the only one of his sons left who hasn't paired off. Clearly, that means I'm deficient. Then again, he's always seen me that way.

"I doubt it," I say, aiming the words at my plate. Not because I'm embarrassed, but because I don't really want to talk about it.

"Why not?" Dad asks, and I cut into my lasagna.

"Because she made it clear she doesn't want to be with me, and I'm not going to wait around for someone who doesn't want me."

He makes a dubious sound that's more disappointed than encouraging. As if he thinks I should wait for her. As if he thinks I can't do any better.

Mom wraps her hand around my arm. "But you loved her, didn't you?"

I'm not so sure about that. I thought I did, but I haven't been crying into my Cheerios about it. In truth, I haven't thought about her much at all besides how much of a pain in the ass it's been to disrupt my life.

"She said she wasn't ready to settle down, and I am. That's it."

Dad heaves a sigh with a shake of his head. "She wasn't ready to settle down, or she wasn't ready to settle down with *you?*"

"Robert," my mom chides, but he ignores her.

"How the hell do you plan on settling down with someone when you're living at home with your parents? What? Are you gonna move them in here with us? C'mon."

I feel my face heat up and I grip my fork tighter, but before I can say anything, my mother smacks her hand on the table, telling my dad, "Knock it off."

He doesn't. He only flashes his irritation at her instead. "You coddle him too much."

"This is our son," she hisses, and I'd rather have my pubes plucked out one by one than sit here and listen to them talk about me like I'm not in the room. I'm thirty fucking years old, and still, they make me feel like I'm three.

Dad rolls his eyes, muttering something about *our son being an idiot,* and I move to stand, but Mom stops me, tightening her grip on my forearm. "Stay. Eat."

I'd rather not, but if I don't, it'll only wind her up more, which will then piss my father off even more. So instead of leaving, I stuff my face as fast as possible and bring my plate to the dishwasher because, unlike Robert Moretti Sr., I respect my mother and the work she does enough to clean up after myself.

When I pick up the sponge to squirt dish soap onto it, intending to wash the glass dish she cooked the lasagna in, Mom stops me, forcibly turning me to her. "You'll find somebody when the time is right."

I nod, pasting on a smile because I don't want her to think she's making it worse. But she is making it worse.

What I really want to hear is *Fuck everything your father said. Fuck him and fuck anyone who's ever called you stupid. You're not stupid. You're perfect.*

What I get, though, is worry about getting married. Since I can't possibly remain on my own. I'm too dumb for that. I need someone to lead me around by my nose.

Even if she doesn't think that, it's what all her hovering feels like.

But I can't say any of that out loud. I'd make her feel like shit and reinforce to my father that I'm some pansy-ass kid incapable of doing anything on my own. I'm too emotional.

Well...I am emotional. There is no argument against it.

And I can't read well. That is a fact.

There is nothing I can do about any of it.

"Go on upstairs," Mom tells me, and I don't argue or insist on staying to do the dishes. I hightail it up to my bedroom and head directly to the bathroom I used to share with my brothers, where I turn the shower spray on hot and strip down, washing away the sweat and grime from the day. But I can't wash away the feelings of inadequacy that follow me like a shadow whenever I'm in this house. It's impossible to ignore it, especially now that I'm back. At least as a child, my father wasn't so in my face about how I'll never measure up to his expectations. I have no excuses as an adult, so he has no reason to hide his disdain for me.

I close my eyes, leaning my forehead against the cool tile, and that's when I think of her.

Taryn.

How she came into work today in tight-fitting pants and a white shirt that hugged her tits underneath a cardigan. And I had a hard time not staring at her.

She caught me a time or two...or ten. Whatever.

She's hot.

It's so easy to recall her naked skin and how shy she'd been at first when I was in her bedroom. How she'd hesitated to take off her top and bra, how she tried to hide her soft belly and the scar on her abdomen with her hands. As if I'd find any part of her ugly.

Good god. The woman is perfect.

Soft all over with thighs and hips that depressed when I squeezed my fingers into them. What red-blooded male who likes women doesn't want to grit his teeth and just fucking... fuck? It was so hard for me to go slow that night, when all I wanted was to flip her over, grab those sweet little love handles of hers, and go to town.

Women spend so much time worrying about cellulite and fat when we only care about pussy.

I mean, really. All the rest is simply gift wrapping.

And what a present Taryn Stone is.

Tall with long legs and big tits I want to bury my face between. Suck on those perfect golden-brown nipples all night. And she can't deny how she liked to be bossed around. I knew it.

Felt it.

A woman like her is in charge of everything all the time. Because she's good at being the boss, and rightly so. She deserves the recognition. But she also needs to relax occasionally. Be treated like the royalty she is.

Wrapping my hand around my straining cock, I recall our night together and the way she felt beneath me, the way she moaned in pleasure and writhed when I put my mouth on her. I can still taste her. Like drinking the most expensive bottle of wine on a perfectly sunny day at the beach. That's what Taryn tastes like. Heaven. Soft and warm, wet and delicious. Earth, salt, and honey.

I give my dick a rough squeeze, groaning quietly when I remember the feel of her fingers in my hair and how her thighs tensed around my head, the way she clenched down on my fingers and my cock when I pushed inside her. How she arched her neck and held me close, urging me on. Taryn knew what she wanted; she only had to allow herself to have it.

After soaping up my hand, I stroke up and down my length, spreading my feet, anchoring myself to the floor even as my mind takes me back to those too-few short hours with her. Teasing and flirting and finally kissing those lips of hers. Bittersweet dark chocolate. She is everything. Curves and confidence and a no-bullshit attitude.

I imagine her beneath me now, her legs wrapped around my waist, her nails digging into my back. I imagine her on top of me, riding me, her head thrown back in ecstasy. I imagine finally getting her on her knees and sinking balls deep.

I stroke faster, my breath coming in quick gasps. I'm close, so close. And then I think about her face, her rare smile, her even rarer laugh. And that's all it takes. I come hard, squeezing my eyes shut to the pleasure and pain of it all.

After a moment, I shift, standing directly under the showerhead, letting the water wash over me, sending the evidence of my orgasm down the drain, before I turn off the water and step out of the shower. I towel off then wrap it around my waist as I walk into my bedroom. And that's when I see it. A text from Taryn.

> In case I don't tell you, thank you for the good work you're doing.

My duchess, such a softie.

Chapter 8
Dante

Since I'm the project manager for multiple sites, I'm not at The Nest every day, but I park my truck outside today to check in with the electricians who are installing all the new equipment after we gutted the place, working as quickly as possible so Taryn isn't left without a kitchen that long. The subcontractors got the new floors in, fixed the small leak in the ceiling, and are now working on the wiring.

With two coffees in hand—I'd learned Taryn has a bit of a sweet tooth and brought her coffee with lots of cream and sugar —I head in through the back, greeting the workers in both English and Spanish. I can't read worth a damn, but my accent for an easy *Qué onda?* is pretty good.

"For me?" Raf asks in his thick accent, jutting his chin to my second coffee, and I laugh.

"Get the fuck outta here. Where's the buñuelos you promised me?"

"Carla is baking this weekend," he says with a smack to my back.

"Yeah, I'll believe it when I see it."

He waves at me with a congenial smile, saying offhandedly, "Jefe is upstairs."

Technically, I'm Raf's boss, like all the other subcontractors, but Taryn is the *big* boss. And she runs a tight ship.

I take the steps two at a time and find her in the hall, speaking to a housekeeper in low tones, and I patiently wait until she's done to hand over her coffee. She accepts it with brows raised up to her hairline, her mouth curved in a surprised little O.

"No one's ever brought you coffee before?" I ask, a little grumpily because that's shit.

"No one besides my brothers."

I still don't like that, and I huff. "I would've brought you breakfast, but I didn't know if you have any food allergies. Do you have food allergies?"

"No, I don't, but you don't need to do that."

"I want to."

She steps past me into one of the bedrooms. "I don't want you to."

I pivot to lean against the doorframe, watching as she sips from the coffee before setting it down on the little table in the corner. "Taste okay?"

"It's good, thank you." She starts to peel back the bedding, her voice sharp as a knife when she says, "You can leave now."

"I'm good, thank you."

I can hear her eye roll as she yanks on the quilt. Next are the bedsheets, my eyes glued to her as she strides around to the other side of the bed so she's facing me when she bends at the waist. It's not my fault I have a direct line of sight down her sweater when it gapes, but I do take advantage.

"Eyes up," she says, and I take my time, meeting her gaze.

I smile. "You look very pretty today."

"Stop it." She straightens and tosses the sheet on the floor, and what I wouldn't give to throw her on top of the building pile. Get rid of that sweater and pull the cups of her bra down. "You promised you'd be professional."

I lift my arm, gazing around innocently. "I think I am. I'm well within my rights to compliment you."

She closes her eyes and takes a big breath, one I hear all the way across the room. "You're incorrigible."

When she flicks her eyes open once again, I lift my coffee to my mouth. "You're gonna have to define that one for me."

"Unable to be reformed."

I waggle my eyebrows. "Accurate."

She can't hide the tremor of her lips, and I take it as a win, moving to step into the room, but I hear a muffled yell from downstairs. "La migra!"

Taryn whips her head toward the window, before running past me. "You know all the workers?"

I follow her down the hall. "Yeah."

"You know who's undocumented?"

"No."

"Get anyone out of here who might be," she says, flying down the stairs, catching the two officers before they can enter her building, one hand on the door, the other on her hip. All the panic in her voice is gone as she straightens her spine and lifts her head. "Hi there. How can I help you today?"

I rush back to the kitchen, noticing Raf is gone, but a handful of other workers are jockeying for space to see what's going on with Taryn. I turn, interested myself, and silently pump my fist as she blocks the door. "Rafael Parilla? I don't know who that is."

I don't hear what the ICE officers are saying, but she stands her ground, a spine of steel.

"No, I'm sorry," she says, loud enough that I think anyone

in a three-block radius can hear. "You gentlemen cannot come in without a warrant."

Behind me, the workers murmur. They're proud of her too.

"We need to look around," one of them says, but Taryn doesn't budge because she's a fucking rock star. Although I can't merely stand here anymore when they shift, attempting to get inside.

And, no. Nope. Not happening.

I clomp across the floor, making each step in my work boots heavier than it needs to be, so I pull their attention. It's two older white guys, decked out like they're going to war as opposed to standing on the porch of a century-old home in the middle of West Chester, PA, "a charming small town with a historic downtown," according to the pamphlet on Taryn's desk. I fold my arms over my chest, making myself as big as possible behind her. "You heard the boss. No warrant, no entry."

They look me up and down and back away, narrowing their gaze on Taryn. The taller of the two juts his finger at her. "We'll be back. With a warrant."

My first instinct is to jump in front of her, but she wiggles her fingers at them, a sarcastic smile gracing her face. "Nice seeing you, fellas. Have the day you deserve." Then she slams the door on them, muttering, "Motherfuckers."

A moment passes before she lifts her focus to me. "That was..."

"Fucking awesome," I finish for her, grinning. "You were incredible."

She laughs, a shaky sound, and walks past me to the check-in desk, and I tell all the guys in the kitchen to take five, leaving Taryn and me alone. She plops down in the chair and yanks open a drawer to find a bag of mixed gummy candies. She rips it open and plucks out two gummy worms. She sticks one between her teeth, stretching it until it breaks in half, and I don't know why I find that so hot.

She's welcome to bite me and break me in half anytime.

Catching me staring, she holds out the bag. "Want some?"

I shake my head. I don't really feel like eating at the moment, too nauseated about what just happened. "You've got your own candy drawer."

"For emergencies." Then she stuffs another worm into her mouth and takes another three. "I have a bad habit of eating without thinking, so I have to hide it. Otherwise, I'd eat a pound of this a day, and I don't have the money to support a candy addiction."

I make a mental note of the Gray's Candy label and decide I'll stop by to make sure she's always stocked up. I check my phone—for what, I don't know—but my nerves are jangled.

Taryn seems okay, at least, going ham on the poor worms. But I can only guess it's her stress relief. After a while, she turns to me. "You know Rafael well?"

I nod and sit on the edge of the desk, close enough that her foot rests against my calf when she crosses her legs. I don't move. Neither does she.

"I've known him for years. He's in his forties, married with kids. His wife, Carla, works in healthcare. She's a home care nurse, I think."

Taryn nods, swallowing another piece of candy. "He's the guy doing the electrical work?"

"Yep. He's the best. I've worked with this electrical company for a long time because I trust them. I trust Rafael."

She looks down at the bag of candy, her fingers playing with the edge. "What do you think will happen to him?"

I sigh, running a hand through my hair. "I don't know. I truly don't know anything about his immigration status, but even if I did, it doesn't matter. He's a good person. He's lived here for...I don't know. At least a dozen years or so, from all the conversations I've had with him. I just..."

She looks up at me, eyes round and worried. "You feel responsible, don't you?"

I shrug, trying to play it off, but I guess I do. This is my site. This is my project he's working on.

She puts the candy away and stands up, inching closer to me. "It's not your fault."

I know that, and yet... "I don't know what to do. I don't know how to help."

She curves her palm around my cheek, lifting my face up, her normally angular features soft. "It'll be okay."

"You don't know that," I rasp, emotion clogging my throat, and she surprises me by wrapping her arms around my shoulders, urging my head down, and I bury my face against her neck. When I accidentally brush my lips over her pulse point, she doesn't move. So I do it again on purpose, her skin warm and too tempting not to kiss, but she stops me before I can, leaning away. Her fathomless dark eyes roam over my face, and I could get lost in them, searching, learning, drawing out every desire and need.

"Dante," she whispers, not quite an invitation but not exactly a reprimand either. I press my forehead to hers, our noses brushing, her breath smelling sweet like the candy, and it's near impossible to stop myself from taking a sip from her decadent mouth.

And yet somehow I do.

I stop.

She wanted me to be professional, and after what just happened, I need to check in with Raf. I need to talk to all the workers. I have a job to complete.

For myself and for her, I wrap my fingers around her upper arms to gently push her back, making room for me to stand up.

So close to each other, she's forced to tilt her head back a bit, and I'd be a liar if I said I didn't like that.

With a smile, I remind her, "You left your coffee upstairs."

She clears her throat, and it's a small consolation to know she's not as unaffected by me as she likes to pretend.

"See you later, duchess."

Chapter 9
Taryn

To say my divorce was contentious would be an understatement. After nearly ten years of marriage, most of which were unhappy, and having two kids, whom he didn't take much interest in, I thought Craig would sign the papers without a fight. But that son of a bitch fought me every single step of the way. Looking back now, I understand cruelty was the point. He wanted to punish me. Make me spend more money on the lawyer fees, extend arbitration as long as possible, and force me into giving him hours of custody, when in reality, he could not give two shits how often he got the kids.

So it is no surprise when I receive a text that he can't pick up Maddie, but it is no less frustrating. At least he texted me, as opposed to up and forgetting about our daughter, which he's done in the past. Straight up left her at McDonald's when he had a work phone call. He was too busy taking care of whatever the fuck to realize he'd walked to his car without Maddie, not even noticing until he arrived at his office. By then, our nine-year-old daughter had been left completely alone, scared and crying.

It was the reason I got her a cell phone and therapy.

We're all in therapy now, but that was the tipping point. I decided I had to stop acting as if he would ever change. He wouldn't. Even for his own children. I've learned to rely on myself—and lean on my family from time to time.

I look up from my work when the front door of The Nest opens to find Ian and Maddie. He tosses his thumb her way. "Found this wandering around outside. Looked familiar. Does it belong to you?"

Maddie giggles at my brother's teasing, and I usher them both inside. With my arm around my daughter, I walk them to the kitchen, which is newly refurbished and back in working order. "Thanks for picking her up," I tell Ian as I retrieve the half gallon of chocolate milk from the fridge to pour some out for Maddie. "Do you want something to eat or drink?"

He shakes his head, his focus skipping around the room. "I can't believe this got done already."

"I know." I brush my hand over Maddie's hair as she gulps down the milk. "Did you finish your homework?"

She nods, and Ian helps himself to a lap around the kitchen. "I helped her with math." Then he notes, "You even got a new ceiling."

When he turns his curious gaze on me, I shrug. "Dante does good work."

Ian smirks. "I bet he does."

"Shut up."

"I'd like to talk to him. It's always nice to have a contractor's name in the back pocket in case of emergencies."

Ever since ICE knocked on the door last week, Dante has been coming every day, not only to check in on the progress, but also to work. With whatever needs doing, he jumps right in.

It's frustrating how good he is at his job, making *my* job of ignoring my attraction to him all the more difficult.

Competent in his skills and kind to everyone. What a considerate pain in the ass.

At that exact moment, the pain in my ass saunters into the kitchen, sweaty and covered in sawdust, wiping his forehead with a bandanna he always keeps in his pocket unless it's wrapped around his forehead like some 1980s action hero. It's gross, really, how cute he is. Like, he shouldn't be. But he is.

"Hey," he says, noticing his audience, and he tucks the sweaty bandanna away before skimming his hands down his jeans. "Sorry to interrupt. I only wanted to grab a water."

"Why are you still here?" I ask, double-checking the time. "It's almost five."

He waves the question away. The crew left around three, as usual. He should have as well.

Charitable asshole.

Ian cuts Dante off, sticking out his hand. "We've never been formally introduced. I'm Ian Stone."

"Dante Moretti."

They shake hands, sizing each other up.

"Seems like you're doing a great job here," Ian says. "You've managed to do the impossible and impress my sister."

Dante flashes an irritating smile my way. "My new mission in life."

Ian slaps his shoulder. "She could use some impressing."

I stick up my middle finger behind Maddie's back as he asks Dante about a business card. They exchange information, and I definitely don't pay attention to the fit of Dante's jeans or how the sleeves of his T-shirt mold to his biceps. Instead, I ask Maddie about her day and what she wants for dinner. We haven't fully restocked the kitchen, but there is enough food for sandwiches with an assortment of chips, dips, and fruit.

After Ian finishes his conversation with Dante, he drops a kiss to Maddie's head and one to my cheek for good measure. "Let me know how Jake does."

"I will," I promise and lean against the counter.

Dante moves toward me, motioning to Maddie. "And who's this?"

"My daughter." I reach out for the pickle jar she can't open, but Dante beats me to it, popping it open without any effort.

I shouldn't swoon.

And yet, I do.

Inwardly, at least.

"Thanks," Maddie says quietly when he hands the jar back, ducking down to her level.

"I'm Dante. What's your name?"

"Madeline. Maddie, I mean."

"Madeline, that's pretty."

That earns him a small, shy smile.

"You mind if I have one of your pickles?" When she shakes her head, he uses a fork to scoop one out, biting into the spear with a crunch. "Mm, my favorite. I love pickles."

"Me too," she volunteers, and of course, the one guy my daughter isn't afraid of is the one I'm trying to stay away from. Maddie has always been on the shier side and is especially distrustful of men—thank you, Craig—but Dante eases into conversation with her.

"So, Mads, what grade are you in?"

"Seventh."

He nods. "I don't remember seventh grade much. You like it?"

She shrugs. "It's okay. It's harder than last year."

After I make Maddie a sandwich, I slide the loaf of bread, along with turkey and cheese, across the counter to Dante so he can help himself. As he builds his sandwich, he says, "I was always so bad at school. Everything was hard for me. I have a reading disability, so I got pulled out of classes a lot for help. I had an IEP—"

"My one friend has an IEP," Maddie cuts in.

"Oh yeah? I used to feel really bad about it when I was in school 'cause I was afraid of what people would think about me, but nobody really cared."

The way Dante so casually talks about something that shaped him as a person is both endearing and worrying. Because no one should feel bad about needing accommodations, but his voice is filled with a forced cheerfulness that I can see right through. I'd like the names of anyone who's ever made him feel less than perfect.

Because that's what he is.

Much to my dismay.

"So, even though school might be hard for you, it's okay," he continues before biting into his sandwich, speaking around a mouthful. "It's okay to ask for help."

Maddie nods. "My cousin, Gracie—she's my best friend, and she's in sixth grade—she's so good at school, she can help me out with my work."

Dante eats like a drunk panda bear, stuffing as much of the sandwich into his mouth as he can. I don't know why I find it so adorable.

"Nice. It's cool she'll help you. You got a lot of cousins?"

"I have..." Maddie rolls her eyes up to the ceiling. "Five cousins."

"I got about that many too." Dante laughs. "You get along with them?"

She nods. "Yeah. It's fun. We have parties and picnics together and stuff."

"Your family sounds awesome."

"What's your family like?"

"Not as cool as yours." He glances my way and smiles, a bite of the sandwich hanging out of his mouth.

I roll my eyes.

What a goof.

Perfect, adorable, maddening goof.

He turns back to my daughter and polishes off his sandwich. "So, what's up? Give me the tea of seventh grade. Who's dating who? Who's having the parties?"

"Oh my god." I pointedly step into his space. "You're as bad as Clara." Then I set my hand on Maddie's back, reminding her, "You have lots of time for dating and parties when you're older."

Dante raises his fingers to the corner of his mouth, stage-whispering, "You can tell me later."

Maddie giggles and agrees with a nod as I sigh. "Finish up, sweetie. We need to leave soon for Jake's game."

Dante leans back, his palms pressing into the counter, the soft cotton of his shirt clinging to the contours of his chest and stomach. As if I needed reminding of how fit he is. "What game?"

Maddie swallows her bite, eager to fill him in. "Jake's soccer game. He's really good."

"Yeah?" Dante slants his curious eyes to me. "Where does he get the athletic gene from?"

Maddie pipes up before I can respond. "Mom used to play soccer in college. She was really good too."

Dante's gaze slides over to me, a slow perusal that has my body heating up despite my best efforts to remain apathetic to him. I can practically see the gears turning in his head, and I don't want to imagine what he's thinking. I'm actively trying to avoid thinking of him the same way, but it's hard when he looks at me like that.

I drag my hands through my hair, lifting the strands off my hot neck. "We should get going. Don't want to be late."

Dante pushes off the counter, putting the cold cuts and pickles back in the refrigerator. "What about you, Mads? You into sports like your brother?"

Maddie shakes her head, her ponytail swaying. "I like dancing and singing."

Dante's face lights up with a genuine smile. "Yeah? That's awesome. You any good?"

Since she's mid-chew, she shrugs. I'm so happy my daughter found hobbies she loves, but the poor kid isn't very good at them. Though what she lacks in skill, she makes up for with enthusiasm. Maddie beams. "I have a recital every year for dance, and my school does a spring musical. I don't know what it is yet, but I heard it might be *The Wiz*."

I hide my grimace. A bunch of mostly kids butchering "Ease on Down the Road." *Great.*

Dante holds his fist out for Maddie to bump. "You let me know the dates, and I'll come check it out." He glances at me. "As long as your mom says it's okay."

Maddie bounces on her toes. "Yeah, okay."

"Come on." I usher her out. "We gotta get going." I toss a quick goodbye over my shoulder to Dante, who's watching us, and I'm not sure I'll ever get used to his steady gaze. Like he's content to merely look. Like he's interested in every little thing I do.

So annoying.

I put on my jacket and loop my purse over my shoulder, calling out to Alec, the night manager, that I'm leaving and head out. Once we're settled in my car and buckled in, Maddie leans forward, casually observing, "Dante's nice."

"Mm-hmm. Yep." *Famous last words.*

At the field, Maddie and I find seats toward the middle,

cheering for Jake as he takes position as midfielder. He's tall and fast with long strides, able to outrun his opponents. My siblings and I all played sports when we were younger, but Roman and I were the only ones to play in college. My little brother was offered a full ride for football. And then blew it. But...whatever.

I'm woman enough to admit it pisses me off that he was given what I wanted and he threw it all away. I would have loved to be offered a free ride, but I had to work hard, study every night, apply for scholarships and grants of all kinds, and still came out with debt. I'm also the only one with a college degree, even though it doesn't mean much. My mother raised all of us to know education isn't about how smart a person is; it's about how willing they are to learn.

Soccer provided me an outlet and a little bit of a scholarship, and while I used to dream of playing at the Olympics and had a poster on my bedroom wall of Brandi Chastain ripping off her shirt after her game-winning goal, that was never in the cards for me. Instead, I sought out a useful degree in marketing and allowed myself to follow my passions with a minor in visual arts from Penn State. It was there I met Craig, a guy who swept me off my feet. A man who had his sights on expanding his family's business of real estate and homebuilding. He was handsome and fun, and after living most of my life without a dad, his ability to pay for everything for me was nice. It wasn't until after we were married that his ability to pay for everything meant I couldn't do anything without his permission.

My mother passed away not long after I graduated college, and in the difficult months of grieving after her death, I accepted his offer to work for his family's company. When I got pregnant with Jake, it was Craig's idea for me to work part time from home, and by the time I had Maddie, I was used to giving in to his whims. To doing all the heavy lifting at home while still working for the company, but because I was "at home," he assumed I should be able to do it all. He never lifted a hand to help. Never went to the grocery store. Never folded a piece of clothing. Never even made dinner while I recovered from my cesarean with Maddie.

He was too busy. Too tired. Too goddamn selfish to ever offer physical support, let alone emotional support. When I finally asked for a divorce, he told me it was my fault. I was giving up. He said he would've gone to couples counseling, so when I offered to do that, he said no, it was too late.

It's comical. The knots some men will tie themselves into simply to make the woman the villain.

I know the moment Craig shows up to the game because Maddie elbows my side, tucking her cell phone away. She got bored and was watching videos, but she probably assumed that would bother her father. Because he's an ass who doesn't care about his kids' wants or needs, only his own.

Craig is six feet tall and lean, and he still looks the same as he did twenty years ago but bald. He started shaving his head as soon as his hair began thinning when he turned thirty. He doesn't acknowledge Maddie or me when he sits down a few feet from us, but he does cup his hands around his mouth, shouting for Jake to step it up. On the field, my son spins in our direction and lifts his hand, but I can see a subtle change in him when he spots his dad. Maddie, I think, still hopes her dad will notice her. Still longs for a relationship with him. But I've had conversations with Jake about Craig since he was younger. About the time puberty hit, I told Jake that even though he might not want to talk to me because I am a woman, he could come to me about anything he was feeling, ask me any questions about the changes happening in his body, but I probably wouldn't be able to answer them as well as his dad could.

Jake told me, quite matter-of-factly, that he would prefer to talk to me, and that if I didn't know the answer, he would ask one of his uncles before he asked his dad.

So.

Here we are.

One big dysfunctional family.

"Don't back down, Jake!" Craig shouts. "Attack the ball!"

Next to me, Maddie shoots me a questioning glance, and I nod. She smiles and moves down the bench. "Hi, Dad."

Craig turns, finally acknowledging her. "Hey, Madeline. Sorry I couldn't pick you up. I had a meeting go long at work."

"That's okay." She's like a little sunflower, always seeking the light, even when the light doesn't shine back. "Since we'll be at your house this weekend, I was wondering if I could go to my friend's house. She's having a Halloween party and—"

"Yeah. Whatever. We'll talk about it later. Let's go, Jake!"

I see the hurt flicker across her face, the way she shrinks back, retreating into herself. I want to reach out, to pull her into a hug, to tell her she deserves better, that she is worthy of love and attention. But I know that's not what she needs right now. She needs her father to see her, to acknowledge her, to love her. And I can't make him do that.

I sigh and refocus my attention on the field, watching as Jake steals the ball from an opposing player, dribbling it down the field with ease before passing it off to the center, who scores. The ref blows the whistle, signaling the end of the game. Jake's team won, 3-1, and his eyes shine with pride as he high-fives his teammates. I stand up, cheering, and Maddie joins in, her earlier hurt momentarily forgotten. Craig stands too, a smug smile on his face, like he's the one who won the game.

Jackass.

The stands empty out as the friends and families of the players meet them. Jake trots off the field, his eyes scanning the crowd. They land on me first, a soft smile playing on his lips. I mouth "Good job," and he nods, his smile growing wider.

Then his gaze shifts to Craig, and I see the tension return, the way his shoulders stiffen, his smile falters. Craig gives him a hard clap on his back. "Nice work, bud."

Jake doesn't respond, moving to my side as my ex-husband goes on, like he's the best daddy in the whole world. "Ready to go home? We'll order dinner."

As if he does anything else besides order dinner. The man suffers from learned helplessness. God forbid he Google how to cook a meal. Or go to the grocery store. Whenever I would ask him to help me, his common reply was, "But I'll burn it." Or, "I don't know where anything is. It would be quicker if you just went shopping."

Jake hugs me, thanking me for coming, and I kiss his cheek. "Of course. You looked great out there. I love you."

"Love you too," he says, his voice stuck somewhere between a young kid and a man. Maddie hugs me goodbye, her arms tight around my waist. I kiss the top of her head. "Have fun with your dad, okay?"

She nods then goes to Jake's side as they follow Craig. He didn't acknowledge me. As usual. I don't exist to him unless he needs me for something. Like not being able to pick up Maddie.

Sometimes it sucks living the life of a divorced single mom.

And I would never go back.

Chapter 10
Dante

"Are you even listening to me?"

I force my gaze back to my father from where I'd been staring out at the window in a daze. "Yeah."

He huffs a sarcastic sound. "Do you have any idea how much your screw-up on the masonry order is going to set us back?"

I do, actually. Because I was the one who brought my mistake to his attention. Not that I expected a different reaction, but he had to know. This has happened before. Me fucking up and him yelling at me. I tune him out as he loses steam so that he can pretend like he didn't treat his employee, let alone his son, like he was a piece of shit.

I'm used to it by now.

And maybe, if I could put my big boy pants on, I'd quit or tell him to shove his company up his ass, but...

"I thought I handled it," I mumble, trying to maintain some semblance of confidence under his relentless glower.

"Thought? That's just it! You *thought*. That's your whole problem. Now we're at risk of missing our deadline and losing the contract!" Dad slams his fist against the table, causing a few family photos to rattle, and I dip my chin, holding back an irritated sigh. We won't lose the contract, and we will meet the deadline because I caught the wrong order in time. The delivery of the stone will be a few days late, but it'll be fine.

I lift my phone, checking the time. I don't have a meeting, but I use one as an excuse. "I need to appointment with contractors downtown."

He waves me away, already busy with something else. I'm a mere irritant. A fly. A bug he'd like to finally get rid of.

I don't say goodbye, but I do offer a smile to his assistant on the way out of the office, and I take a full, deep breath once I'm back in the truck. What I'd really like to do is go take a ride on my bike and relieve some of the tension in my bones, but I can't. I need to check in at The Nest. With the kitchen finished, we've moved on to tearing down the walls and opening up the space, before we'll go on to the bedrooms next month.

I take my time driving downtown with the windows open, letting the cold air cool my overheated skin and stop at Cuppa Jo for Taryn's coffee order then hit up Gray's Candy for a couple bags of gummy bears, worms, and Swedish Fish.

When I arrive at the B&B, I take a minute to talk with the workers. I'm informed Raf has had trouble renewing his green card, and he hasn't been back to work since ICE showed up. I hate that he's losing all those wages, but I'd been told he found an immigration lawyer to try to help. For now, he's lying low. I've spent a lot of nights thinking about him, and I still feel bad, but I've had to push through, finding a new electrician to work on this project and finish it on time for Taryn.

Walking through The Nest now is second nature. After three weeks, I've learned where every squeaky board is and that Taryn takes her personal phone calls in the laundry room, which is where I find her, stomping around. She huffs and puffs, tossing bedding around with more force than necessary, banging the dryer door closed. She pivots around, finally spotting me, leaning against the doorjamb. Her chocolate eyes scan me from head to toe and then back to my hands holding her coffee and candy. I know she wants them even as she folds her arms over her chest. She's got on an oversized sweater, soft and woven, and I'd like to put my head on her tits. Take a nap.

"What's wrong?" I ask, offering her my gifts.

"Nothing." She reaches for the candy first, tossing a bunch of Swedish Fish into her mouth. "Thank you."

"You're very welcome. Now, wanna tell me why you're in here beating up the laundry?"

"Not particularly."

I step into the room and close the door, shutting out the sound of the crew working, keeping out the lingering smell of sawdust and paint, leaving only Taryn's soft breaths and the smell of coffee and sugar. I close the distance between us and set her coffee down on the washer behind her then place my hands on the machine, boxing her in. Her mouth parts, pupils dilating, and it would be so easy to duck my head and taste the skin of her throat, suck on that spot under her jaw that makes her moan so sweetly.

She is so sweet.

Even when she's angry.

"What's wrong?" I ask, and she shakes her head.

"It's not a big deal."

"You're a terrible liar, duchess."

"Don't call me that."

"Don't tell me everything's fine when it's not. How can I help?"

"Jesus," she snaps. "What is your deal?" She shoulders past me, bumping me out of the way, and turns so her back is to the door. "Why are you so pushy?"

I don't expect her to trust me implicitly, but after working together, I would think we're at least on friendly terms. More than acquaintances. And after I fucked her in her bed, I would hope she believes I wouldn't hurt her.

But whatever series of unfortunate events has led her to be this untrusting can't be undone in a few days, so I try again. "Listen. If you really don't want to tell me, you don't have to. I just want you to know that if it's something about this place—" I circle my hand, encompassing the whole of the bed-and-breakfast "—I'll help you with whatever you need. And if it's something else, I'd be happy to lend an ear to listen or a shoulder to cry on or a fist if we need to go take care of business. Know what I mean?"

The corner of her mouth twitches, and I smile, chucking two gummy worms her way. She catches them, biting into one viciously. She chews and swallows before twirling the bottom half in the air as she explains, "My tenant got engaged last night."

"And we're not happy about that?"

She stuffs the rest of the worm into her mouth with a cute little growl. "No. I'm happy for her."

"Yeah. Sounds like it."

She throws her second worm back at me. "She wants to move in with him now, which is great, I guess."

I muffle my laugh by eating the candy. "So great."

Much to my satisfaction, she crosses the room to stand next to me, picking up her coffee, sipping from it with an even more satisfied sigh. Her shoulders drop, eyes close. And I feel eighteen feet tall for how I'm able to provide her even a few seconds of comfort. I wait, silently observing, her throat working as she drinks, the shake of her right foot that she has crossed over her left, and I wonder if the action is her nervous tic, her sign of stress.

"I was counting on that money," she says eventually. "I'll need to find a new renter."

I wrench away. "You need to find a new renter?"

She frowns at me as if she doesn't understand my sudden grin.

"I can be your new renter."

"What? No. Uh-uh. No. *What?*"

I move in front of her, my hands on her shoulders. "I can be your renter."

She shakes her head, adamant. And, honestly, does she not know me by now?

"Come on, babe, you need the money. I need a place to stay. It's a win-win."

"First of all," she says, knocking my hands away, "don't call me babe."

"You prefer duchess? Me too."

"I can't fucking stand you," she says with no heat in her voice. In fact, I think she likes me. More than *likes* me.

Especially because she asks, "Why do you need a place to stay?"

I am immeasurably happy that she's curious about me, but my living at home isn't exactly a topic I want to explain, so I skip over it. "I broke up with my girlfriend a few weeks ago, and I need a new—"

"You *cheated* on her with me?"

Without thinking, I grab her shoulders again. "No. I would never and have never cheated on anyone."

"When did you break up?"

I can't help my growing smile. "Are you concerned for her or me or you?"

She wiggles out of my hold, scrunching up her nose. "*Not* me."

"No? There was no tinge of jealousy in your voice just then?"

She steals the bag of candy and sees herself out of the laundry room. I, of course, follow her. "I'm a great tenant. I'll mow your lawn, take out your trash. Hell, I'll even cook you dinner if you want."

She stops abruptly, pivoting to face me. "Cook me dinner?"

"Yeah." I lean against the wall, casual as can be. "I'm Italian. Make you sauce from scratch."

She rolls her eyes. "I can't have my contractor living in the apartment above my house. It's not appropriate."

I push off the wall, taking a step closer to her. "There's nothing inappropriate about it. I work for you, not *under* you."

Immediately, my mind goes to working under her. Fuck yeah, I'd work so hard.

I think she's imagining the same thing—her sitting on my face—because her cheeks flush pink.

And she struggles to reply, her jaw flapping up and down. So I cut her a break. "You won't even know I'm there. I'll be so good. Scout's honor."

I hold up three fingers, giving her my best innocent smile, and she shakes her head. Though, I can see her resolve wavering, lips twitching, and I press my palms together, silently begging. She eventually closes her eyes with a delightful little growl. "I'll think about it."

I can work with that. I tweak her arm and head over to the crew to see what I can help with.

By lunchtime, we've made good progress inside, so I head

outside to refinish the porch. Which makes Taryn completely incensed when she realizes.

"Why are you doing this? I can't pay for it. This wasn't in the contract or on any list of items we discussed."

I shrug. "Yeah, but the exterior could use some love too."

"It's not in the budget."

"It's on my dime," I tell her, and she fumes.

"This better not be some quid pro quo situation."

"I literally have no idea what that means," I say, adjusting the bandanna I have tied like a headband to catch my sweat. "But this'll be loud, so..."

I hit the power on the sander, and she clamps her hands over her ears, shouting something at me that I can't hear. Though her ass sure does look good as she stomps away from me.

Later, I help carry in a pallet of wood, waving at Taryn to catch her attention. "Look at me being professional at work."

She scowls.

"I can be professional as a tenant too." I waggle my eyebrows, but she doesn't think I'm cute.

A shame.

I thought it was a good line.

And even later, when it's time to punch out, I tap my knuckles on Taryn's makeshift desk until we're done with the renovations on this floor and smile when she glances up. "I'll see you tomorrow. Or, maybe, earlier if you want me to move in upstairs."

Her exhale is pure vexation. And maybe it's my need to please her that has me leaning down, catching her chin between my fingers. "I'm bringing you breakfast tomorrow. Do you want hash browns or potatoes on the side?"

It takes her a second to answer, her brows drawn down, eyes unfocused as they roam my face. "Uh, potatoes."

"You got it." I touch the pad of my thumb to her lower lip, remembering what it was like to touch her clit. Make her mouth pout so prettily in pleasure. "Later, duchess."

Her voice is still dreamy when she answers. "Bye."

I think I won that round.

Chapter 11
Taryn

The doorbell rings, and I curse under my breath. I haven't gotten my "Take One" bowl ready yet, and already, the trick-or-treaters are arriving. I grab my giant mixed bag of chocolates and tear it open, some spilling on the floor in my haste, but when I open the door, it doesn't matter. It's not kids in costumes. It's a package delivery.

I pick up the small box and set the candy down on the kitchen counter, noticing it's from my brother Roman. More than curious, I swiftly and carefully cut through the packing tape and peel back the side to find a Post-it with big sloppy words written out. *Sorry it's late. Happy Birthday*.

I haven't directly spoken to him in a long time, and I'm beyond surprised to receive a gift from him. My breath catches when I tug the item out of the bubble wrap, a small ceramic vase in the shape of Lucy Ricardo from *I Love Lucy* with an opening where her red hair would be for a flower or plant. It's so cute and perfect, and I'm...touched.

A mixture of warmth and melancholy spreads through me as I trace the outline of her painted face, a smile tugging at my lips. Mom and I used to watch *I Love Lucy* together all the time. It was our favorite show, and in a house full of boys, it was our special time together. We cuddled on the couch, eating popcorn and laughing at the ridiculous antics Lucy always pulled off.

This vase isn't just a gift. It's a reminder of those treasured moments.

And for how much I am still so mad at Roman, I will always love him. I pull out my phone and send him a text. **Thanks for the vase. It's perfect.**

I don't expect a reply—Roman's never been one for long conversations or quick responses—so I pocket my phone again in time for Jake to saunter through the front door and into the kitchen, dropping his bag on the floor. He's still sweaty from soccer practice, and I point to the slow cooker in the corner. "Sloppy Joes."

He loosely pumps his fist in the air a few times before moving to help himself, making three sandwiches and taking the entire bag of chips over to the table.

"What are your plans tonight?"

He shrugs.

"Are you sure you don't want to come with us?"

He nods, mouth full.

October 31 falls on a school night this year, and while I think it's totally fine for high school kids to continue trick-or-treating, Jake is much too cool to go. So he'll probably stay home and sleep or do homework or whatever it is fifteen-year-old boys do in their room that I don't want to know or think about.

"Andi's coming over with the twins, and Mari and Clara will probably stop by, and can you please stop shoving whole sandwiches in your mouth like that? You're gonna choke."

He doesn't listen, stuffing Sloppy Joe number two down his throat like he's never eaten in his life. Frankie sits at his side waiting for something to drop, and when it doesn't, he whines until Jake places his plate on the floor for him to lick up before diving into the chips, nearly finishing the whole bag. He is the reason I need to have a renter—to support his appetite.

By the time I've finished breaking down the cardboard box from the delivery, throwing away the garbage, and finding a place for the vase to sit, Jake is done eating. He rushes away without a word. "Hey," I call after him. "Get your bag."

He reverses a few steps, picks up his bag, and then continues. I'm told by the time he graduates he'll find a personality again.

Fingers crossed.

Just as I hear the water turn on upstairs, the doorbell rings again, and I open it up for Andi and Griffin's twins. Logan is his father's mini-me from his hair to his posture, but he's much more gregarious, though he's got blood painted on his face now. I'm not sure what exactly he is, but I'm guessing it's a zombie. Grace painted her face green and has her hair braided underneath her black witch hat with matching dress. The Elphaba to Maddie's Glinda. They're obsessed with the movie. Spent an entire weekend in my living room learning the dances from *Wicked*.

"Thanks for inviting us to tag along with you," Andi says, wearing all black with a cat-ear headband and whiskers drawn on her cheeks. She's young and cute, a little sprite with a Texas twang and really great eyebrows. Meanwhile, I'm an old curmudgeon who can't be bothered to be cute. It's tough enough to find pants that fit. Searching for a costume? No, thank you.

"Yeah. Of course," I reply, knowing my brother is on shift tonight. It's Andi's first Halloween in West Chester, and while she is by no means incapable, my brother specifically told me to invite her and the kids tonight since he couldn't be with them to trick-or-treat. You can take the man out of the SEALs, but you can't take the SEALs out of the man, and "the bigger the group, the better."

I nudge Frankie to stay inside to place the Take One bowl out and then shout upstairs. "Mads! Time to go!"

She races down the steps, passing me by with a quick hello to Andi. She, Grace, and Logan all head out to the sidewalk with their bags, while I call to Jake that we're leaving and lock up. My neighborhood is close to downtown and always has more trick-or-treat activity than Griffin's cookie-cutter development that isn't very walkable.

Once we get going, with the kids leading the way, I turn to Andi. "So, how are you?"

"Good, busy. Logan and Grace are keeping me on my toes with their schedule. I've been trying to write more music, but this year feels a lot different with school. It's a big change for them. And for me too. Settling in has been...challenging."

I nod, understanding. "It's hard to find time for yourself when you're a mom. But you're doing great. The kids are happy, and that's what matters most." A bright smile lights up her face like she might fly away, and I don't understand why. "What?"

"You called me a mom."

I lift my shoulder. "That's what you are."

She bites into her lip, trying and failing to dim her clear and utter happiness as she shakes her head. "Yeah. I am. I guess hearing someone else say it... It feels validating." She glances at me, eyes glassy. "Thank you." She sniffs and waves her hand over her face a few times and takes a big breath as if we're starting the conversation over from the beginning. "How are you? How's the B&B?"

"It's fine. I'm fine."

"You'd say you were fine even if you weren't," she says, and

I hear those words in my head in Dante's voice. Sounds exactly like something he would say. "How are you, really?"

I zip up the vest I have on over my hoodie and stick my hands in the pockets. I suppose this time is as good as any to become better acquainted with the woman I know my brother plans on marrying eventually. "How am I? Tired. A constant state of exhaustion."

"Physically or emotionally?"

I huff, chagrined that she would be able to discern the difference. Then again, I'd guess all women feel perpetually exhausted. Holding up half the sky with less than half the recognition, even though the weight on our shoulders feels a fuck-ton heavier than what I notice men carrying most days.

"My bandwidth is pretty narrow lately," I admit eventually, and she nods, waiting for me to continue. So, I do. "My brothers always tell me to take a nap. As if that'll solve anything."

"I'd venture to guess your brothers are in the top one percent of men, and they still don't get it. Pretty as they are to look at."

That pulls a surprised laugh out of me. I like Andi more and more every time I talk to her, and I don't hesitate to answer her when she asks about the renovations at The Nest. She doesn't act as if she has any knowledge of what happened between Dante and me, and that is one positive of Griffin's personality being that of a brick wall. He knows how to keep his mouth shut.

We continue chatting as we follow the kids down the sidewalk. They run from house to house, filling their bags with candy as we trail behind at a leisurely pace. It's a cool, clear night, and I'm enjoying the fresh air and the company. I can imagine Andi at our monthly wine and whine nights at Tabby Cat with Marianne and Clara. They already love her, so we might as well invite her. But I am not the includer one of the group. That's Clara's role and responsibility.

After we loop back to my house, the kids eagerly dump their haul onto the living room floor. More pounds of candy than any of them can reasonably eat, but they dive in, giving it a good go.

Marianne and Clara show up right as Jake meanders downstairs, and he greets his pseudo aunts with hugs before pilfering a few Snickers bars from Maddie to bring back to his room. When they spot Andi, Clara claps excitedly and takes Frankie's front paws to dance with him, singing a made-up song about candy and girl time.

"All right, hand over the goods," Marianne says to the kids, holding out her hands. "We've got to test it to make sure it's safe."

This is our tradition. Every year, Marianne and Clara "sample" a few pieces of candy to check for tampering. It started when the kids were really little, but now, it's mostly an excuse for them to eat a quarter of the pot.

When the four of us have each stolen some candy, bargaining with the kids for our favorites, we move into the kitchen. Clara starts up her bullshit immediately while unwrapping a blue Jolly Rancher. "Soooo, a little birdie told me you're considering letting Dante rent the apartment."

I heave a sigh. Since I haven't disclosed that information to anyone yet, the little birdie could only be Dante himself.

I will strangle him with his own measuring tape.

"You should do it!" Clara says enthusiastically. Too enthusiastically. "I mean, you need the extra income, and Dante's a great guy."

I scowl at her. "You know this is all your fault."

Her eyes go wide in innocence, hand to her heart. "*My* fault?"

"You pushed us together that night, and you're pushing us together now."

"I wouldn't say *pushing*," she says, poking around the candy in front of her.

Marianne gestures around us. "It feels like you're auditioning for a new Netflix show about matchmaking, and yet there are no cameras."

"Oh my god! I would *love* that."

"I know. You'd be good at it." Marianne smiles at her wife indulgently, and I roll my eyes. Clara and Dante both have that same annoyingly endearing thing of being terribly likable.

Which I hate. As an unlikable woman.

Clara absently places her hand on Marianne's thigh, while the other flits through the air. "All I'm saying is you two had chemistry—"

"Chemistry?" Andi looks between us for an explanation. "With this Dante guy? Who is that?"

"No one," I say, but Marianne jumps in to explain in simple terms.

"He's the contractor of The Nest renovation."

"And one of my best friends from high school," Clara says then lowers her voice, adding, "Tar and Dante hooked up a couple weeks ago."

"I had no idea." Andi gasps, playfully scandalized, and I chuck a Tootsie Roll at Clara. Marianne picks it up to eat.

"Because we don't talk about it," I say, shooting pointed glares at my so-called friends.

Andi leans in to whisper, "Talk about it to other people or right here, because... What's the deal? Are you into him?"

"I am definitely *not* into him."

Marianne eyes me like she doesn't believe me, while Clara shakes her head. "Oh, come on. How could you not be?"

"Easy. It was a one-time thing, and he now works for me. I

told him that it has to be professional between us. No flirting or anything."

Clara snorts. "Good luck with that. That boy can't help himself."

"He's been good so far," I say defensively. "Mostly," I amend, thinking of a few moments that would not be categorized accurately as completely professional.

"And he wants to rent your apartment?" Andi asks, still trying to piece it all together.

"Yeah."

"Well..." Andi pops a Twix into her mouth. "Speaking from experience. Kinda hard to ignore the other person when you're living under the same roof."

Clara clucks her tongue as if that's been her evil plan all along, and for some reason, I find myself justifying it. "Technically, we wouldn't be under the same roof. The apartment is a separate unit. He would have his roof, and I'd have mine."

Marianne props her chin on her hand. "So then, you'll rent to him?"

"Aren't you supposed to be on my side?" I ask, offended. "Thirty years of friendship lost over a man who wears a red bandanna like a headband."

Marianne laughs. "It's more than thirty, and that's actually kinda cute."

That's the whole problem. It *is* cute!

Goddamn it.

"What's he like?" Andi asks to no one in particular, and I assume Clara will jump in, but she doesn't. Merely stares at me instead.

I focus my attention on carefully balling up the empty candy wrappers. "He's competent and surprisingly thoughtful." I recollect the conversation he had with Maddie the other day. "He's patient and..."

"Kinda hot," Marianne cuts in when I trail off, my mind on his smile, glistening wet after he went down on me during our night together. When he sucked and licked and fucked me with his tongue like it was his job.

"Very hot," Clara adds, and I lift my gaze to find all three of them staring at me.

"Yeah. He's hot. Whatever. But he's also a good person. Just, like...intrinsically good." From how he cares for his workers to how he treats a young girl to how he was and still is a stand-up friend to Clara, he's *good*.

While I don't know everything about Dante—hell, I don't even know an eighth about him—I doubt there is anything I could learn about him that would make me dislike him. As much as that fact annoys me.

"Maybe I should give him a chance," I say slowly, and Marianne places her hand on Clara's leg, keeping her in her seat, as if silently telling her to sit still as Frankie dances around. He can feel it too.

The energy shift.

Maybe he can subliminally understand his pal is going to be around again.

So, I suppose, the decision is made.

I thump my fist on the table, conceding the fight. "All right. I'll let Dante rent the apartment."

Marianne nods as if she's known all along. Andi smiles and sticks a lollipop into her mouth. Clara, that she-devil, takes out her phone, and I snatch it away.

"I don't need any more little birdies flying around. I'll send Frankie to kill 'em."

She bends, accepting the dog's kisses when he licks her cheek. "Frankie's not a killer. No. No, you aren't. You're the best boy, aren't you? Yes. Yes, you are." She peers over at me, her perfect teeth glinting under the kitchen lights. "At least until Dante moves in. Then he might become the best boy."

Chapter 12
Dante

Taryn informed me I could move in at exactly 9:04 a.m., and I had my head on a pillow in my new place at 9:07 p.m. There is something to be said for not owning a whole lot. Just me, my work boots, and Torts. Tortellini Arturo Moretti, my pet tortoise.

The apartment above her house is one room with appliances that are older than I am, but in relatively good condition. Big windows span the entire front wall, so I can't beat the sunshine in the morning. Although, when I have the time, I'm gonna see what I can do about those wooden shutters that have obviously been painted over multiple times.

I've been living here for a few days, and I'm trying my damnedest to be the perfect tenant for Taryn. I've been careful about moving around at night, not wanting to disturb her, and I have a reminder on the fridge for the garbage and recycling nights. Can't have my new landlady thinking I'm a slob.

So far, we haven't seen much of each other at home, even though I ran into her son yesterday. Jake seems like the average fifteen-year-old, and he was in a rush to get out of the house, so we didn't exchange much more than a hello.

The Nest is coming along well, and with only about a month left, we're on target to finish for the holiday season. Taryn appears to be happy with it, and that's all I care about. Now, if only I could get some alone time with her. Since I've been proving how professional I can be, I'd like to show her how professionally unprofessional I can be.

Which is why I leap off the beat-up futon near the windows when I hear a car door slam. By now, I know the way Taryn Stone closes a car door. Like she doesn't have time to deal with its shit today. Smiling, I watch as she opens her trunk, and I take note of some boxes, so I throw on my sneakers and a coat and head on down to the sidewalk.

"Hey." When she glances at me, muscling a big-ass crate, I reach for it. "Let me help."

"I'm fine." She blows a puff of air out of her lips, aiming up to get the wayward lock of hair out of her face, but when it doesn't budge, I tuck it behind her ear.

"Are you sure?"

The ponytail on the top of her head is barely hanging on, and from the way she's hunched, I don't think she'll be able to handle the weight much longer.

"Yes," she says stubbornly. "I got it." Though the thump and clank of whatever is in those crates doesn't sound very encouraging.

I don't wait. I go for the other crate, and it is pretty heavy. "Whaddya got in here? Bricks?"

She shuts the trunk, hits the fob to lock the doors, and shakes out her arms, readying to pick up her box up from the ground. Then she squats and lifts with her legs. Good girl. "My pottery."

"Your pottery? Like pottery you bought?"

"Pottery I make."

"Oh, no shit?"

She tips her head, a silent order to follow her. As if I'd dare to do anything different. She leads me up to her porch and unlocks her front door, where Frankie greets us happily. I set down the pottery then kneel to accept his kisses, nuzzling my face into his neck. "You remember me? Yeah? I remember you. Yes, I do. Yes, I do. Are we gonna be friends? You gonna hang out with me?"

"No," Taryn answers for him, hanging her purse and coat in the closet, but I ignore her.

"Yes, we are. We're gonna be good friends. And you can play with Tortellini. You guys are gonna be buds. I know it."

"Tell me Tortellini is a sentient being and not a piece of pasta you speak about like it's alive."

God, I love her. "Tortellini is my tortoise. He's the best. Super fun."

"Your turtle...is super fun?"

"Tortoise. And yes. I made him a little skateboard, and he loves to scoot around. He's got a lot of energy, actually."

She narrows her eyes in suspicion. "I...have so many questions."

I grin. "And I'd love to answer them for you."

She shakes her head. "No. I am sure it would only make me like you more, and I don't want to do that."

I grin even wider. "Aw, babe. You going soft on me?"

"Absolutely not." She snaps her fingers. "Get the box."

"Yes, ma'am." But when I don't hear anyone else in the house, I ask, "Where are the kids?"

"With their dad."

"So, you're all alone?" I take the time to observe more of her house now than I did when I was here weeks ago since my attention had been pretty much focused on one thing. Now, I let my gaze coast around at the framed photos of her children, the random collection of what I think are *I Love Lucy* knickknacks all over the place, the clean yet haphazard space of a home that is used well and full of love.

"I'm gonna need you to stop that line of thinking right there," Taryn says, forcing my eyes to her then down to her ass in a pair of leggings.

"You don't know what I was thinking."

"Yes, I do. You were about to try to talk me into having sex with you."

I gasp. "You scandalize me! I was going to ask if you wanted to play Monopoly."

She sniffs an impatient sound as she uses her hip to nudge open the door to the basement then hits the light with her elbow. Literally, she would rather break an ankle falling down these steps, carrying a box, than she would ask for help. When I finally get downstairs, I find it a real mess. It's cluttered with toys that I doubt teenagers would play with, laundry all over the place, sports equipment, and in the middle of it all, a setup for pottery. A table, wheel, stool, and bins of...stuff. The plastic tubs are labeled with "mail" and "clay" and "paint" and "sponges."

"So, you *do* pottery."

"Yeah. I have a small online shop."

I make a circuit of her setup, noting what I assume are completed pieces—a few vases, coffee mugs, matching plates and cups, a really big bowl that my mother would love to have for Seven Fishes on Christmas Eve, and a cute little ceramic Christmas tree. "Taryn..." I turn to her. "You're really talented."

She ignores me and opens one of the crates, beginning to pull out her art, but it's easy to see she doesn't have much room to work with everything else she's got going on.

"You make it all down here?"

She nods. "I don't have much of a choice."

Until now. "Can you walk me through the process?"

She freezes with her hands in midair, halfway to the box to take out another ceramic dish. "You want to know how to make pottery?"

"Yeah."

"Really?"

Her voice is high and squeaky, and I'm not sure why she's so surprised. "Well, I don't want to do it. I just want to know how *you* do it."

"Oh...kay." She proceeds to explain how she throws her pieces on the wheel first, letting them set up to dry before adding decorative elements. She shows me where she stores her clay and the different tools she uses to cut and shape the pieces. As she talks about it all, I can tell she loves it by how confident and animated she is, more than I've ever seen her.

"Do you fire everything here too?" I ask, using the opportunity of moving the now-empty crates to step closer to her.

"No. I take them to a studio downtown that has a kiln. It's the only way I can get them properly fired."

This woman is seriously talented. And doing it all in a cluttered basement? Even more impressive. "How long have you been doing this?"

Taryn thinks for a moment, her dark-chocolate eyes focused on some point in her mind as her bittersweet mouth purses. "I've always liked to draw and paint, and I loved art in high school. In college, I minored in it and fell in love with pottery. I love using my hands to make something beautiful."

It's so hard not to wrap my fingers around her neck and taste those lips of hers, swallow her words, pull her love and energy into my body, and keep all her dreams safe. That's what I want for her. From her.

"I understand that," I rasp, unable to be anything other than myself at this moment. A man at her feet. Mesmerized. Beholden. "I love seeing something old and making it new again or having nothing and suddenly...something."

She slants her face toward mine, and she must have been chewing on candy at some point because her breath is sweet as it gently wafts across my mouth, warm and inviting. It would be nothing to close the last inch between us, but I want her to come to me. To offer what I want so badly, I feel it in my bones.

"I guess we're both creators," she says quietly, and I fist my hands at my sides, forcing myself to take a step back from her, putting a foot of space between us. Then another, two feet. Three feet. Until I can no longer feel the warmth of her body, smell the candy flavor on her tongue. Tempt me to do something I know she wouldn't like.

My woman needs to make all the decisions on her own time.

I blink a few times to clear my head. "So, you said you have a shop?"

She stares down at her feet, as if she's working through a fog too. "Uh, yeah. When... When I was married, I, um..." She clears her throat before lifting her gaze to me, and I can physically see her put on her metaphorical armor. The change in her body is immediate. How she tips her chin, sets her shoulders like she's readying for combat. "When I was married, I did it as a hobby. It was something I did for myself when I didn't have much that was mine. I still do it for myself now, but I also make money from it that is *only* mine."

My breath leaves my lungs in a rush. My beautiful warrior.

I can't begin to guess what she's been through, but I will make sure the way forward is paved in gold from here on out. She won't need to fight for anything.

"I know you don't need to hear this because you already know, but you are incredible."

Her cheeks redden as she shakes her head slightly.

"You don't believe me?"

"Anyone can make an okay-looking ceramic dish. Even preschoolers."

"Yours are more than okay-looking, and it isn't only your pottery. It's everything. Everything you do, everything you are. You're incredible, and I am truly sorry because it seems like I was wrong. You do need to hear it. You haven't heard it enough." I lick my lips, reaching for her shoulders even though I know it's a bad idea. "You are wildly talented and smart and so interesting that I look forward to what new fact I can learn about you every day. I'm sorry for whatever has happened in your past, but you have to know... You are more than a mother or an artist or a badass businesswoman—you are fucking remarkable. Truly."

Her eyes water like she doesn't know exactly how special she is, and I have the sudden urge to hammer something. Instead, I tighten my hold on her and bend, pulling her close, barely a sliver of daylight between her lips and mine. Every second, every millimeter of space between us is too much, but then she goes and whispers two heart-achingly soft words, vulnerability pouring out like water from a broken levee. "Thank you."

I hate it.

I hate whoever made her believe she isn't wonderful and perfect.

I hate every minute that she second-guesses herself.

I hate that she'd accept an organ before she'd accept a compliment, and unfortunately for both of us, I've got more compliments than I do organs. But I'd happily hand over the one rattling around in my chest right now.

I settle for kissing her cheek instead of her mouth then back away, fingers tingling with the need to return to her. Even my nerves know what I think my heart has known since I first laid eyes on her.

That I was meant to be with her.

That one, my heart said.

That one, my head agreed days later when the universe granted me another chance.

That one, my blood tells me now, rushing thick and fast through my veins, urging me back to her.

And all I can do is try to calm myself. Soon. Hopefully, soon, she'll be mine.

"Thanks for letting me in on your workspace."

She blinks away any lingering emotion and nods. "I'll see you tomorrow at work?"

I wink. "Mm-hmm. Yep."

Chapter 13
Taryn

It's cold, but Dante appears unaffected as he works outside in only a hoodie and jeans. And his bandanna, of course. He knocked on my door this morning to ask if he could use the backyard to build a project, and I easily agreed, although I'm not sure how exactly he's going to move that...shed —I think—wherever it needs to go. He's been hauling wood, sawing, and hammering all day, but it's only since reheating my coffee for the third time that I've been here at my kitchen table. Watching.

It started out of curiosity, but I stayed for the Billy Joel soundtrack and the way his jeans fit his ass. He's so at home in his body, flipping the hammer end over end as he plucks a nail from between his lips before pounding the pieces together. It's a dance. The way he works is beauty.

How he understood what I meant when I said I loved making things with my hands. He does the same thing. We both are artists. Creators. Making the world beautiful one ceramic mug and refinished porch at a time.

The renovation at The Nest is coming along well, and here, as a tenant, Dante has been incredibly easy to have around. I had my reservations about him, but once again, he's proven me wrong. By his looks, anyone might assume he's all brawn and no brains, but he's so much more than his face. He's a good listener and an even better friend. He's thoughtful, funny, charming as hell, and masculine without being toxic.

A true unicorn.

With a six-pack, thick thighs, and the ability to actually build a girl a house, if they asked.

Not that I would ask.

I have a house already.

But...if someone else wanted one...

Which makes me wonder about that girlfriend he'd broken up with. What happened there? Because everything I've seen of Dante is all green flags.

Much to my dismay.

He squats down, eyeing something on the wood, then takes the pencil from behind his ear to make a mark before sticking it back in place. He stands and moves the 2x4 over to the circular saw. I blow out a breath and force my attention away, suddenly a little warm from all the competency porn.

Needing a break from leering at the man a dozen years my junior, I meander into the living room, where Maddie is sprawled out on the couch, her eyes glued to the TV, her phone clutched in her hand. She glances up as I enter, a small smile playing on her lips.

"Hey, Mom," she says, her voice soft and squeaky like an elf. It's the voice she uses when she wants something.

"Yes?"

"Can we order Benny's for dinner?"

I cross my arms, playing at annoyance. "You paying?"

"Pleeeeaaaase. I'm so hungry for it. PMS."

I huff. She got her period over the summer and uses PMS as a reason for everything with me now. If she wants something special or as an excuse to get out of something. It's smart, really. But I caught on quick enough to her evil plan.

"Yeah, all right. Only because I'm PMSing too."

She wiggles back and forth, giddy. "I was going to watch *Wicked* later. Wanna watch with me?"

"Again?"

"Director's cut this time."

I shrug. "Lemme talk to your brother and see if Holden's staying for dinner."

Holden and Jake have been best friends since they met last year on the soccer team and they hang out a lot, so I assume he's going to stay for dinner and don't even think before I open the door to my son's room to find them kissing.

All three of us freeze.

My jaw hits the floor, my brain shutting down for a moment as Holden yanks his hand off Jake's thigh, both of them jumping away from each other. Jake stands, face bright red. "It's not... It's not what it looks like."

"I, uh, was coming to see if you wanted to stay for dinner, Holden."

Jake's best friend shoves his feet into his sneakers and snatches his coat from the floor. "I don't think so. I'm gonna go."

I open my mouth, but no words come out. I'm not sure what to say, what to do. I'm not even sure what I'm feeling, but I chase him down the hall. "Hold, it's okay. You can stay. I—"

I'm not sure I know what words are anymore, but I know I don't want either one of these boys to think I'm mad. Because I'm not. Only surprised.

"No. I should go," he says, barely audible as he races down the steps to the front door.

"Do you need a ride home?"

"No, I'm fine."

"You're wearing shorts."

"It's cool." He refuses to look at me. "Bye."

The door shuts, and Maddie's eyebrows rise to her hairline while I hear Jake come to stand behind me. "Mom?"

I turn to my son, his eyes filled with a mixture of fear and defiance, clearly at war with himself. I am wholly unprepared for a conversation about what just happened, so I skip over it and place my hand on his shoulder, hoping to reassure him. "Maddie wants Benny's for dinner. You okay with that?"

He nods silently, seeming relieved with the way his body droops.

"Okay. I'll order it in a little bit, and, maybe, we can talk after?"

He nods again and spins around, jogging up the stairs. I glance to Maddie, but she's focused on her phone, unaware of what's going on.

Not that there is anything going on.

And yet...I can't ignore what happened. Jake and I will have to talk, although I'm not sure what about.

I absently reach for my cell phone and open my text thread with Marianne. We've been best friends since grade school, and I spent a lot of nights at her house, reveling in the wholesome vibes of her home. While my mother was amazing, and I would never have wanted her to be any different, it wasn't easy growing up with an absentee alcoholic father and a mother who took on part-time jobs after her full-time work of teaching to provide for my brothers and me. Marianne's parents were different. They didn't struggle like my mom and are still alive and well. They've always been supportive of everything their daughter has done, from switching majors multiple times to bringing home girl-friends to marrying a white woman a lot younger than her.

Marianne confided in me during college that she had feelings for another woman in one of her classes. It didn't change our relationship one bit, nor did it make me curious about my own sexuality. Maybe because I'm straight as an arrow, or I'm so stuck in my heteronormative world view, but I never considered one of my children might be queer.

I love Jake. I love both of my kids so much, nothing they could ever do would make me not love them.

Yet I worry about him. About his confidence and turning sixteen and learning to drive. I worry about his mental and physical health. I worry about what my divorce did and continues to do to him. I worry about him growing up into a kind and caring person, and standing up for those who cannot stand up for themselves.

Above all else, I want him to be happy.

Slipping on my coat, I step out to the backyard, intent on dialing Marianne to download all of this, but I stop in my tracks, having forgotten about Dante in my flood of thoughts.

"Oh, hi," I say when he pivots to me with his pencil between his teeth.

He pulls it out and tucks it behind his ear to brush off sawdust from his hands and sweatshirt. "Hey. How—what's wrong?"

I don't know how he does it. How he always knows when I'm upset. But I'm not sure where exactly to begin, and I shake my head to try to clear it of the jumble of thoughts as well as the tears from my eyes.

Dante immediately closes the short distance between us. "You're all right. Come here. Come here." He wraps his arms around me, pulling me into a hug, and I go willingly, taking comfort in his warm breath against my temple and the way he locks his hands at my back. "Came charging out of here like a bat outta hell, so do I need to beat somebody up or get some tissues?"

A reluctant laugh unfurls from the knot in my throat, and I hate that he can calm me down so easily. I've spent the last ten years building meticulous defenses to make sure no one can ever hurt me again—not my father or my ex-husband or the world, for that matter. I've hardened myself to the cuts and slights women experience every single day, and I think I've started to believe that made me better somehow. I could crush a needle of emotion at the earliest prick. I didn't need to feel things. I had risen above all that bullshit.

And yet a man with an eager smile dragged me back down to earth. Showed me I'm no better than anyone else for supposedly being above it all. That, maybe, I do need a hug and someone to tell me they have my back before even hearing the problem.

"Neither," I say, blinking the sting out of my eyes as I step away from him. "It's...something with Jake."

Dante's brow furrows. "He okay?"

"Yeah. Yeah, he's fine. I'm fine. We're all fine."

He presses his lips together, fighting a grin as he nods seriously. "Of course."

I swipe my hand over my forehead. "I'm...not sure what to do. There's..." I sigh and meet Dante's steady gaze. "Promise me you won't breathe a word of this to Jake, because I haven't talked about it with him and I have no idea how he's feeling about anything and I'm so afraid to fuck this all up. I don't want to fuck up."

I don't realize I've started crying until Dante takes off his bandanna to wipe it over my cheeks. My breath hiccups. "I don't want to fuck up."

Dante soothes me, once again taking me into his arms, tucking my head against his neck. "You're not going to fuck it up. You never could, and I know you love your kids more than anything. Your kids know it too. They feel it. Everything's going to be okay."

He hands me his bandanna to use as a tissue then cups the back of my head, his fingertips making soft circles against my scalp, tangling in strands of my hair, lulling me into a state of quiet. In myself and in the world around us. I don't hear the rustle of leaves or the squirrel skittering off somewhere in the distance. There is only him and me and this sense of rightness.

"What happened?" he asks, drawing my attention to his eyes, solemn and captivating in how dark they are, almost black. Makes every quirk of his mouth all the more playful, although he's not smiling now. I place my hands on his sides, curling my fingers into the cotton of his hoodie, partly for heat but mostly for solace. He's not going anywhere.

"Jake had his best friend over, and I went upstairs to ask if he was staying for dinner, but I interrupted them."

At first, he frowns then tips his chin up as it dawns on him. "Inter—ohh."

"I didn't know what to say, but I feel bad because I probably embarrassed both of them. Holden couldn't run out of the house fast enough, and I don't know if he's okay. Jake was... He seemed shocked and mad and mortified. I mean, if my mom ever walked in on me with someone when I was in high school, I would have been scarred for life."

Dante agrees. "My mom did walk in on me once. With Annalise Schaffer. I had my hand up her shirt."

"What happened?"

He chuckles with a shrug. "My mom told Annalise to go home and then smacked me upside the head."

"That's it?"

"Basically. And not to make her a grandmother that young."

I had Griffin and Ian talk to Jake after Craig and I agreed he would give our son "the talk." I came to find out he'd tossed Jake a box of condoms and said, "Use them," and that was it. I've also had conversations with Jake, reminding him to treat girls how he would want his own sister to be treated and harped on consent and consequences, though I've never thought about it in terms of same-sex relationships.

"I told Jake we'd talk later," I explain to Dante, "but I'm not sure what to say to him. Like, first of all, do I need to put rules in place now about Holden in his room? Or other boys? Do we need to have more talks about sex and health? I don't know."

Now that I've started talking, I can't stop, spitting out every thought that's been swirling in my mind for the last few minutes. "As much as I know no one in my family will treat him differently, I can't say the rest of the world won't. I think of Marianne and her journey of coming out, but Jake's will be different. He's an athletic white kid, and does it make me a terrible person for being glad about that?" I shake my head, eyes on the ground. "It does, doesn't it? That he can move through the world easier because of what he looks like than other queer people. I'm such an asshole. The worst kind of person."

"No." Dante stops me from backing away from him with my shame. "You're not an asshole. You're a person who knows we have certain privileges, and, yeah, guys who look like me and Jake sometimes do have an easier time with everything. I'm sure every mom wants their kid to avoid pain at all costs, and I think all me and you and Jake can do is try to make the road easier for other people."

I nod, sniffling, letting out the last of it. "I just want him to be safe and happy, and I'm afraid he might be hurt for being who he is."

Dante kisses my forehead. "I'm not sure anything I say can

take that worry away, but I'm really happy Jake has you as his mother. He's a lucky kid."

I blow out a breath, tucking my hair behind my ears, hoping I don't look too raccoonish. Dante's hands follow, his fingers tracing the same trail with my hair and under my eyes. I like it better when he does it anyway. He's more careful about it. More appreciative. Touching me as if he can't believe I'm allowing him to.

"You know," he starts with a shrug, "this might all be nothing. Could be a couple of kisses to experiment. He might not know what it is either."

I tip my head, studying this beautiful yet work-roughened man. He's coarse but refined, like he's been carved from a pine tree by the hand of God. And that's how I know God's a woman. Because She would make sure her creations understood social justice.

"Why does that sound like it's coming from experience?" I ask, and he offers me a sheepish smile.

"I may have done a little...experimenting in the past."

"Yeah?"

He leans against his worktable, tugging me next to him. "It's not a big deal. I can't speak for all guys, but I feel like we're all a little curious. You know? Like if I could suck my own cock, would I? And if I did, what does that say about me?"

I can't help it. I laugh. He does too.

"And, I don't know... I really do think sexuality is a spectrum, and we're all fluid in some respect."

"I've never been with a woman or have even wanted to try."

He hums curiously, his eyes roaming over my face as if in search of an answer, but I don't know what the question is. "Never wondered what pussy tastes like?"

My skin heats, my cheeks on fire, and the way he licks his lips lets me know he knows.

"I feel bad for all the people who've never tasted yours. Sweet like honey. Hot like fresh coffee."

Before I can stop myself, I admit, "That's the entire world, except for two."

He inhales sharply and turns to fully face me. "You're telling me I'm one of two people who have ever had the pleasure of eating you out?"

When I nod, he goes positively wolfish, baring his teeth like he might bite my neck. I might let him.

"Fuck me, Taryn. I shouldn't like that so much, but I do. I really fucking do."

I ignore how blood pools between my legs, my core tingling with desire. "You were saying you did some experimenting...?"

He moves to stand in front of me, caging me in with his hands on the table on either side of me. I briefly worry about the kids seeing us, but we're mostly hidden by whatever he's building. Besides, I can't concentrate on much of anything other than what it feels like to be the center of his attention.

I think I'm starting to crave it.

The moment when his pupils expand.

The way he watches me so closely.

His gaze is a phantom touch everywhere it glides over me.

I'd always worried about addiction running in the family. Who knew it would be the way this man makes me feel— wanton and lustful—that is my new habit?

"I used to hang out with this guy who was in my one community college class," Dante tells me, forcing my attention to his voice and away from the painful way my nipples have pebbled beneath my shirt, how my blood has pooled between my legs.

"It was this required writing course, and I was failing, of course. So, he said he'd help me out, and..." Dante lifts a careless shoulder, even though his gaze is set on my mouth. "One night, one thing led to another, and he gave me a blow job. I liked it, so I returned the favor, but I've never really thought too hard about what that makes me. I've never felt the need to label myself."

He shifts, his hands slipping under my coat to my waist, hips pressing against mine. "An orgasm is an orgasm, right? Does it matter how you get it or who gives it to you?"

I swallow thickly. I've never thought about it like that. Although I have no time to answer, because he goes on, his lips grazing my ear. "Unless it's the best orgasm you've ever had. Then it matters, huh? When you've had a taste of heaven, you want it again." His thumb finds my bare skin under my shirt. "I want to taste heaven again, duchess. Let me taste it."

I almost—*almost*—let him. But as much as I want to say yes, I have to say no. I need to provide dinner for my children and then have a discussion with Jake.

I have my whole life to consider.

He doesn't have the same constraints, and it's easy for him to play it off as only sex.

I can't do that.

Before I even speak, Dante knows my answer. He backs away, his fingers trailing my hips until they completely fall away. "If you need anything, I'm here for you." With a glance to the house, he adds, "And the kids."

"I appreciate you," I say, avoiding touching him as I pass by, heading for the back door, when I remember his bandanna that I have stuffed in my coat pocket. I lift it, ready to throw it to him, but he holds up his hand.

"Keep it. I've got, like, seventeen of them."

"Of course you do," I say more to myself than him, chewing on the inside of my cheek to refrain from smiling.

Inside, I order a few cheeseburgers and fries from Benny's

then head upstairs to Jake's room, where I knock on the door. His voice is weary. "Yeah?"

"Can I come in?"

"Yeah."

He's splayed out on his bed, a soccer ball in his hands. He keeps his eyes on the ceiling when I sit on the end of the mattress. "I ordered dinner."

He doesn't answer.

"Got you the double bacon cheeseburger, fries, and milkshake."

"Thanks," he mumbles.

"Do you want to talk now?"

He shrugs.

"I hope you know you can tell me anything. I hope I've never made you feel like I would get mad or shun you or anything like that."

This gets his attention, and he sits up, shaking his head. "No."

I pat his knee and take a deep breath. "I was worried that you felt like you couldn't talk to me about this."

He pitches his gaze toward the wall. "I don't really know what to say. It's...confusing."

"Okay. That's...probably hard for you, but it's okay to be confused or not have the answers right away. Or, ever, really."

He runs the side of his fist over his mouth and then plows his hand through his hair. It takes him a while to look at me again, and when he does, I see the baby who made me a mom. The tiny screaming thing who lay on my chest in a blue cap. The toddler who refused to be potty-trained until I told him he couldn't go into the swimming pool unless he stopped wearing diapers. I see him on his first day of school with his Iron Man backpack. I see the middle schooler who twisted his ankle in a game and refused to cry until he was home with me. I see the man who he'll hopefully become, one who works hard and leaves the world a little better than he entered it.

And I have no other words for him besides the ones that have always been true. Will always be true. "I love you." I brush my hand over his head then down the side of his face. "I will never stop loving you. No matter what."

His eyes well with tears, and I tow him into me. He's no longer my little boy, yet he'll *always* be my little boy. Even when he's taller than me. I kiss his cheek, his temple, his ear, wherever I can reach. "I love you so much. Always and forever."

His breath is shaky, and my shoulder feels wet when he lifts his face, though his cheeks are dry. "I love you too."

"When you're ready to talk more, we can. Okay?" I stand, pointing to the door. "But for now, when anyone is over, your door is going to stay open."

He easily agrees, and I drop one last kiss on the top of his head. "I'm going to pick up dinner. Your sister wants to watch *Wicked* again. I'd really like it if you watched it with us."

It's a fifty-fifty shot, and just when I think our lovely little family moment will carry over into a lovely little family evening, he scoffs. "No way."

Like I asked him to hold a tapeworm for me.

"Then why don't you go outside and ask Dante if he wants help?"

Jake rolls over to peek out his window. "What's he building?"

"I don't know. But go tell him I ordered him dinner too."

My kid doesn't need any more prodding. He pulls on a hoodie and steps into his sneakers before heading outside, and I watch from the window as he exchanges a few words with Dante, who easily strikes up a conversation that I can't hear.

Though it's not long until Jake's got a hammer in hand and Dante's instructing him.

And an hour later, after we've all shared dinner at my kitchen table, Maddie invites Dante to watch the movie with us in the living room, and when he decides to stay, so does Jake.

That's how I get my lovely little family evening.

With Dante.

And my kids.

And Frankie eating leftover popcorn between us.

Chapter 14
Taryn

Over the last week, Dante has become a staple at my house. Like we're living some old-school sitcom, with the funny upstairs neighbor poking his head in the window to toss out some wisecrack. Except, instead of the funny upstairs neighbor being a sarcastic old man, he's an annoyingly handsome young man with a penchant for sexual innuendos and a bad habit of providing me candy.

Jake has developed a special affinity for Dante, who is unsurprisingly capable at teaching my son stereotypical paternal lessons that he misses out on with Craig. Between soccer practice and meals, Jake has been outside hammering away on Dante's project even after the sun has set.

It is incredibly heartwarming. And even more disturbing.

Because I can't deny how I turn all gooey inside when the two of them clasp hands, smiling and laughing. Or hear how excited Jake is to hang out with Dante, clearly missing that kind of relationship in his life.

Worse yet, Maddie is always included. She's learned the difference between a flathead and Phillips screwdriver and has told me about the importance of girls knowing how to perform household maintenance. "For their independence," she said, according to Dante. As if I've never told her that before. As if I haven't always harped on her knowing how to do everything on her own so she didn't have to rely on anyone else.

It's impossible to pretend my children aren't falling as fast and hard for Dante as I am.

Even for his stupid turtle.

That he's brought down to show us how the thing gets around on his stupid adorable skateboard, lying on his belly and pedaling with his hands and feet... Or whatever you call a turtle's feet. Paws? Claws? Stumps?

I don't know, but those are questions Dante is making me consider. Going to the grocery store and buying extra carrots so Maddie can take them up to Dante's apartment to feed Tortellini and discuss the latest episode of *Gossip Girl* since they're doing a rewatch together.

Honestly... I hate how much I like him.

Every single day, I look forward to seeing him, acting like I'm not actually hanging on his every word. It's pathetic how I've started dressing for his compliments and finding moments I can be alone with him, which are much too far and few between. Because everyone wants his attention—the crew at work and my kids at home. He's everyone's favorite, but I want to be *his* favorite.

And it makes me feel out of control.

I never expected nor wanted to be attracted to anyone after my divorce. My life is a series of spinning plates, and one misstep could send them crashing to the floor. I put these plates in motion years ago, but lately, they seem to be moving faster and faster, and I fear Dante's unrestrained force will send them all careening away. Yet I can't stop it. The inevitable spill.

Which is why I spend a few hours downtown. After

meeting with Ian and Griffin for coffee, I waste another hour at Lux & Lace, being talked into buying a fancy petal-pink bra that I don't need and swear up and down to Marianne and Clara that no one will see besides me. Especially a *Jersey Shore* cast member knock-off. Then I buy a gratitude journal at Chapter and Verse, convincing myself I will start using it—I swear—before popping into Stone Ink for a quick hi to my nephews, Jasper and Jaybird. They're both tattoo artists like Ian but could not be more different. Demonstrated by how they're in the middle of an argument about something I don't care to referee, so I skip right on over to Sweet Cheeks, where I buy myself a cinnamon bun. The mental and emotional gymnastics I've been putting myself through lately are quite taxing on the system, and I need a good jolt of sugar to keep up my stamina.

Good thing, too, because when I arrive back at home, I discover Jake kicking the soccer ball around with Dante in the backyard while Maddie watches, and I absolutely do not take a picture. Even though that was my first instinct. To document all three of them laughing.

Ugh. Even I'm sick of myself.

So, I do the only thing worse than mental and emotional gymnastics and decide to physically work out.

I let out all that pent-up frustration on an imaginary target while I follow a cardio kickboxing YouTube video until my T-shirt is ringed with sweat and my hair sticks to the back of my neck. Since having kids, finding and keeping a workout routine has been difficult, but even more since I turned forty. Everything about perimenopause sucks, but the worst part for me has been how my vagina has suddenly revolted. We'd always had a relatively good relationship until recently, when she became a mercurial bitch. Some days, she's dry; others, she smells weird. My periods are out of whack, and I've had so many blood tests done, I'm on a first-name basis with all the phlebotomists at the testing center. But what I really detest is how I sometimes pee when I cough or sneeze or land a roundhouse kick to a pretend attacker.

Which is why I purchased a "pelvic floor strengthening course."

I have no idea if I'm actually doing anything as I complete these exercises, but the perky blond lady leading them certainly thinks it'll help, so I've been faithfully doing them every week.

I grab the two yoga blocks I need and position myself on top of them before hitting play on the video, and I close my eyes, as instructed, imagining an elevator shaft in the middle of my body, inhaling and exhaling to send that elevator up and down.

I hear the back door open and assume it's one of the kids, so I don't press pause on my exercises. They've heard and seen this all before.

"Now, take those breaths further. Zip up those transverse abdominals with every exhale and suck up a blueberry with your lady parts. That's it. Big inhale and exhale, let it go. Drop the blueberry, set the elevator shaft down, unzip the abs."

I hear a big exhale next to me, and since I know Frankie is outside, it can't be him. I open my eyes and shoot my arm out in reflex at the intruder.

Dante catches my wrist, grinning. "Sorry, babe, didn't mean to scare you and your blueberry-picking lady bits."

I growl and lean over to grab one of the yoga blocks I'm sitting on, whacking his shoulder with it. "You asshole."

"Hey." He laughs, stealing the block from me to put under his butt as he sits down. When I hit the pause button, he has the gall to act affronted. Like *I* interrupted *him*.

"We were just getting to the good part." He moves to play it, but I nudge my shoulder into his, knocking him off-balance. He takes me with him, down to the floor, my breath stolen when he rolls us so I'm on my back, and he pins my hands above my head. "Mm. Now, *this* is the good part."

"What are you doing in here? Besides annoying me?" I ask, though there is no actual ire in my voice. Only breathless anticipation.

"I came in for a drink but then heard some real interesting stuff happening in here. Seems like a really good workout. What else can you pick up with your lady bits? Grapes? Cherries?"

I attempt to wiggle away from him, but it only settles us more in place, his trim hips fitting snugly between mine. His stomach against mine. Our chests so close that every one of my inhales sends chills across my skin at the way my hard nipples rub against him. It's torture, even through the multiple layers of fabric. They're so sensitive and needy. Ever since the night he ordered me to feed them to him.

I won't ever forget that.

And from the way Dante stares down at me with heat in his eyes and filthy words I know are gathered on the tip of his tongue, I don't think he will either.

"I like you like this," he murmurs, and my body responds of its own accord. My thighs bracketing his hips, back bowing to bring us even closer together. "All flushed and sweaty."

His grip tightens, thumbs digging into my wrists, and I remember that too. Those slight reminders of who is actually in charge, and the visceral memories are too much. The scent of his skin then and having him so close to me now. The feel of his tongue on me with his mouth so close to me now. The full and throbbing echo of his cock inside me taunts me with his hardening length resting against the cleft of my sex now.

It's all too much.

I can't breathe.

"Please," I gasp, "the kids are right outside."

The slow and wicked twist of his lips sends a shiver down my spine. "Then you better be quiet."

I buck my hips, trying to dislodge him, but he's too heavy, too strong. "Dante, I mean it. We can't do this here, not now."

He leans down, his breath hot on my ear. "You say that, but your body is telling me something different, duchess. I can feel how much you want this."

I can't deny it. My body is a traitor, my nipples hard, my core pulsating with need. An ache that only he can satisfy.

But I can't give in. I shake my head. "We can't do this here."

He pulls back the tiniest bit, enough to allow me a deep breath that only fills my lungs with his now-familiar scent of freshly cut wood and clean cotton. "But you *do* want to do this."

I do. I really fucking do, but I push against his chest, my voice firm. "No."

He searches my face, his expression softening. Then, with a sigh, he rolls off me. I sit up, adjusting my clothes, trying to regain my composure. But it's no use. The idea is in my head. My nipples are hard points through my sports bra and T-shirt. Heart racing.

"We can't," I tell him, narrowing my eyes to slits, hoping he'll let it go. Leave me and my spinning plates be.

But of course, he doesn't. He huffs a rough sound and rakes his hand through his hair before pointing at me. "Don't look at me like that."

"Like what?"

"Like you're fooling me. You're not. You certainly aren't fooling yourself either." He waves his hand up and down the length of me like it's proof enough.

It is, and I hate him for pointing it out. Even more for continuing to tell the truth.

"You want to be thrown around. I know you do. I know you want me to fold you up like a pretzel and fuck your pussy until you can't breathe. I know, so don't look at me like it doesn't turn you on when I talk like this. You forget I've already done it. Fucked you so good, you felt it the next day."

With my tongue stuck to the roof of my mouth, I am unable to reply. He simply nods to himself then stands, silently holding his hands out to me, helping me up as well. He tucks the loose strands of hair that fell out of my ponytail back behind my ears then steps back. "I'm ready." His searing gaze marks my skin, leaves a scorching trail down my throat, over my chest, down my stomach, to settle between my thighs before it glazes over. I don't know what he's imagining, but I can guess. Then his eyes are back up on mine, honest and open, so I can see how much he wants me. Even without his promise. "I'm ready when you are."

Chapter 15
Dante

I'm knee-deep in drywall at The Nest when Taryn's voice slices through the hum of construction work around me. She's on the phone, her tone sharp enough to cut glass. My hackles rise. Because I know the differences in her voice, when she's giving shit to someone and when she's ready to actually murder them.

And I don't have the money for bail in my account right now.

"No, that's not good enough. You do this all the time, and it needs to stop. I—" She stops abruptly to listen for a few seconds and then explodes again. "You really think they give a shit about that? Because they don't. This is supposed to be your time with them, that you *fought* me for, and now you're canceling. *Again.*"

I stand, creeping closer, but my boots are heavy and I wince at my footfalls, but she doesn't notice me, too busy pacing the room.

"No. I can't just leave. I'm not like you. I can't do whatever I want without thinking of the repercussions," she says, and while I assume she's speaking to her ex-husband, I'm surprised at the level of vitriol.

"Oh, fuck off. I'm not the one constantly letting the kids down. That's not my doing. It's yours, and you're eventually going to have to face the consequences of the choices you've made. So, don't worry about it. I'll take care of it. Like always. You enjoy your make-it-or-break-it dinner that you can't possibly get out of for our children."

She lowers her cell phone from her ear and stabs her index finger on the screen to end the call before lifting it like she might throw it. And I literally just finished these walls. She can't go putting holes in them now.

I catch her wrist, muttering a quiet, "Hey, hey, it's okay. It's okay."

She spins on me, though she lets me take her phone and set it down, her chest rising and falling with quick, angry breaths. "I'm so fucking mad," she seethes, her jaw so tight, I'm surprised she hasn't broken any teeth. "He always does this shit. I don't know why he insisted on dragging me to family court when he doesn't care. He doesn't care!"

She shoots her arms out, whirling around like she wants to scream and yell, but keeps it all bottled up.

That's her whole problem. She's always so contained.

She needs to let it go.

"Come here," I say, holding out my hand. She doesn't take it, but she does follow me downstairs and outside to where I have extra plywood. Neither one of us has a coat on, but with how pissed she is, she clearly doesn't feel it. I hand her a pair of work gloves and safety glasses then offer her one of the planks of wood. "Go ahead. Smash it, bang it, whatever."

After a moment, she accepts the wood and proceeds to go to town. She takes a running start toward a big oak tree on the side of the property lining the drive and repeatedly thrashes the wood against the trunk. It breaks and splinters, and when it's no longer usable, she throws it to the ground then gets another, pummeling that one too. Then a third and a fourth, until finally she runs out of steam and bends over with her hands on her knees.

I stroke my hand up and down her back. "That was awesome."

She takes a couple of deep breaths and straightens, pulling off the gloves and glasses. "Yeah. Yeah, it was."

"You wanna talk about it?" I ask, opening up the bed of my truck.

"That was my ex."

"I guessed." I take her by the hips when she's close enough to lift onto the back of the truck, then I hop up next to her. "What's the story there?"

She dabs at the sheen of sweat on her temple and upper lip. "He's in construction, too. His family owns a real estate and home construction company."

"What's the name?"

"Barrett Homes."

I wrench back. "You married a Barrett?"

She sniffs in irritation. "Yep, Craig."

Oh, I've heard of him. A huge asshole who thinks his shit doesn't stink. He overcharges and does shoddy work, but he's a smooth talker. A real slick businessman.

What a douche.

"That family is terrible," I hedge, and Taryn outright laughs. Though it's not a joyful sound.

"Yeah. I figured that out eventually."

"I'm sorry."

"It's not your fault."

"Yeah, but now, you've got to deal with all this bullshit."

She sighs and tucks her hands between her legs, her shoulders drooping, all the fight wrung out of her. "I don't care about how he treats me or what he says to me, but the kids... He treats them like they're disposable."

I curl my hands around the edge of the truck, my usually good temper being challenged. First, because Jake and Maddie don't deserve a shitty father, and second, because Taryn doesn't deserve whatever shit Craig put her through.

"What do you mean when you say you don't care how he treats you or what he says to you?"

She won't meet my gaze, and already I know whatever she's about to tell me will make me want to work up my own murder charge.

"It took me a long time to come to terms with the word abuse. You hear it and think it's black eyes and busted lips, but what he did to me was abuse too."

I'm almost afraid to ask, my stomach in knots, my muscles tense with the need to find this motherfucker. "What did he do?"

She shrugs. "Little things at first. We met in college, and he started suggesting I wear different things. I thought it was nice... He wanted me to wear things he liked, and I wanted to do that too. I wanted to look good for him, make him happy. But then it was comments about my friends and gradual control of my schedule. He never yelled at me or said anything overt enough to catch my attention. It was slow and insidious."

I drop my chin to my chest and close my eyes, imagining my duchess feeling controlled by anyone other than herself. I don't *want* to believe. I don't ever want to believe she did or does anything that is not wholly her choice.

"My dad was never around, so I thought Craig's attention was love. I thought it meant he *really* loved me. He was there for me when my mom died, and when he asked me to marry him, I didn't hesitate. Then he suggested I quit my job and work for his company, and I did. Then he suggested I stay home when I got pregnant, so I did. Then when I started to sell my pottery, he called it a cute hobby. When I had Maddie, he was barely around. I couldn't lift her up after my C-section, but I was so 'capable,' he told me he didn't think I needed him. I could handle it all myself—the kids, the house, the cooking, cleaning. I got no help, but he still asked me to work from home for the company part time. And it was only a few hours a week," she says, finally turning to me, sarcasm arching her eyebrow, though there is nothing except sadness in her dark eyes.

"Only a few hours a week, on top of everything else you were doing," I fill in, and she nods.

Her voice is low and reedy, long-held pain surfacing. "So when I got mad and upset, he turned it around like it was my fault. He wasn't asking much of me."

"Only everything," I mutter, hating Craig Barrett for a host of new reasons. Not the least of which is making Taryn Stone cry.

She holds up her hand, counting off her supposed sins with her fingers. "I was selfish. I was nagging. I was cold. I was a bitch. But if I ever got angry at him for calling me a bitch, he'd come back with, 'Well, I never *called* you a bitch. I said you're *acting* like one.'"

"Taryn—"

"I know. I know I'm not a bitch. I'd just started standing up for myself, but to him, that's acting like a bitch. But, you know what? I'd rather be an actual bitch and happy than ever be put in that same position again."

I don't know what else to say besides, "I'm so goddamn proud of you."

At that, her self-defense melts, her eyes lighting up, lips curling into a smile I've never seen out of her. This is no hint of amusement or a fighting tremor. No, this is a full-blown grin that I feel so deep in my body, it lights up my soul.

This is my duchess. My *proud* girl.

Makes me want to jump down from this truck bed right now and kneel in front of her, kiss her feet. Worship her inside and outside, for everything she is and everything she gives to the world.

She deserves nothing less than utter devotion.

I was baptized in the Catholic Church. Received Holy Communion in second grade, Confirmed at fourteen, but this woman—this goddess—is who I pray to now.

"So, what do you need help with?" I ask, happy she doesn't try to argue or fight with me.

Instead, she tells me, "Craig was supposed to pick up Jake from soccer and Maddie from Girl Scouts. Now he isn't, but I can't leave to get them."

"I'll do it."

"Are you sure?"

I hop down to the ground. "Yeah, of course. It's no problem."

Tension leaves her shoulders, her breath whooshing out in relief. "That's...amazing. Thank you so much."

I wave her off. "It's really not that big of a deal, Tar."

But I can see it is to her. She nods, gratitude shining in her eyes. "I owe you one."

I clamp my hands on her hips to help her down from the truck. "I only take my payment in orgasms."

She snorts, lightly punching my arm, and I offer her a grin. "I'll get the kids home and fed."

By the time I've cleaned up my tools, Taryn has texted me the addresses of the locations and forwarded Jake's and Maddie's cell phone numbers, as well as included me on a text thread with the kids, informing them I'm on pickup duty.

When I get Maddie, she's a chatterbox, talking nonstop about Girl Scouts, her really hard math test, and this girl who is in her science class and after-school dance class. She apparently has Blair Waldorf vibes and is sometimes friends with Maddie and sometimes not. I tell Maddie to drop this girl like yesterday's news. She tells me to stop sounding so old.

Next, I park in the high school lot, waiting as the soccer team guys all file out, Jake hanging back with some other player, talking really close together. Could be nothing. Or could be something, and I resolve myself to let him know at some point, I'll be in his corner.

Back at home, I raid the cabinets while Maddie does her homework and Jake splits upstairs for a shower. I don't consider myself much of a cook besides a few recipes my mother taught me, but seeing as Taryn doesn't have any ingredients for home-made sauce or chicken parm, I find a couple of frozen pizzas, which I heat up like a pro. And after we've all eaten, Maddie and I settle in the living room to watch more *Gossip Girl* as Jake disappears to his room.

Taryn gave me no instructions about if or when they have a bedtime, and I don't have a lot of experience taking care of kids, but much to my appreciation, Jake and Maddie pretty much take care of themselves. At nine, Maddie declares she's going to go to bed, and I follow her upstairs, offering her a high five before knocking on Jake's bedroom door.

I assume a lot of people dream about marriage and kids when they think what they want to be when they grow up. Like it's a package deal. A rite of passage. But now that I'm thirty and no closer to marriage or children, I don't feel like I'm missing out on anything. Especially when I have my sights set on a woman, and I'm given the opportunity to hang out with her kids.

I don't know where I fall on the responsible adult scale, but

I suppose I'm doing okay in terms of my relationship with Jake and Maddie. We have fun, and Taryn trusts me with them. I would take care of them with everything I have, like I would take care of Taryn the same way.

They are my package deal.

Can't have one without the other.

Which sounds pretty perfect to me.

"Hey, what's up?" Jake asks when he opens his door to me, and I shrug, glancing behind me to make sure Maddie can't hear.

"Your sister's going to bed, and I just wanted to check in with you. I don't know, uh, know what the procedure here is."

He laughs. I like that he does so easily. He's not jaded. "There is no procedure. I usually stay up later than I should, talking to friends and stuff."

"You play video games at night?"

"Sometimes. Sometimes, we're Snapping each other or whatever."

I nod. "Yeah, well, I think at some point around, like, twenty-eight, your body starts to go, hey, whoa, you should go to bed now. I swear I used to be able to stay up until two in the morning all the time, and now, I'll fall asleep in the middle of watching a game at nine. Pathetic."

"Pathetic," he echoes with a chuckle, and I slap my hand to his shoulder.

"All right. Well, I'll be downstairs until your mom gets home." When he nods, I try to slip in a little nuance. "But I also wanted to let you know if you ever need someone to talk to, about anything, whatever it is... I'm here, all right?"

He shifts his gaze around, and I remember high school. Being nervous and suspicious about everything and everyone. Even when I didn't have much to be nervous or suspicious about.

"Yeah." He clears his throat. "Cool. Thanks."

Then I head back downstairs and make myself at home on the couch until Taryn arrives home an hour later. Frankie greets her with enthusiastic kisses, and I would like to be able to do the same, but I'm sure she'd still fight me on it.

I inform her of the evening's events as she hangs up her coat and purse. "Thank you so much. You were a massive help."

"It's not a big deal. They take care of themselves."

She flips on the dining room light and pauses. "It's so bright in here."

"Oh yeah. I changed out your lightbulbs. They were all dim and shitty."

She turns to me, stunned. "You didn't have to do that."

"It was nothing."

She shakes her head at me, brows furrowed, her mouth open as if she wants to speak, but she doesn't. Moments pass in silence, and I wonder if I maybe overstepped.

Then she's really not going to like what else I have for her.

I follow her to the kitchen, where she washes a red apple before cutting it up into slices and placing them on a plate along with peanut butter and a few little pieces of cheese. It's not a very good dinner for someone who worked over twelve hours, but I've got to pick my battles.

And I fear this might be a big one coming up.

I wait until she eats a few bites to point to the bottom corner. "I also fixed that baseboard. It was sticking out, and I didn't want anybody to hurt themselves."

She pauses mid-chew, staring at me in wonder again. She swallows her food, her voice barely above a whisper when she says, "I kept meaning to fix that."

I wave her off. "Took me less than five minutes."

"Yeah." She puts her plate down with a thump. "You have to stop doing all these things for me."

"Why?"

"Because."

"It's really not that big of a deal."

"It is, though," she whines, facing me with a frown. "Don't you get it?"

I mean...kinda. It took me no time at all to change a few lightbulbs and fix a baseboard when it might've been on her list for a long time, and maybe she's mad at me for taking away her independence. But also, maybe she's happy for the help because she could use a little bit of it, whether she wants to admit it or not. And for all of her previous experience she disclosed to me today, it's clear she never had someone helping her with all this day-to-day stuff.

"Can I show you one more thing?" I ask with a playful wince, and she heaves a sigh, rolling her head back on her shoulders.

"I guess."

I take her hand and lead her outside to the shed. "I finished it."

"Great. How are you going to get it out of here?"

"It's not going anywhere."

She tips her head to me. "What do you mean?"

I open the door so she can see inside. "It's yours."

She gasps, covering her mouth with her hand as she steps inside, turning in a slow circle. It's not very big. I couldn't make it as large as I would've liked with the size of her backyard, but it fits snugly in the corner, and I painted it a robin's-egg blue at Maddie's suggestion. I hung the twinkle lights at Jake's insistence since he thought she might want to come out at night and work.

Taryn's eyes fill with tears as she takes in the wooden

shelves with her pottery supplies, the space for her wheel, clay, and containers of glazes and paints, as well as the kiln in the corner so she doesn't have to transport her pieces in her car to and from the studio. She can do everything right here.

She touches the hooks on the back wall for aprons and towels then tilts her head back to the skylight that'll be perfect for sunny days. Hopefully inspiring whatever art she wants to create.

Finally, she meets my gaze, wiping the back of her hand over her cheek. "Dante, I...I don't know what to say. I can't believe you did all this for me."

I let out a huff. As if this isn't the least I can do for her. "You deserve it. Whatever you want. A place to work. Help with the kids. The moon, the stars. Just tell me, and that's what you'll get."

She parts her lips, blinking the wetness from her eyes until there is nothing left in them but fire. And I can't breathe. Barely have time to do anything except brace myself when she launches at me, arms around my neck, legs around my waist, lips on mine.

"You," she whispers. "I want you."

Chapter 16
Taryn

This is all too much.

Dante Moretti is all too much.

And yet there is nothing I want more than to gobble down every bite he offers me.

I am greedy.

Gluttonous.

And so damn tired of fighting it.

I dig my fingers into the soft strands of his hair and lock my feet at his back, earning a growl of approval from him. He pushes me up against the hard wooden wall, and my bottom lip stings from his teeth, but I love it. *Need* it.

I claw at him, any place I can get at, his neck, the slope of his shoulder, his back after I hike up his sweatshirt. His skin is hot and tastes like salt when I skate my tongue over it, sucking on his neck. I've never been particularly into vampire stories, but I suddenly want to know what his blood tastes like. Would it fill me up? Quench my thirst?

His hands are everywhere, in my hair, gripping my ass, digging into my sides. We are anything but graceful. Messy and raw, all clashing teeth and searching tongues. I can't hear anything besides his panting breaths and my racing heart. But God, I feel *everything*.

The pulsing desire settling between my legs and the relief of finally giving in. It has been agony.

I feel his trembling hands and his fading self-control as he accidentally rips my shirt. I don't care.

Because I am just as desperate.

"Fuck, duchess," he groans, trailing his lips over my cheek and ear, rolling his hips so his hard length pushes against my clit. "I think I might come in my pants."

"No, don't," I laugh, my head thumping against the wall so he can pay attention to my throat, but he doesn't. He stops, his eyes reflecting the twinkling lights above us as he smiles.

"I love your laugh."

Then he thrusts against me, and I close my eyes. "I'll be laughing at you a lot if you finish before we've even started."

He grunts and spins around, moving so fast I'm disoriented, so I don't understand what's happening when he turns me away from him. I've barely found my balance or breath when he pops the button on my gray slacks, tugging the zipper down to slide his hand inside my panties. "You should know by now..." His teeth graze my jaw. "I take fucking you very seriously."

Then two thick fingers find and press on my clit as he wraps his other hand around my throat, forcing my back against him and tilting my mouth up, taking no prisoners. I am utterly at his mercy.

But I don't want to be anywhere else, and I reach behind me to hold on to his hips, rocking back against his cock impatiently, earning a hiss and another scratch of his teeth. Though he can't lose the trace of laughter in his voice. "Yeah, yeah, we'll get there."

Then his mouth is on mine once again, his tongue invading me like his fingers do, pushing in, curling and thrusting. With him wrapped around me, I don't feel the cold November night air, but I shiver when he shoves my pants down, giving him more room to work his fingers in and out of me. I'm a panting, delirious mess, my nipples hard points beneath my bra and shirt, and I'm clearly out of my mind, not thinking as I tear the rest of the buttons away, letting my favorite oversized shirt fall to the floor. In some far-off part of my brain, I think I should be upset I ruined it, but I don't care. I don't care about anything except the crackling fire in my belly and Dante's breath against my ear.

He yanks the left cup of my bra down to pinch my nipple, but my ragged cry is too loud, and he slaps his hand to my mouth, rasping, "I didn't insulate the walls, and you have the tendency to get noisy."

"Fuck you," I mumble under his palm, and I feel his smile against my temple.

"No, *I'm* fucking you. Now, come on my fingers, so I can fuck you with my cock."

It's a neat trick how my body responds to him, going off like a bomb, and I'm glad his hand is over my mouth to muffle my shout as I convulse under the weight of pleasure that has been building and bearing down on me for all these weeks.

I deserve a trophy for even lasting this long.

Or maybe he deserves one for bringing me to my knees.

Tearing apart my self-control with well-timed smiles and well-placed touches on my shoulder and back, ever supportive. Always a memory.

And now, here, in this tiny hideaway he made me, it is better than I remember.

I blink my eyes open to find him sucking on his wet fingers, the ones he had in me moments ago, before using those same fingers to drag my pants and underwear down to my ankles, and my skin pricks with goose bumps. He barely spares a glance down my body before he tears off his hoodie with a rough, "Bend over. Hands on the table."

I do as he says, but I keep my gaze over my shoulder as he quickly undoes his jeans and pulls out his erection, the tip wide and glistening. "I don't have a condom, but I've been tested, and I swear to God I'll pull out. I swear, Taryn."

It's completely reckless and absurd, but the words are out before I consider any other answer. "Do it."

I brace myself with wide feet, having already waited too long. I have no chance of getting pregnant, and I trust him when he makes promises.

The voice in the way back of my mind calls me every name in the book: stupid, idiot, fool. But I don't care.

Never in my life have I cared less about the consequences of my actions. Because there is a fire inside me, and the only thing that can put it out is Dante.

"Please," I whimper, and he shakes his head slowly, as if he can't believe his good luck.

"Look at this," he whispers, almost to himself, his left hand gripping my hip so tightly I know I'll have marks tomorrow. Then he's at my entrance, and he spits, a long drop of saliva hitting the seam of my ass. He mixes it with my own arousal to coat his length, and all at once, he thrusts in, wrenching the breath from my lungs. When I can inhale once again, I moan at the perfect fullness of him. Like he was made for me. Or I for him.

I'm not sure which or if it even matters. Only that nothing has ever felt as right as this.

He rocks back and in again, hitting me so deep, I gasp, my hands scrambling for purchase on the rough wood of the table as he mutters curses behind me. Something about "sweet pussy" and "fucking good." I can't concentrate with how amazing it feels, how the intensity of our connection overpowers everything else. All logical thought ceases, leaving only animal desire.

And suddenly, images of all those nature documentaries I used to watch with Jake flood my brain. Lionesses stripping the flesh from prey. That's how I feel now.

Vicious.

Feral.

Like I would do anything for Dante.

Tear anything and everyone to pieces.

Even myself.

"Please, please," I whine, pushing back against him with each of his thrusts. And I'm so close to the precipice that all it takes is a look over my shoulder at him, with the bottom of his T-shirt between his bared teeth, lines bracketing his mouth as if he's in pain, but I know he's not. There is a sheen of sweat on his flexing stomach, and he releases a soft grunt with every plunge of his cock.

My lion.

The orgasm hits me like a freight train, and I fall to the table, shuddering as wave after wave of pleasure crashes over me. I smother my sounds with Dante's sweatshirt as his thrusts become erratic, and then, suddenly, he pulls out. A moment later, warm ropes of liquid hit my back as his left hand settles beside me.

We both breathe heavily in the silence that feels too still after the frantic hurricane of lust that passed through here. Eventually, the cold starts to actually be too much, and I straighten up on shaky legs. Dante hands me a new roll of paper towels from one of the drawers he stocked for me, and I clean myself up, while he rights his clothes and picks up my ruined shirt from the floor, including each button that he pockets.

"You've worn this a few times," he notes as I finish zipping up my pants.

"It's my favorite."

"I'll get it fixed."

I start to argue that it's a few years old and not worth it—I think I found it on the clearance rack at Old Navy—but he stops me with a quiet, "Arms up."

He puts his hoodie on me, and I bury my nose in it, soaking up the scent of him. Then he tugs me close, smoothing my hair and cupping my face. "You okay?"

I admire the angle of his cheekbones, the shape of his mouth, the scruff on his jaw. "Yeah. I'm great."

"You sure?"

It's unlike him to be so insecure. Normally, he's overly confident, arrogant even, and I arch my brow at his question.

"I don't want you to regret this in the morning." The ache in his voice makes me want to wrap him up and never let go. Dante has an aura about him, a shield like mine, except his is made of laughter and smiles. I arm myself with sarcasm and resting bitch face, while he puts on this sunshine facade every day. And I don't know why, but I do know there is so much more below the surface. A man wanting to be loved. To be chosen.

"I'm not going to regret this in the morning," I say, and his throat works on a swallow.

"Good. Because I will never regret you." He inhales through his nose, his thumbs stroking my cheeks as his tongue drags along his bottom lip. Like what we just did is only the appetizer. "I remember you telling me over and over it would only be that one time."

I roll my eyes. He would bring that up.

"I hope you don't tell me now that you needed one more to get it out of your system."

I bite the inside of my cheek, sticking my hands into the front pocket of his hoodie, refusing to admit I doubt he'll ever be out of my system. Or if I want him to be.

Instead, I say, "You should know better than to give a girl your hoodie."

"Why? You plan on stealing it?" When I nod, he grins. "Start a collection. I want you to."

Then he leans down to kiss me, slow and sweet this time, his tongue teasing mine, anchoring me to earth with his playfulness. I never expected to fall for anyone. Let alone a giant golden retriever of a man. Yet, here I am, tripping over my heart.

He rolls his forehead against me, whispering, "I had to have you. I couldn't hold back anymore."

I agree with a soft hum. "I couldn't either." But reality sets in. "I should get back inside."

He nods, brushing his nose against mine. "Of course."

We step out of the shed, and I spend another few moments taking in what he made for me, thanking him with a quick kiss to his cheek. "You're amazing."

His answering smile is brighter than the moon, and he twines his fingers with mine to walk the twelve steps to my back door, where he whistles. "Long commute."

"Yeah, but you seem able to make it over every day."

"Damn right." He slides his hand around my waist, drawing me in for one last searing kiss that has me leaning against the doorjamb for support when he steps back.

"Thank you for tonight. For...everything." I gesture to the shed and then to my house.

"Anytime, duchess." He gently drags his index finger down my jaw then tugs on the collar of his sweatshirt as if I'm the one who needs the warmth when he's left with only a T-shirt.

"I'll see you tomorrow."

I bite my bottom lip to keep from smiling too big as he pivots away from me and quietly turns to the side of the house, where his soft footsteps take him upstairs to his apartment. Only then do I finally whisper to the night sky, "See you tomorrow."

Chapter 17
Dante

I barely slept last night after the way I took Taryn so hard and fast in the shed. It's all I could think about. So much so that I masturbated at two in the morning, recalling every detail. The way she threw herself at me, heels at my back, fingernails dug into my skin. How her back bowed against me when I touched her swollen clit, the way she mewled and begged and whimpered as she came on my fingers. I don't think I'll ever forget how she shamelessly bent over, her wide hips swaying back and forth, her thick thighs spread, and how she shivered when I spat, making her pussy soaking wet.

Something happened yesterday.

Something I can't quite name, but Taryn transformed before my eyes.

She opened herself to me, put all her vulnerabilities on display, and let me take care of her. I know that's not easy for her to do. She's been taking care of herself and everyone around her for so long, I'm not sure she knows how to give up control. But she did for me.

Her trust and the pride I take in it kept my head in the

clouds all day, which pissed off my father during our Moretti Construction meeting this morning, and I had a lot of trouble wiping the smile off my face during lunch with Clara, so she gave me a ton of shit about it.

Since that fateful night at Tabby Cat, we've renewed our friendship and picked up right where we left off after high school. Which is why I decided to come to The Nest. Even though I don't need to be here today, I have to warn Taryn.

With only two weeks until Thanksgiving, we're in the home stretch of the renovation, and I've got the plumber working upstairs today. After that, it's all finishing touches, and then it'll be ready for the big party in December. Adding to my high, I spoke with Raf this morning. He's doing well, and he finally got his paperwork sorted. The legal system is a hellscape, but I'm happy he's doing well and staying here with his family.

I stroll into the bed-and-breakfast through the kitchen, spying a familiar head of hair as she passes through the new sitting room to the reception desk in the corner. I pause at the doorway, admiring her as she types something into the computer, humming mindlessly. She's a terrible singer but fucking adorable all the same.

Taking a chance, I step behind her, my hands finding her waist, pressing a kiss to her neck, inhaling her scent that's a mix of coffee, candy, and feminine grump. My favorite.

She spins around, hand raised, but immediately relaxes when she realizes it's me. "Oh," she breathes, a symphony in that one tiny sound. Surprise and relief and something deeper that tugs at my very soul.

I love that "oh." It's layered, complex, like she is, and I want to peel it apart, understand every nuance. But more than that, I want her. I need her body against mine, her breath on my skin, her voice in my ear.

"Dante," she starts, but I cut her off, my lips on hers. She melts into me, her hands gripping my shirt, pulling me closer. I walk her backward to the nearby closet I'd built for extra storage space she'd requested. And perfect for what I have in mind.

I press her against the door, my hand reaching behind her to turn the handle, and we stumble inside, surrounded by shelves of linens and cleaning supplies. It's cramped but private, with a door that locks.

I hit the light—which she doesn't fight me on—and flip the lock, then drop to my knees, sliding my hands up her thighs. "You ever consider wearing a skirt or dress?"

Taryn Stone does not need to change one goddamn thing about herself. Every inch should be worshipped, and it would be my honor to do so anytime she wanted.

But.

It would be easier to do so if I didn't have to take her pants off every single time.

"No," she says, staring down at me with wide eyes. "We can't do this here. I'm working."

"You can spare me ten minutes." She opens her mouth to argue, and I bite her upper thigh once I've got her tan plaid pants down around her ankles. They shouldn't be as hot as they are, but they hug her hips and ass so nice. Plus, she's got this tight beige turtleneck on like a librarian. And I'm so hot for it.

For her.

"Dante!" She hisses, pushing at my shoulder. "Don't bite me."

"Stop talking, or I'll do it again. You want us to get caught?"

Her panties easily slip down her legs, and she grits her teeth, seething at me even as she steps out of them. "You're going to get me fired. And then I'll hate you forever."

"You couldn't." I lick my lips, mouth watering in anticipation of her taste on my tongue. I push her leg up to my shoulder, hooking my arm around it so she's steady.

"Dante, no. What are you—?"

"Shh," I murmur, my nose buried against her already damp curls. Using my thumbs, I spread her pretty pussy wide, putting her clit on full and clear display—finally—and I tilt my head back. "Let me take care of you, duchess."

Then I kiss her.

Lick her.

Love the very center of her.

"Oh my god," she whispers to the ceiling, bending her standing knee, and I wrap my left arm around her hip, gripping a handful of her ass to keep her upright. "Oh my god, Dante," she whimpers, and I really might come in my pants.

I was so close last night, but hearing her say my name like this... It sends me into overdrive. My cock is already rock hard. Ever since my knees hit the floor.

It's not like I didn't enjoy eating pussy before, but I can't get enough of Taryn's.

It's my favorite meal.

And the sounds she makes drive me wild. Like she can't contain herself.

Except here, she has to.

It's all the more exciting. Because it's illicit.

Every low gasp of breath feels like she's exhaling right on the tip of my dick, teasing it, and I need to finish *her* off before *I* finish. "You gonna come on my tongue? Let me lick up all that sweet honey?"

She arches her neck, fingers tunneling into my hair, gripping it tight enough to send another jolt of pleasure to my cock, my balls drawn up tight with the need to orgasm, and I pick up the pace, my tongue flicking against her clit as my skin flames, fighting myself. My own goddamn animal instincts to fuck this woman. Mark her. Make her mine.

The idea of her as mine draws a hum of satisfaction up my throat, and Taryn sucks in a sharp breath at the vibration, refocusing my attention on what I need to do. Make her come so fast and hard, she won't be able to recover quick enough to tell me no. She'll be mine.

At least, that's what the savage part of my brain thinks.

I let go of her ass to slide my index and middle fingers inside her. She's hot and tight, and her walls clench around them, ready for release. It brings me even closer to release too.

Every squeeze of my fingers, every tensing of her thigh, every barely audible groan is sweet torture. "I'm so close," she whispers, tugging on my hair. "I can't... I can't..."

I hum against her again, louder and longer, and she finally sails past the edge, curling her lips over her teeth, swallowing her moan as she orgasms.

I can't stop my own.

Both of us lost to this otherworldly experience.

I imagine this is close to what heaven feels like.

And I can't even be embarrassed by the mess I've made in my underwear because Taryn is still riding out her orgasm as I tenderly stroke my fingers in and out of her, placing kisses on her hip, thigh, and all along her scar. When she finally blinks her eyes open, she caresses the side of my face with her hand, fingertips trailing over my temple and jaw, and before she lets go of me, I place a kiss on her palm.

She smiles.

So do I.

Then I stand and reach for a small folded towel. Taryn gets herself dressed as I open my fly, cleaning myself up to her snickers. "You really did come in your pants."

"Yeah, well, I love the taste of your pussy, and your moans are hotter than any porn I've ever seen. So... It's your fault."

She huffs, although she sounds quite pleased with herself, and takes the dirty towel from me when I finish, tossing it into a bucket with other dirty rags. "You're a hazard to my work environment."

"Absolute terror," I agree, pulling her to me with my hands on her waist. "Should keep me locked up."

"Not a bad idea."

"In your basement."

"You'd love that, wouldn't you?"

I cluck my tongue. "Kinda hot thinking about you keeping me tied up except for when you want to come sit on my face."

She turns away from me, mumbling, "I don't know why the fuck I ever said yes."

Me either. But she's stuck with me now.

And I remember why I'm here in the first place. "Wait, hold on a sec. I gotta talk to you about something."

She pivots to lean against the door. "I have to get back out there."

"I know, but I wanted to give you a heads-up. I told Clara about us."

Taryn freezes, the whites of her eyes huge. "What do you mean, you *told* her about us?"

"We had lunch today, and she figured it out. That we hooked up."

"She already knew."

"Yeah, but...I told her we did again." I motion to the floor, where I'd been on my knees to fuck her with my tongue. I plan on doing it again. And again.

Taryn dips her chin, jaw working back and forth. "What exactly did you say?"

I rub my hands on my jeans, keeping it light and casual so I don't scare her away. "Nothing really, but you know her. It sorta slipped out when she was giving me shit about me smiling."

She inhales an audible breath that makes me think she's mentally counting to ten. Like I'm an annoying child. Then she opens her eyes to me, the playfulness from a minute ago completely gone. "You're *always* smiling."

I flop my hands out at my sides, trying for a joke. "Maybe I'm smiling differently."

She rolls her eyes and swipes her hand over her face, grumbling my name. "Dante. *Why?* Why would you tell her?"

"She's my friend. Why wouldn't I?"

"Because," she growls. "It's not... This isn't..."

The hairs on the back of my neck stand on end. It is. This definitely is... "What?" I ask, forcing her to spit out the lies I know she tells herself. "What is it?"

"Nothing!" She mashes her lips together and closes her eyes like she didn't mean to say it, but she did. I know she did. But I also know it's not true.

What I felt—feel—transpire between us is real. It's honest. The most basic truth between us.

"Nothing?"

She releases a noisy breath then focuses her gaze on me. Though it doesn't last long. She can't look me in the eye while she lies. "I don't want you making a big deal about this. Because it's not, and now, Clara is going to get it in her head that it is. You know this is just...a one-time thing."

I can't say it doesn't sting, but I ignore that pain for now, determined to show her I'm not afraid of her past. I can't be run off by her present. I want her future. All of her. "Technically, three times now."

She glares at me in return. "You... This... Fuck." She grits her teeth and spins toward the door, taking a few breaths that lift her shoulders. "I don't want either of us to get hurt, okay?"

"Okay," I agree because I do not plan on ever hurting her.

"So, let's agree to leave feelings out of this...whatever it is. I'm a mom and have this place to manage. I don't—can't be in a relationship. Especially with a guy twelve years younger than me. That's..."

"Got nothing to do with anything, but sure, whatever you say, Tar. You wanna be friends? We'll be friends. Doesn't mean I can't give you a few orgasms now and then."

She stays silent, only tosses a glance over her shoulder before opening the door like nothing happened.

I don't move, staring at her back as she walks away from me.

A feeling that I assume I'm gonna have to get used to.

She's not an easy one to crack. But she's also not easy to let go of either.

I'll simply have to be patient and keep showing up. Keep showing her she can trust me. That I'm here for her, in whatever way she needs.

Because what we have, it's real. Special. And I'll wait as long as it takes for her to see that too.

Even if that means pretending we're only "friends."

Chapter 18
Taryn

I remember the day I realized Dad wasn't coming back. It had been a few weeks. Ian had been acting weird, grumpier. Mom had been acting the exact same as always. In control. Smiling. Cool as can be.

That day, I'd been riding bikes with Marianne for a while, but I was tired and felt like going home. As usual, Ian was playing with Roman outside, Griffin reading, so I went upstairs to my room.

And that was when I heard it.

Mom crying.

My mother *never* cried. Not when she was happy, and certainly not when she was sad. Although I didn't know for sure because she never let us see her be sad.

She was strong, always knew the answers, and never let on that the world wasn't exactly as she made it out to be.

Until I opened the door and saw her on her bed, head bent over, tissues scattered all over, hands covering her face. She didn't even hear me enter the room.

I remember her shoulders shaking. The pale blue sweater

she wore and the dark droplets on her jeans from her falling tears.

"Mom?" I said, and she shot up with a gasp. The sight of her red cheeks and the lines from her mascara are seared into my memory. But I didn't even get to say anything else before she hugged me to her, apologizing.

She apologized to *me*.

As if she had anything to be sorry for.

Her husband, my father, was the one who didn't appreciate what a good thing he had with her. He didn't value the life he had. He was the one who thought he could do better, blamed everyone else around him for his failures. He was the one who chose to drink away the money my mother made then got mad because one of us kids dared ask him to act like our father.

The folklore is Clifford Stone had his eyes set on the NBA in college but needed tutoring for a class. That tutor ended up being a pretty, dark-haired girl named Violet, daughter of an Iranian immigrant father and artist mother. Clifford, the middle son of strict Irish Catholics, had never met anyone like her.

The NBA never worked out for old Cliff, but Violet was there at his side and they married right after college. Got pregnant almost immediately.

But poor Clifford couldn't hack the simple life. He was meant for bigger and better things, and off he went, leaving Violet alone with her toddler. But she made it work on her teacher's salary and the occasional check he'd send from whatever the hell he did in Atlantic City or New York.

Years later, he came crawling back with apologies and promises to be better. And for a while, I suppose it was, because Griffin was born. Then me. And then Roman.

And, wouldn't you know? Cliff still couldn't handle it. The life of husband and father or his liquor.

But when he left that second time, he left for good, and I let my mother comfort me, when I really should have comforted her.

She was the one who maintained our family unit. Who scrimped and saved and held us together with Band-Aids and kisses. She was everything to me and my brothers, but as a grown woman and mother now, I understand how she must have felt.

Like she was never enough.

Because that's how I feel.

Like I was not enough for my father. I wasn't enough for Craig. And I know I won't be enough for Dante.

Which is why I reacted the way I did the other day with him in the closet. After he literally got on his knees for me, I told him it meant nothing.

It was a shitty thing to do, but I don't have any other options.

He is far too good, and I am far too scared for us to become anything, let alone make it for the long haul. We're not meant to be.

And that is why I'm out here, in the shed he built for me, working my stress out on the wheel. The spinning clay centers me, helps to calm my mind. I can lose myself in the repetitive motions, forming, lifting, smoothing. I can forget about every-thing else except what I'm creating.

Usually.

Today, though, I can't get a pair of intensely dark eyes out of my head. The scratch of work-roughened hands on my skin. The familiar smell of wood and cotton. I can't help but replay the scene in my head, the way he stared up at me and told me he'd take care of me, then buried his nose between my thighs and inhaled, his raw yearning palpable.

Never had a man ever orgasmed simply because I did.

That needy desperation we both share for each other sends a shiver down my spine, even with the small space heater wafting warm air through the shed.

Dante really did think of everything.

And it's as if I conjured him from my thoughts, jumping slightly when his voice cuts through the white noise in my head. "Hey, duchess."

I look up, my hands still molding the clay, and there he is, leaning against the doorway. His dark hair tousled like he's been running his hands through it, his gaze fixed on me, a small smile playing on his lips, and gray sweatpants hanging low. As if I don't have enough reasons for being out here, reminding myself why being with him is a terrible idea.

Add another to the list—those sweats don't hide how he's a shower, not a grower, and hangs slightly to the right.

Motherfucker.

"Hey." My throat is sandpaper. "What are you doing here?"

"Kids are with Barrett this weekend, right?"

I don't miss the slight sneer when he says Craig's last name. My kids' last name too. I didn't want to change my name. Not because of my father but because of my mother. Craig always hated that I never did. Even brought it up that she ditched her Persian last name for her married one. Why couldn't I?

One more thing added to my list of transgressions.

"I figured you could use some company," Dante says, and I raise an eyebrow.

"Company, huh? Or are you here to distract me?"

He grins, that charming, lopsided grin that never fails to make my stomach flip. "Can't it be both?"

I roll my eyes, but a reluctant smile that tugs at my lips.

He steps into the shed. "You feel like teaching me how to do this?"

"You want to learn how to throw?"

"That's what you call it?" He is utterly delighted, rubbing his hands together. "Yeah, I want to *throw* pottery."

I eye him, already knowing where this is headed. Nowhere I can hide.

It's not safe.

Not for him. And definitely not for me.

But I know he won't leave. Once this man gets an idea, that's it.

"Okay." I stop the wheel, mashing the clay into a lump—it wasn't turning out the way I wanted it anyway—and tip my head back. "Come on. Sit down."

He settles himself behind me, thighs outside of mine, his chest against my back, and it makes me think of that first night when I rode on his motorcycle. The one he rides a few nights a week. The one he's asked me to get on the back of no fewer than fourteen times in the last week. The answer is always the same. *No.*

But, this? I can do this. Feet on the ground, his big, warm body wrapped around mine.

"What are we making?" he asks, reaching for the clay, overeager.

I slap his hands away. "A flowerpot. You need to be gentle."

"I can be gentle." Though the way he rubs his five-o'clock shadow along my neck is not at all gentle.

"First things first. We have to make sure the clay's wet," I say, and his chest expands against my chest for a comeback that I cut off because it is surely filthy. "Scoop some of that water onto it."

He dips his hand into the bowl next to the wheel and douses the clay. "This good?"

"A little more. Yeah, that's good. Now we mold it."

His arms come around me, caging me in as his large

hands cover mine, our fingers intertwining as I guide them up and down, shifting the shape of the clay. His breath feathers over my ear, making me aware of every point our bodies connect. Hip to hip, his chest to my back. It feels dangerously intimate.

Together, we form a dome, and I try not to think about his strong hands roaming my body instead of clay.

"Okay, now we open it up," I say, and I feel more than hear the rumble of his chuckle against my back, the amused puff of air against my neck. "You're such a child."

"I didn't say anything."

I move our hands to the top, crooking my thumbs, and he copies the action. Together, we press down and out, hollowing out the middle.

"Perfect. Just like that."

His lips ghost over my neck. "I like the sound of that praise, duchess."

I swallow hard, determined not to let him fluster me. But it's so hard.

He is so hard behind me. From his pectoral muscles to what I know is his dick against my ass. His sweatpants don't hide anything.

"Don't get smug. We've still got work to do."

"Yes, ma'am."

I walk him through the next steps, lifting the side, shaping the rim, smoothing out imperfections. His fingers follow mine the whole time, his easy inhales and exhales keeping rhythm with the spinning wheel.

As we continue, his touch grows from tentative to more confident until he's doing most of the work. I wet the sponge, squeezing water over his hands and the clay, and he hums behind me. "This is like that movie."

"*Ghost?*" I guess.

"They do it on the pottery table," he says, and I sputter a laugh.

"That is not at all what happens."

"Then what does happen, smartass?"

"He dies."

His fingers reflexively squeeze a little too hard, and our flowerpot becomes a candy dish. I snort, my head flopping back to his shoulder. "That's why it's called *Ghost*. He's a ghost."

"But... They don't do it?"

I stifle a laugh with my forearm, and he heaves a sigh. "I really thought they did it." When my snickers subside, he slants his head back, smiling at me. "Can we still do it?"

He's impossible, and it's impossible to say no to him. "Not here."

He kisses me, dragging his hands up to my wrists and forearms, painting me with wet clay. I scowl at him. "Now we're definitely *not* going to do it."

"Famous last words," he murmurs into the slope of my neck, and he's right.

I'll give in. I probably always would.

Which is exactly the problem.

"You ever make a sculpture?" he asks as I stop the wheel to clean up.

"I've tried. I'm not very good at it."

He makes a curious sound. "Okay, but what if you, like, make a copy of something?"

I put the clay away and wipe off my hands. "I don't understand what you mean."

"You know how famous people put their hands and feet in the sidewalk at that theater in LA?"

"Yeah." I smile. That was on an episode of *I Love Lucy*. One of my favorites.

"Can you do that?"

"I guess." I shrug, standing, and he follows me.

"You should make one of your tits for me."

I slug him in the shoulder, and he chuckles, rubbing at it.

"It was just a suggestion."

"I'm not making a mold of my tits."

"But they're so nice. They should be immortalized."

"I can't stand you."

He snakes his arm around my waist, towing me into him, his grin doing more to soothe my weary soul than hours at the wheel. "You love me."

"I don't," I say, even as my heart clangs around in my rib cage.

He strokes my cheek with his thumb. "You got a bit of clay on you."

I lean into his touch, my breath hitching slightly. "Because you made me a mess."

He smiles, his thumb tracing a path down to my lips. "I like messy."

Before I can respond, he leans in, capturing my lips in a soft, slow kiss. I melt into him, reaching my hands up to tangle in his hair as he glides his down my sides to my thighs, squeezing, urging me up. I wrap my legs around his waist so he can carry me to the house. "Let's get you cleaned up."

He doesn't even sound strained when he says it either. I'm a solid woman, in height and weight, but he might as well be lifting a feather.

I hate that I'm impressed by a gym bro.

But it doesn't stop me from sucking on his throat, nibbling on his earlobe, earning a smack to my ass cheek before he sets me down on the sink in the bathroom upstairs and proceeds to turn on the water in the bath. He aims a stern pointer finger at me. "Do not move."

Curiosity wins out, and I don't. He disappears for a few

minutes as the tub slowly fills up, steam rising. Right when I start to get up to turn off the water, he returns. "I told you not to move."

"I—"

He points at me again. "Only good girls get rewards."

My brows shoot up, a mixture of irritation and...excitement flooding my veins. But he doesn't notice how my cheeks turn pink and hot because he's too busy filling the tub with bubbles and lighting candles. He even produces a bag of candy, places it on top of a long piece of wood that he sets across the width of the tub, along with my favorite flavor of sparkling water and a headband that matches a new fluffy robe.

"Dante."

He turns to me like he puts together professional baths every day.

"You... Did you buy all this?"

"Yeah."

"Why?"

He waves his hand like it should be obvious.

"For the off chance I'd take a bath?"

He nods. "For the off chance I could provide you with a nice, relaxing bath, yes. I bought this stuff. It's not that big of a deal."

My throat clogs and my eyes sting. "I wish you'd stop saying that. This all... Everything has been a big deal. A big fucking deal."

He frowns. "Why do you sound mad about it?"

"Because! Because you don't need to do it."

"I know." He closes in on me. "I want to do it."

I close my eyes to the tears threatening to spill out, and he kisses my temple, murmuring, "Get in the tub. Relax. I'll be back in a bit."

Chapter 19
Dante

I n the half hour I've let Taryn soak in the tub, I have emptied her dishwasher, played a few rounds of tug-of-war with Frankie, and took some measurements of the living room. But I can't stand the idea of her naked and wet without me anymore, so I knock twice on the door before opening it.

She lifts her head, appearing a bit dazed, and maybe my plan worked a little too well. I wanted her to enjoy herself, but I still need her to have a bit of life left in her for what comes next. She can't be a wet noodle.

That's my job. To make her boneless.

"How're you feeling?" I ask, noting the gummy bears are gone and all of the bubbles have disappeared, allowing me a clear view of her glistening skin, her light-brown nipples, the dark triangle of hair between her legs, and the roundness of her kneecaps poking up out of the water.

Maybe I'll add a bathroom renovation to my list. Because Taryn deserves a tub she can fully lay out in. I'd have to rearrange everything in here, since three people share it. Then again, if she ever wanted to get rid of the top-floor apartment, I could convert it to another level with bedrooms for the kids and really give her a bathroom fit for a duchess.

I remove the plank from the tub and hold out the fluffy robe as she stands up, quickly covering herself. It's clear she's still uncomfortable being naked in front of me. As if I'd be suddenly turned off.

Could never happen.

My dick would fall off first.

Once she's wrapped up in the robe, I hug her to me, trailing kisses up the side of her damp neck. "How do you feel?"

"Mmm."

"Mmm?"

"Mm-hmm."

"I got something else for you."

I guide her to her bedroom, scented with the few lavender candles I lit. I also kept the lights on, hoping she wouldn't mind. After shucking off my shirt, I lean back against the headboard and invite her to lie down between my legs.

"What are you doing?" Her voice is breathless as I uncap the little bottle of oil.

"Taking care of you." I nudge the sides of the robe down so I can massage her shoulders, working my thumbs up her neck. She exhales a long, audible breath, so I focus there for another few minutes, making sure all the knots release from her muscles. Then I trace over the small purple flower tattoo on the back of her shoulder. "This is pretty."

"For my mom," she says quietly, rolling her head to the side, granting me better access to her neck. "Her name was Violet."

"Ah, violets for Violet. Tell me about her."

"She was wonderful, kind, and so smart. She loved to laugh. Her favorite show was *I Love Lucy*."

"I assumed it was your favorite, with all of the memorabilia you have."

"Yeah, I loved it. Mostly because Mom did. She would make us a bowl of popcorn, and we'd watch a few episodes on weekend nights. She worked so hard, and my brothers and I fought over one-on-one time with her, but those were my nights with her. Laughing on the couch at Lucy."

I nuzzle my face into the crook of Taryn's neck. "I wish I could have met her."

This earns a slight pause, a barely noticeable tension in her muscles before she relaxes again and admits, "Yeah. Me too."

"Will you take off your robe?"

She shoots me a glare over her shoulder, and I raise my eyebrows in innocence.

"I can't keep massaging you if not."

Our first night together, she fought me on the lights and seemed to find it laughable that I'd be really fucking physically attracted to her. The night in the shed, it was relatively dark with only the soft glow of the twinkle lights. And the other day in the closet at The Nest, it was bright, but I only had her naked from the waist down.

Here, now, she can't hide from me. The lights are on, and there is nothing for her to cover up with.

But I see the moment she overcomes her insecurities.

From the second I laid eyes on her at Tabby Cat, I wanted her. It had nothing to do with her body. I don't care about stretch marks or surgery scars or the size of her thighs. All those small details add up to the person she is. And I want her, whole and forever.

Fuck.

I want Taryn forever.

The realization makes me break out in a sweat, and for a

moment, I almost miss how the stress bracketing her mouth fades away. *Almost.*

Because even the idea of spending the rest of my life with this woman is not enough for me to ignore the gift she's offering me.

"Good girl," I murmur as she slides the robe off her arms before leaning back against me, completely naked. With our position, I have a perfect view of all her hills and valleys, the slope of her breasts with tight tips, the roundness of her belly, and the flare of her hips and thighs, leading down her long legs to her cute little toes. "Put your head on me, beautiful. Relax."

She does as I say and rests all her weight against me, arms at her sides, legs partly spread, nice and even breaths raising her torso. I pour more oil into my hands and skate them up and down her right arm, making her skin shine. "Feel good?"

She nods. "You're going to spoil me."

"That's the point." I pinch the webbing between her fingers then roll each of her digits out before giving the same attention to her left arm. By the time I finish, her chest and throat are flushed with color, and I'm not even sure she knows she's wiggling back and forth.

I turn the bottle upside down, drawing a line of oil from the dip in her collarbone to just below her belly button and smooth my palms over the same path, rubbing it all in, luring soft moans out of her, and honestly, I don't know who's enjoying this more. Me or her.

With both of her breasts in my hands, I plump and play, brushing my thumbs over the stiff peaks, rolling them between my fingers, watching goose bumps dot her skin. She pushes against me, arching her neck, silently asking for more. And I will never deny her anything. I caress and massage, learning she likes it when I scratch my blunt fingernails in circles around her nipples, but never quite touching.

She hisses and throws her hands around my head when she eventually can't take it anymore, digging her fingers into my hair. "Dante."

I smile against her cheek at her sweet whine. "Yes?"

"Stop teasing me."

"No, I don't think I will." I glide my hands down her stomach and hips to her thighs. "Keep your hands where they are. Don't move your legs."

"I can't," she says on a gasp when I brush my fingers over her pussy.

"Yes, you can. You can do everything, anything you want to. Especially be my good girl, can't you, duchess?"

Her answering groan sends my lust into overdrive, and I concentrate on the way my fingertips leave tracks on her skin with the oil, pushing her thighs open farther so I can part her slick flesh. The scent of the lavender candles and her arousal is a heady mixture, and I inhale deeply before dipping my chin, rubbing my lips back and forth across her shoulder, my fingers echoing the motion as I drag them over the lips of her pussy, then slip along the crease of her thighs, gripping them hard, putting her in the position I want. Knees bent, legs open.

I squirt another few drops of oil on my fingertips then use my left hand to expose her clit. We both watch in rapt attention as I circle it with my right index and middle fingers, slow. So slowly, she whimpers.

But we have a long way to go.

Even if my cock is hard as steel in my sweats and I already know how good it'll feel to be buried balls deep in her.

I add a little more oil to make her really wet and then speed up. Since our first night together, I could tell Taryn needed a little extra moisture to get her going, and it was pretty easy to buy this almond oil.

In bulk.

She squirms in my hold as I add a third finger, rubbing that sweet spot faster and faster until her moans become long and loud. Then I back off.

She huffs. "What... What are you doing?"

"Playing."

"*What?*"

I pinch her nipples. "You've never been edged before?"

She shakes her head.

"Well, babe, your only job is to lie here and enjoy it."

"I'd rather have an orgasm."

"You'll get one." I scrape my teeth over the shell of her ear and keep rolling her left nipple between my fingers, moving my other hand down to her clit. "Eventually."

I laugh when she curses me, but I swiftly lose my humor as I work her up again into a writhing mess. Then immediately back off. She growls my name. I merely massage her hips and belly.

Then I start again, stroking her clit until she's trembling, her breath coming faster. So close to the edge.

And stop.

"Oh my fucking god!"

I pour more oil into my hands, rubbing her tits, fingertips drawing circles around her nipples.

"Dante, please."

I love hearing her beg, love knowing I'm the one making her feel this way. Because I've been begging her for weeks.

She's got me on a tight leash and doesn't even know it.

I slide my hands down, thumbs tracing her now soaking-wet sex, her clit swollen and sensitive. And I give it a light smack.

She jerks but groans softly, so I do it again. This time hard, and she sucks in a sharp breath, hands slamming down on the mattress outside of my hips, as if she's out of control of her body. Then she hits me with a request. "Again, please."

Fuck me.

I can't come in my pants again. Once was a funny story. Twice is an embarrassment.

I slap her clit again, and I know she's riding the edge hard, so I soothe the sting with my fingers, and she plants her feet on the bed, hips lifting up.

"Fuck," she swears, chasing my touch and orgasm.

I'm chasing my own.

She is just so hot.

This is so hot.

Being with her, I lose my place in space and time. All I hear is her gasp, all I feel is her heat, all I smell is her desire, all I taste is her skin, all I see is how she loses herself. In me. In us.

Knowing I can give this strong and independent woman pleasure, make her beg, bring her to her metaphorical knees while I get on my literal ones...it is all-consuming.

When I'm with her, nothing else matters.

Nothing but her and me and this ever-growing fire between us.

Ashes to ashes, dust to dust, that's what they told us in church. And that's what I am. Ashes without Taryn.

She shakes, muscles twitching, body pink and practically leaping off the bed with every pass of my fingers over her clit. She's ready, and so am I.

"You want to come, duchess?"

"Yes," she sobs, hands fisted in the bedsheets.

"How bad do you want it?" I fondle that sweet little button again, not giving her enough to send her over the edge, but enough to keep her right there, on the brink.

"So bad," she says, her voice barely audible, her jaw tight. "Please, Dante. Please let me come."

I give her what we both hunger for, circling my fingers faster and harder until she cries out, her stomach contracting, her pussy pulsing against my hand. I can feel her come, can feel the wetness, the heat. It's fucking beautiful.

She collapses against me, limp, and I wrap my arms around her, her pulse racing against my lips when I kiss her throat, my own heart beating so hard against my chest, she can probably feel it.

Once she comes down, I tip her chin toward me, kissing her mouth as I roll us both to our sides, my chest against her back, her ass nestled in my lap. My cock is straining so hard, it's poking out of the elastic of my sweats, and after I have them off, it twitches reflexively. I wrap my fist around the base, willing my excited member to cool it. We just put Taryn through the wringer; I can't fuck her like a farm animal.

I slide my arm under her neck and kiss her throat, earning a soft smile and whispered, "You're gonna be nice to me now?"

"I'm always nice to you," I say with a nip to her ear.

"Yeah, that's why I like it when you're a little bit mean."

I exhale a harsh breath because my lady knows exactly what to say to get what she wants.

"You ready for me to fuck you?" I ask, but I don't wait for an answer. Instead, I skate my palm up and down the length of her rib cage then between her legs. She's still wet, still ready for me. "Yeah, you are."

I push in, moaning into her neck at the stretch and pull of her body accommodating mine, not being particularly careful or slow, thrusting in and out how I want.

But she likes it and twists to kiss me, her tongue finding mine, welcoming it into her mouth, and it's not lost on me how special it is that she has invited me not only into her bed but her life as well. I know enough about her to know she doesn't put her faith in a lot of people. And I won't let her down.

Not ever.

I wrap my arm around her, start to move fast, rocking in and out of her with enough force to earn a choked sob with every thrust. I roughly squeeze her breast and hip and waist. Anywhere I can reach that will keep her as close as possible to me. Her most intimate muscles clamp around my cock, and both of us lose the kiss, unable to coordinate. We merely pant into each other's mouths.

She arches her back, and I pinch her nipple.

She meets my plunges, and I hold her leg up.

Both of us climbing higher and higher.

"Come for me, duchess. Come on my cock. Let me feel you."

She does, her body convulsing, yet I can't luxuriate in the pulsing of her pussy, because I need to pull out. Barely making it in time before I come on her robe trapped beneath us.

"Oh fuck," she mumbles, sounding half asleep already.

I can't argue. I hardly have the energy to toss the robe to the floor and turn off the lights. Taryn doesn't say a word when I slip back into her bed, naked and wrapped around her, my sweat-slicked chest against her back, my palm on her belly.

And I know, without a doubt, that she is it for me.

The one. Taryn Stone.

She's gonna hate it when I tell her.

Chapter 20
Taryn

I haven't woken up beside someone since Maddie finally transitioned out of needing to sleep next to me. After that whole nightmare of Craig forgetting about her in McDonald's, she spent almost a full year in my bed.

Now, with a muscled man arm around my middle, I can't get out of bed fast enough. I've been experiencing night sweats for months, random times when I'll wake up with soaked pajamas. This time, I'm naked, but no less dripping with sweat.

I leap out of bed, snatch a bunch of tissues to dab at the skin of my neck, armpits, and backs of my knees. Behind me, Dante yawns noisily. "What time is it?"

It's still dark out through the windows, and I blink over to the digital clock in the corner. "Five fifteen."

"What are you doing? Come back to bed."

"I can't."

Sheets rustle, but I'm too busy to pay attention as I use more tissues to wipe away the sweat. Then his hands are on my waist. "What's wrong?"

"Nothing."

"What are you doing?"

With all the lights off, we can't see each other very well, and he feels around for my arms, eventually taking the balled-up tissues from my hand. "What's this?"

"Tissues. I'm sweating. I—"

"Come back to bed."

"I can't."

"What are you—"

I shriek in frustration. "I have night sweats! You had your big man body all over me last night, and I don't know how you didn't feel it. I sweat all over the sheets. They're soaked."

He turns me to face him, and I can barely make him out in the shadows. "Is that normal? Are you okay?"

"Yes. I'm just old."

"You're not old."

"Old enough to be in perimenopause."

"Don't you go through that when you're, like, sixty?"

"And this is why men should not be legislating women's bodies," I grumble with a push of his shoulder to pull the sheets of the bed.

He helps. "I don't disagree. But in my defense, I'm one of three boys, and I've never had experience with a woman in perimenopause."

"Because you're thirty, and I'm forty-two." When he doesn't respond, I yank the sheets from his hand and throw them to the floor. "You might as well go home."

"Nah. I'm still tired." He curls his arm around my waist and pulls me down to the bare mattress. It feels so good on my overheated skin. Dante moves so we're facing each other on our sides and yawns again. "I wouldn't care if you were fifty-two or sixty-two. I'm here because I like you."

"You would definitely care if I were sixty-two. There is

such a thing as being in different places in our lives, and sixty-two is hip replacement surgery age."

"I'd get you one of those scooters so you could zoom around."

"You're ridiculous."

"So are you if you think a little bit of sweat is going to scare me away."

It's more than a little. It's buckets. Gallons. An ocean.

"I can't have kids anymore," I tell him because it is too early for my brain to be fully functioning, but it seems important he knows that I am at a different place in my life than he is. I've been married and divorced with two kids. I've buried my mother. I'm solidly in the middle of my life, while his frontal lobe only reached maturity a few years ago.

"Cause of perimenopause? I'm gonna need you to explain all this after I've had some coffee because—"

"I had my tubes tied after Maddie."

He's quiet for a moment, his hand sliding under his pillow. And then, "Okay. Again, are you trying to scare me away or...?"

"I'm trying to explain that I'm too old for you. Whatever we're doing here... Don't get any ideas. It's not going to work out. It can't."

His hand brushes my hip, like he's going to settle it on me, but then he must feel how hot I am because he places it back on the mattress between us, shifting his pillow, resetting his head, getting comfortable.

Almost as if he's ignoring everything I said a moment ago.

It's infuriating.

And I'm about to tell him so, but then he says, "I think you know, but to be sure you really do know... I can't read. I mean, I can, but not very well. School was always hard for me, but I wasn't diagnosed until third grade. I have both a visual processing and reading comprehension disorder, and I hate reading. *Hate* it. I've never read a book in my life."

"Not even as a little kid?"

"No."

"What about it being read to you?"

"I get bored. I've tried audiobooks, but I make it twenty minutes and then find something else to do. I'd rather do literally anything else than read a book."

"That's okay. Some people aren't readers."

"Yeah, but most people can read."

"Debatable. I don't know the statistics off the top of my head, but most people in America read at a seventh-grade level."

"I'm one of those people."

"So?"

He puts his hand on my arm, squeezing gently as if he wants to shake me but stops himself. "*So* don't you get it? You could be with someone smarter than me. You should be with someone who doesn't fuck up order forms and doesn't need the computer to read things to him. You should be with a guy who's been to college like you and reads books and has discussions about, like, philosophy and shit. You *should*, but I don't want you to because I want to be here with you. Fuck that guy who can read six-hundred-page books and explain what actually happened in the First World War because I still don't know, but fuck that. I want you, and I want to be in this bed with you whether you're sweating in it or not, whether you still have your ovaries or not—"

"I still have my ovaries."

"See? You're smart and have shit to teach me, so don't hold it against me, okay? Whatever you think I *should* have, fuck it. Because I want you." He molds his hand to the side of my face, fingers in my hair, thumb stroking my cheek. "Don't try to scare me away. You can't."

Maybe not, but sooner or later, this will come to an end, and I'd rather cut it off before we go too far for us to walk away without one or both of us hurting. Especially after he's opened up this wound I know hasn't healed. And beyond my own doubt about us, I need him to know he is more than someone who struggles to read.

"I don't like that you say you're not smart."

"I'm not."

"Maybe not book smart, but you are in so many other ways. Intelligence comes in many forms."

"Tell that to my dad," he jokes, except there is that underlying pain in his voice I've heard before.

"I will. Is he the one who said you aren't smart?"

"Mostly."

"He's wrong." I place my hand on his face, mimicking his position. "You're incredibly smart, the most competent person I've ever met when it comes to construction and labor. You're also really good with people, and that takes a special emotional intelligence not many people have."

"Doesn't make the company any money, though."

"Doesn't it?" I trace his cheekbone with my thumb. "You think people want to work with assholes?"

"People work with Craig."

"Because he's a two-faced snake who will charm a client and then come home and take off his mask."

"Like my dad."

"I'm sorry," I whisper, laying my hand over his on my cheek to move it to my mouth, kissing his palm then placing it on the bed between us, lacing our fingers together. "My ex-husband being an asshole to me is one thing, but a parent being one to their child is something completely different—and worse, in my opinion. Children are born innately loving their parents, and for it not to be returned is devastating."

"Sounds like you know," he says, twining his legs with mine. Now that I've cooled off, I don't mind.

"My dad was an alcoholic and left when I was five."

"Oh shit, Tar, that's awful."

"On the one hand, I'm glad because I'm sure our lives would have been worse if he'd stayed. But it still wasn't easy. It was really hard. My mom worked herself to the bone to provide for us, and my brother Ian never had a life. If he wasn't taking care of my younger brother Roman, he was doing oil changes for extra cash for us. I knew that if I wanted to go to college, I was on my own. I needed a scholarship to pay for it."

"So you got one?"

"Partial for athletics, partial for academics, and I worked in the library all four years to help with the rest of it."

"I wish you didn't have to," he murmurs, speaking the things I tell myself. Money isn't everything, but it sure makes a lot of things easier. I was always so jealous of the kids who didn't have to work or keep their grades up to maintain their scholarship. They got to fool around and do whatever they wanted. Growing up was the same. Kids with new clothes, backpacks, and shoes. Girls with makeup and perfume. I wore a lot of Griffin's hand-me-downs when I could get away with it, which was often because I played sports, and thrifted my clothes or bought strictly from clearance sections.

Which is why Dante's thoughtfulness is so unexpected and difficult for me to accept without feeling like I need to work for it.

I shift closer to him. "I wish your father didn't make you feel like you're anything less than brilliant at what you do."

He makes a noncommittal sound. "Maybe we can agree

that we're a couple of kids trying to outrun the shadows of our fathers."

True. And I could be better about showing my gratitude. "Maybe I can learn to say thank you more often when you're sweet to me."

He lifts his hand to my mouth, dragging the tip of his finger over my lips. "Sucking on my dick would be fine."

I slap his shoulder. "There you go, ruining the moment again."

He pulls me into him, pressing my naked chest against his, and I don't fight him when he kisses me, rolling me to my back. Instinctually, I wrap my arms and legs around him as he roams his hands up and down my sides. He grows hard against me, but there's no urgency in his touch. It's lazy, both of us caught somewhere between awake and sleep. I let out a soft sigh, pressing back against him, inviting more.

He cups my breast, his thumb brushing my nipple until it hardens, as his tongue finds mine in a deep kiss that lulls me into a stupor. So much so that I tell him, "You don't need to pull out. I told you I can't get pregnant, and I trust you aren't sleeping with anyone else."

"Never," he swears into the skin of my chin. "Are you sure?"

I snake my hand between us, wrapping my fingers around his shaft, notching the head at my opening. "Positive."

He freezes, gazing down at me in the dark. "Wait, you didn't even come yet. Are you wet enough?"

"Make me."

I hear more than see him spit on his fingers before he swipes them up and down the length of my pussy, pressing and rubbing my clit, making sure I'm ready to take him. Then he slides in slowly, inch by inch. He's right, of course, I am not as wet as I need to be, but he doesn't stop getting me there, kissing my neck, licking my nipple. Eventually, my body gives way, allowing him to seat himself completely, and we both moan into a kiss.

His pace is languid, each thrust deliberate and controlled. It's a different kind of pleasure, a slow burn rather than a raging inferno. His tongue slides against mine in time with the glide of his cock, this slow and sweet sex more intimate than anything we've done before with only our breaths as our soundtrack and the wounds of our past hovering over us. But each one of our shared heartbeats closes them. Each soft sigh is a promise to be tender. Each kiss takes away the sting.

My orgasm is a steady climb, and soon, I'm gone, dissolving under the pleasure like sinking into a warm bath. There are no stars in my vision, but my heart is not where it used to be. Instead, it's floating above me, straight up to Dante's chest as he rocks his hips one last time.

"Taryn," he whispers, voice hoarse with emotion. It's not a question, not a demand. It's a statement, a declaration. My name on his lips is a secret of devotion in the early morning.

"Yes," I reply, my voice barely audible. It's all I can manage, all I need to say.

Yes, I'm here.

Yes, I'm with you.

Yes, I feel this too.

He rests his weight on top of me, our bodies still connected, pressed together, entwined.

I let him hold me. I let myself feel this, whatever it is. I let myself be in this moment, in this place, with this man. And for now, that's enough.

For now, that's everything.

Chapter 21
Dante

My mother is a phenomenal cook, but only if it's Italian. For the fifth year in a row, she's ordered Thanksgiving dinner, picture-perfect browned turkey, piled high mashed potatoes, and green beans that are so shiny and angular, they look fake.

It's almost a shame to dig into it.

I did a double workout this morning so I could eat double tonight, and I plan on stuffing as much sweet potato pie as possible down my throat.

So, it's another goddamn shame when we're barely a few minutes in, and my father opens his mouth to tell me, "Rumor has it this apartment you're living in is owned by the same broad that runs The Nest."

Broad? As if he's Frank Sinatra in some Atlantic City nightclub.

Across from me, Johnny snickers like an asshole. I'm sure he's the rumor.

I set down my fork and wipe my mouth. "Yeah. She does own it, and her name is Taryn Stone."

Dad raises his hands up like he meant no offense when I know he did. He lives to humiliate me in any way he can. I'm not sure why... Is the disappointment of his middle son so great he has to prove it to everyone? Is it some contest he plays with himself, seeing which kid he can pit against the other and who will come out on top? I don't understand, and I'm getting tired of it.

"Just don't shit where you eat," Johnny warns me, and I roll my eyes.

"Next time I want advice from my little brother, I'll ask for it."

"You're the only one sitting here alone." Johnny places a possessive arm on the back of Emily's chair. She offers him a smile, weak and mild. Johnny's going to walk all over her.

"I don't think so," Lauren, my sister-in-law, snaps down at the other end of the table, taking the small plastic fork from her kid's hand, gesturing for Robbie to do something since it looks like the toddlers—Kassidee and Everleigh—are about to start a food fight.

Mom comes to my defense, but it does nothing except circle the sharks. "Dante will find someone when he's ready."

Dad sniffs. "He's thirty years old. If he's not ready now, he never will be."

"Statistically speaking, most people find their spouses in college," Robbie says academically and completely unhelpfully since I'm the only one of us three who did not attend.

"But being thirty isn't old," Lauren adds, almost like she's trying to convince herself she's not old. Because if I'm old, then so is she. God forbid, we age.

The kids bang on the table, rattling the dishes, and Dad waves his fork in the air.

"The real problem is we've been babying him too much."

My face flames hot, and I curl my fingers into a fist,

sneering at Dad and then Johnny. "I think you're right. You have been babying Johnny too much. Poor guy's never done a full day's work in his life. How will he ever learn?"

"Fuck you. I do more for the company than you've ever done."

"No fighting at the table," Mom chimes in. "It's Thanksgiving."

I split my ire between my father and younger brother. "While you sit in an office all day, I'm the one in the field. I'm the one doing *real* work. You would be nothing without me, and I'm getting real goddamn tired of having to defend myself."

"We'd be nothing without you?" Robbie says, wiping mashed potatoes from his sweater, an attack from one of his kids. "That's a bit hyperbolic, don't you think? I was the one who helped Dad expand it from Grandpa's side hustle to an actual corporation."

Mom flaps her hand. "Yes, you've all done a lot to help. Now, let's move on. Lauren, you said you were going to put the girls in gymnastics?"

"Oh yeah, your big math brain, crunching ones and zeros all day, is what's keeping us in business. You're an overpaid accountant." I slap my hand to my chest. "*I* manage all the sites. I keep us on schedule. I'm the one bringing in new clients because you all and your lunch meetings sure as shit aren't. People want to book with us because of me and my work, not because of you!" I can't help the rise in my volume. Hearing Taryn speak about me the other night has unleashed something in me that I can't and don't want to rein in. "I'd really appreciate some acknowledgment every once in a while."

Across from me, Emily has melted into her chair while Lauren is full-on fighting with her kids to stop them from climbing over her and the table. Robbie is silently fuming like he can't believe I'd actually tell the truth, while Johnny's looking to our father for help because he knows I'm right. He barely does anything. He's a yes-man to Dad, who balls up his napkin and throws it on the table, pointing his stubby finger at me, the one he nearly lost in an accident years ago with a saw. I was the one who wrapped a towel around it and drove him to the hospital so he didn't lose it completely. "You ungrateful little shit. You should be lucky I keep you employed. Don't come into my house and tell me I need to show you appreciation. I am your father and your boss. You are nothing without me and what I gave you."

Yeah, that's right. What *he* gave me. Not like Mom had any hand in raising me. Not like I became who I am *despite* his lack of faith and confidence in me.

And I'm suddenly not very hungry anymore. I stand up so fast, my chair falls backward, but I don't bother picking it up. Mom watches slack-jawed as I grab my coat from the closet, but when she stands to come to me, I hold up my hand. "Not now. I need to get out of here."

Her eyes well with tears, and she nods silently. I'm texting Taryn before I'm even out the door.

> Where are you right now?

DUCHESS
> At my brother's. Why? What's up?

> I need to talk to you

DUCHESS
> Ok? Is everything all right?

> not really

DUCHESS
> Come to Griffin's. Dinner's almost ready.

She sends me a pin as I put on my helmet then rev my

engine extra long just to piss them all off inside. The drive is about fifteen minutes to a development of homes probably from the '80s or '90s, all of them built in the exact same way, with siding and stone, attached double garages, and neat front yards. I park my bike behind a row of cars out front of the house with an American flag, mums in pots, and a big yard sign that reads *My favorite season is the fall of the patriarchy* next to a bunch of turkeys stuck in the grass.

After I ring the doorbell, a woman about my age answers, smiling widely with long light-brown hair, ripped-up jeans, a sweater falling off her shoulder, and bare feet. "Hi, you must be Dante. Come in."

When I step inside, she takes my leather jacket, hanging it in the closet, and I perform a quick appraisal of the house. It's a well-maintained Colonial with pictures all over the walls and stacks of shoes next to the door, so I shuck off my boots.

"I'm Andi," the woman says. "It's nice to finally meet you."

"You too," I say reflexively, surprised she knows who I am, and she must see something on my face that makes her explain, "I'm Griffin's girlfriend. I think you met him in passing."

"Oh yeah, yeah."

She waves for me to follow her. "Everybody's here, but don't worry about remembering anyone's name, including mine. I won't be offended."

I'm good with names and faces, but I don't tell her that as I round the corner to the living room and kitchen, where a dozen people are scattered around. Maddie jumps up from where she was on the floor and pulls on my hand. "You're here! I didn't know you were coming."

"I didn't know either."

She smiles. "Are you gonna eat with us?"

"I guess so."

"Mom! Dante's here!"

I wave to Taryn at her place by the sink, and she waves back with a knife. It's more threatening than I think she means it to be, and I muffle a chuckle with my hand before Jake holds his hand out for a dap. I'm reintroduced to Taryn's older brothers, the men from that day at The Nest. There is Griffin, a guy who could legit play a superhero, and Ian, the tattooed and grizzly bear of a man. There are also a bunch of kids besides Taryn's. Griffin's got twins, and Ian has a bunch, biologically and a few who just hang around, apparently.

With all the talking and laughing and arms slung around shoulders, it feels like a family. One that accepts and loves as much as they give one another shit. I don't sense any competition or jealousy. Only affection. Clear and obvious affection.

"Dinner's ready," Griffin announces eventually, and I hop in line behind Jake to fill my plate. The food is set up as a buffet in the kitchen, and Taryn stands by the sink, answering questions on where to find extra napkins or to retrieve some ice from the freezer in the garage. It's not her house, but it might as well be from the way she takes charge.

"What the fuck are you doing?" Griffin asks, pushing her toward me. "Get a plate and sit down. Your hovering is annoying."

I hold out a plate for her with one hand while tucking her in front of me with the other, her ass brushing up against my groin. No one notices except for us—Taryn, me, and my dick. I shake my leg out like I'm a twelve-year-old with his first boner as she arches her eyebrow. Which, of course, makes her look meaner and hotter. "You all right?"

"Mm-hmm. Yep."

"Famous last words," she teases, and I love her.

I love her so much my bones ache with it.

"How are you, really?" she asks, and I exhale the stress

from my family dinner and inhale the delicious scents of the food spread out in front of us.

"Better now."

"Good." Then she scoops me the biggest serving of mashed potatoes, and I am putty in her hands.

Multiple folding tables are set up in the living and dining rooms, and we find open seats between one of Ian's tatted-up sons and Andi, who animatedly tells stories about her recent time spent in LA. She's a songwriter, and she names a bunch of people I've never heard of, but they are her idols. Griffin sits across from her, staring at her like I imagine I stare at Taryn.

Like she's a double rainbow.

The northern lights.

The sunrise and the sunset.

Throughout the conversation, I learn there is a fourth Stone sibling, living in upstate New York, who hasn't been home in years. Taryn is highly respected by her brothers and also protected, if their reaction to a throwaway line about Craig was any indication. Both Ian and Griffin go off on a four-letter-word-fueled tangent about him as soon as the little kids leave the room.

I decide I really like them both.

I like them all.

After dinner, board games get pulled out, along with Andi's guitar, and everyone finds spots to lounge, helping themselves to second and third servings or pieces of pie. I play a round of Clue with a couple of the kids, Andi, and Taryn, who is, predictably, a *terrible* loser.

But once nine o'clock hits, everyone starts making plans. Maddie asks to sleep over with her cousin and best friend, Grace, and Jake heads out to a late-night movie with Ian's boys, which means Taryn will be home all alone tonight.

And what a coincidence. So will I.

Chapter 22
Taryn

After packing up some leftovers, Dante followed me home on his bike, and I spent no less than three-quarters of the time checking my rearview mirror. The idea of riding a motorcycle is super-hot. The reality is that I'm terrified he'll hurt himself. By the time he parks it and removes his helmet, I'm a sweaty mess beneath my coat, ignoring all my good sense when I stomp right over to him. "Do you know what the fatality rate of motorcycle accidents is?" I do because I looked it up a few nights ago. "One in about eight hundred."

He combs his fingers through his messy hair. "Yeah? You've been doing research?"

"Don't be so flippant! That's almost eight times higher than car accidents."

He steps up so close I have to tip my head back to hold his gaze. "Sounds like you're worried about me."

"Yes, of course I am, you big oaf." I add a punch to his shoulder for good measure. He has to know how unsafe it is and how precious his life is. "I don't like it."

"No?"

He's so smug. His mouth quirking, head tilting to the side. He likes me like this. Losing my mind about his safety. But I don't. I have enough to worry about without adding in the possibility of having his guts spilled on the side of the road. "No, I don't like it, Dante. I..." My breath fogs between us when I let out a rough exhale. "It scares me."

He loses his arrogance and curls his hands around my face, pressing his cool lips to my forehead. "I'm sorry."

My eyes sting, and I'm appalled at the level of fear I have about the mere possibility of losing this man.

I don't love him.

I don't.

I don't care about what he does. He could move out tomorrow, and I wouldn't care.

I wouldn't.

"Look at me, duchess..."

I lift my eyes and try to convince myself again that he is nothing more than my renter, the renovation project manager, a good lay.

He's...

Fuck.

He stares down at me with a tenderness that makes pretending all that much harder. I didn't realize how impossible it would be to ignore these big feelings when the other person doesn't.

He lets everything shine through his gaze, passion and honesty and a promise I'm not sure I have the strength to turn down.

"You that upset about my bike?" he asks, and I shrug, all nonchalant, and he rumbles an amused sound. "It's okay to say so, you know. I won't hold it against you. In fact, might make me think twice about it."

"You're going to stop riding just because I threw a fit?"

"You didn't throw a fit." He sighs like the weight of the world is on his shoulders. "What bothers me most is being the guy to come after the one who fucked you up so bad you think showing a little bit of emotion is *throwing a fit*." He holds my chin in a hard grip, making a point. "Sometimes I wish you would throw a fit. Everybody's got to break at some point. I like to know you're actually human and not an android made to take my cock."

"Dante!" I slap at his chest, and he quickly sobers, smile fading.

"I'm serious, though. Barrett made you think speaking up was bad, but I want to know what's in your head. I want to know what you're feeling. Always. No hiding from me, all right?"

"All right," I agree, and he kisses me on the mouth, his thumb pushing on my jaw, urging my mouth to open and accept his searching tongue, and with the swift rise of my body temperature, I'm reminded of how cold it is. I yank on Dante's leather jacket to follow me inside.

Frankie dances in circles when I open the door, and Dante accepts a few kisses before heading to the kitchen, opening the back door to let the dog out, like he lives here. Like he does this routine every day.

Dante keeps his gaze out on the backyard as he removes his jacket and slings it over one of the kitchen table chairs without looking. As if he is so familiar with the placement of everything, he could walk around with his eyes closed.

Then, after Frankie trots back inside for a treat, Dante puts the leftovers away in the fridge, save for the plate with pie, helps himself to adding an entire can of whipped cream to the pieces of pumpkin pie, and plucks two forks from the drawer. One for me, one for him.

Biting back a smile, I shake my head, enjoying the sight of him here way too much. This cozy little domesticity.

I scoop up a forkful of pie, the whipped cream piled high, and shove it into my mouth to keep from acting on the appeal. Dante does the same, and we eat in comfortable silence, even as my mind is anything but. I keep thinking about how he ended up here, with me, instead of with his family.

"Wanna talk about whatever happened today?" I ask, trying to keep my voice casual.

He swallows his mouthful of pie. "Same old shit."

"Your dad?" I guess, and he nods.

"As soon as we sat down to eat, he started making comments, and I couldn't take it anymore. I usually try to ignore it, but..." He turns to me, licking his lips like he's lathering up the courage to admit whatever is on his tongue. "After talking to you, I guess I didn't want to keep quiet anymore. I don't want to keep taking his shit. So, I said something back."

"Good. Good for you."

"But then my brothers jumped in and..."

"And what?"

He sighs, leaning to set his elbows on the counter, and it takes him a minute to continue, his gaze down at where he scratches his fork's tines along the crumbs on the plate. "In the moment, I was pissed. But now I feel shitty, you know? It's not easy being the family fuckup."

"You are not a fuckup. Is that what he said? Did he call you that?"

"Implied it."

"That's bullshit." I toss my fork down and tug on Dante's shoulder until he faces me. "You're amazing, and it's not your job to convince him of anything, but he's an asshole for thinking you need to. You're hardworking and kind, and if he can't see that, that's on him. Not you. He's the asshole. He's the fuckup.

Not you." I poke my index finger into his hard chest to prove my point, and he catches my wrist.

"You really believe that, don't you?"

"Of course I do," I huff, my anger growing. "I hate him. I hate him for making you feel like this. I hate him for not seeing what I see."

Dante's responding laugh is not one of amusement. "Hey, it's okay. You don't have to get all riled up on my account."

"No, I will." I push away from him. "You deserve to have someone in your corner, and when the chance comes to tell your father off, I will. I promise you that."

He tows me back to him again, his hands around my neck, fingers under my hair, thumbs bracketing my jaw. "I'd pay good money to see that."

He thinks I'm kidding. I am not. One day, I'll tell that man exactly what I think of him. But for now, I want to make Dante feel better. I want to show him that he's worthy, that he's desired.

I dip my index finger into the dollop of whipped cream on the pie and lift it between us. Dante watches me with a heated gaze as I suck it off, moaning quietly. His nostrils flare when he inhales audibly. "What are you doing, duchess?"

"Showing you what I think of you." With one hand, I work on his belt buckle and zipper, gathering more whipped cream with the other before sinking to my knees.

"Oh Jesus," Dante mutters, closing his eyes, and I grin. The way he goes from zero to one hundred never fails to delight me. I'm not sure if he's always been like this—so easily pressed—but I like to think it's me. I'm the one who turns him on so much, he literally cannot handle it.

When I finally pull out his already hard cock, I paint the tip with the whipped cream, rubbing it around the ridge of the head and over the weeping slit. He slowly dips his chin, his eyes on fire when they meet mine, and I offer my fingers up to him, sticky with the residue of the cream. He holds on to my wrist to lick each finger into his mouth, sucking on each tip, grazing the pads with his teeth, and I know that's what he wants me to do to him.

When he releases me, I wrap my hands around his tense thighs and lean in to lick off the white cream, circling my tongue around and around before wrapping my lips around him. He's thick, and I have trouble taking him to the back of my throat, so I use my right hand to help, encircling the base, squeezing and pulling while I suck on the wide head.

He heaves in a breath, hand slapping on the counter to hold himself up. "Taryn, oh Jesus, please, babe. I'm dying. That's so good. Fuck."

His senseless, slightly slurred words spur me on, and I concentrate on the things he likes, long pulls of my mouth, fingers prodding at the sensitive place behind his sac, and soon, his fingers are in my hair. More mumbling. More heavy breathing.

"I'm gonna come," he warns, fingers tight against my scalp. "You have ten more seconds before I come down your throat."

I'm not sure if that's a challenge or not, but I take it as one. I suck harder, stroking him in time with my mouth, then chance walking my other fingers back farther between the seam of his ass and press against the hole there. He coughs in surprise, heaving a low, "Oh fuck. I'm coming."

He doesn't have to tell me. I know the moment before he releases, his muscles trembling, and I relax my jaw, accepting his hot orgasm in my mouth. His cock jerks and spurts a few times, a mix of salt and sweet on my tongue, but before I can swallow, he grips my chin, sticking out his own tongue, a sign I should do the same.

And like our first night together, he stuns me with how

much I enjoy his crude actions. He bends, kissing me, all tongue and teeth, sharing the taste of him between us. It's intoxicating, and I barely realize how he pulls me up to standing, wrapping his arms around me tightly.

"Fuck, Taryn," he rasps, voice raw. "That was... Fuck."

I bury my face into the slope of his neck, where his wood and cotton scent is always strongest. And I know there is not much this man could ask of me that I would not give him.

He swallows, his Adam's apple moving against my mouth. "I don't know what I did to deserve you, but whatever it is, I'm glad I did it."

"But that's the thing," I say, lifting my head. "I'm the one who doesn't deserve you. Don't you see? I'm the mean one. You're the nice one."

He wrenches his head back, a growing smirk aimed at me. "I'd say what you just did was very, *very* nice." Without looking behind him, he grabs the can of whipped cream. "And it's your turn now."

He squats low and throws me over his shoulder, forcing a shriek out of me. "No whipped cream on the bed! I just changed the sheets this morning."

"I'll change them again." He smacks my ass. "Small price to pay for eating my favorite meal with dessert."

Chapter 23
Dante

It's the first Friday in December, and The Nest is buzzing with a warmth that has nothing to do with the twinkling lights or the crackling fire in the hearth. The scents of a freshly cut pine tree and homemade gingerbread fill the air, and the hum of conversation is a pleasant thrum against the backdrop of the soft volume of holiday classics.

This is it. Everything Taryn and I have been working toward, and it's already packed. I've barely had an opportunity to talk to her, only a minute when she introduced me to the owners, singing my praises about my work. In turn, I made sure they knew how amazing Taryn is, a one-woman show who turned their popular but kinda dumpy B&B into a picturesque getaway.

So many people are here, a few I know, including Clara and Marianne, as well as most of Taryn's family that I met on Thanksgiving. Jake and Maddie are around here somewhere, but I've been using the time to meet as many people as possible. This is what I meant when I said Moretti Construction wouldn't be anywhere without me, because every company needs a face. Someone to actually go out there and find new work, and that person is me. I had new business cards printed for the occasion and gladly hand them out to anyone who wants one once word spreads about me being the project manager.

I'm in the middle of popping a few pieces of cheese onto a toothpick when a hand smooths up my back, and I turn, expecting it to be Taryn.

It is not.

It's Kim.

My ex.

I step away from her, right into the food table, causing the plates to clink together. I barely save a tower of chocolates from falling over. "What are you doing here?"

She smiles, one that I used to find so lovely. Now, all I can think about is how I hated the taste of her lip gloss. She always had so much on. Taryn doesn't wear anything on her lips. I much prefer that. I think I'd prefer anything Taryn wore.

Kim sweeps her gaze around. "I saw the open house advertised everywhere, so I thought I'd pop in. Especially after I heard you did the work on it. Looks great."

I'm no longer interested in my food and set the small plate aside. "Thanks, but I didn't do much."

"Sure, you didn't," she says with a laugh, her hand curling around my bicep. "I can always see the work you've done."

That's a lie. We were together for two years, and in that time, she wasn't much interested in any of my projects. I don't believe she's here on a whim.

Kim's three years younger than me, and when we first got together, it was only to hook up. But that turned into me staying at her place most nights, until I was there every night. I assumed that meant we were headed toward the things I wanted, marriage and family, but she didn't. Which was why we broke up. She wasn't ready. She wanted to explore.

And hey, I'm all for exploring. But only if we do it together.

I suspect she realized what a good thing she had with me: loyalty.

"Can we go somewhere and talk?" she asks, but I shake my head, pulling away from her searching hands when she attempts to twine our fingers together.

"Nah. I'm good."

"Honey," she says with a laugh, like I'm joking.

I am not.

She pouts when she realizes. "What's wrong?"

I huff, coasting my gaze around the party, confused about what is actually happening. "Why are you here? We haven't talked in months."

"Because I..." She takes a deep breath, moving closer to me so I can still hear her when she lowers her voice. "I miss you, and I'm sorry. Okay? I just want to talk to you. Please?" She wraps her arms around me, standing on her tiptoes to brush her lips against my jaw. "Please, Dante."

That's when I spot Taryn across the room, frozen in place, glowering as my ex-girlfriend winds her arms around me. Trying to kiss me. I shoot my hand up, blocking Kim's face as Taryn's features flicker through so many different emotions: hurt, anger, jealousy, and back to hurt, her shoulders slumping slightly.

Shit.

What bad fucking timing. I set my focus back on Kim, so there is no equivocation. "I'm not interested in hearing what you have to say. I've moved on."

Her face falls. "You've moved on?"

"Yes. I've moved on with someone else, and I'm not going to go somewhere to talk with you. I'm sorry, but no thank you."

I slip away from her, following Taryn out to the kitchen and through the back door. "Wait, Tar. Wait a second."

Of course, she doesn't. She struts right outside like it's not freezing.

"You're not even wearing a coat." I catch her by the wrist to stop her. "What are you doing out here?"

"Needed some air," she snaps, refusing to face me.

I remove my blazer and slip it on her shoulders. "I'm sorry about that."

She folds her arms over her chest, snagging the lapels of my jacket to pull it closer around her, and I rub my hands up and down her arms. She doesn't push me away, but she still won't meet my gaze either. "Taryn, talk to me."

"Who was she?"

"Kim. My ex."

"The one you were with before me," she says. It's not a question, but I nod anyway.

"It was nothing. I haven't seen or spoken to her in months, and I had no idea she'd show up here tonight. I don't want anything to do with her."

"Didn't seem that way from where I was standing. Appeared pretty cozy, actually."

"Hey." I step in front of her, ducking my head, forcing her to meet my eyes. "You know I'm not interested in her anymore, right?" When Taryn doesn't respond, merely presses her lips together, I take her by the shoulders. "I'm serious."

"Why did you break up?"

"Because she didn't want the same things I did. I wanted to get serious, but she didn't."

"Did you love her?"

The inquisition is harsh, but I don't mind. It makes me sure that Taryn has feelings for me. She may not be ready to admit them yet, but they're there. They're strong.

I shrug in response to her question. "I thought I did. We were together for almost two years, and it was a slow grow. It started out as something fun, and then suddenly, we were together all the time, and it made me realize that I was ready for more. I'm ready to love someone."

I hope Taryn understands what I mean. That I love her. I am ready for everything that comes with her.

I want a life with her.

"She wasn't ready," I continue, squeezing Taryn's shoulders. "And she broke up with me, but now she thinks she made a mistake."

Taryn cants her head to the side. "Did she?"

I slide my hands from her shoulders to her neck, fingers in the back of her hair, thumbs at her jaw, nudging her eyes back to mine. "No. Whatever she does or doesn't feel is none of my business anymore. She wanted to talk, but I don't. I have nothing to say to her. The only woman I'm interested in is standing right here in front of me."

She rolls her eyes even as the corner of her mouth twitches. "Nice line, Romeo."

"Goddamn." I breathe out a frustrated chuckle. "It's not a line. I want you, no one else. Is that so hard to believe?"

Her features soften a little, so I press onward, pulling her into me.

"You're the one I think about first thing in the morning." I push a lock of her hair behind her ear. "The one I want to talk to all day long. The one I wish was waiting for me when I get home."

"Dante..."

"It's you, Taryn. Only you." I lean in slowly, giving her time to back away if she wants. But she doesn't. Our mouths meet, and god, it feels as perfect as the first time. All the times. She tastes like chocolate and feels like silk. She is everything.

"What do you say we do something this weekend?" I

suggest, nuzzling her cheek and ear. "You, me, and the kids. We could take them ice-skating or to the Christmas market."

"Like a date?"

I grin into her hair. "Sure. Like a date."

"No, I can't." She tries to step back, but I don't let her get far. Only a few inches.

"Why not?"

"I'm not going on a date with my kids there."

"Okay, so we don't have to call it a date. It'll just be a hang-out. Come on, it'll be fun."

Taryn wiggles out of my hold and shakes her head, crossing her arms again. "I don't think that's a good idea. I don't want to get anyone's hopes up."

Whose hopes? Mine? Hers? The kids?

Because as far as I'm concerned, my hopes have always been up. I'm merely waiting for her to get with the program. And, all right, I understand not wanting the kids involved if—god forbid—what we have doesn't work out, but it's not like I'm proposing a vacation together. Only a few hours.

"Besides," she says, "it's Craig's weekend with the kids."

Well, that puts a small wrench into the plans, but if there's a will, there's a way. "What time are they going?"

"He was supposed to pick them up at ten, but he had to change plans. Again." Her breath fogs in front of her. "He's picking them up at six."

I have more questions. Like how often does he change plans? Do the kids like going to his house? Where does he live? Can I kill him?

But before I can utter any of them, she returns my blazer to me. "I should get back. I have guests."

She hurries inside, leaving me to take a few deep breaths, my attention on the dark night sky, keeping myself in place to prove I'm not the *biggest* simp in the world. But maybe the second.

I make it exactly five seconds then head into the party. I don't see Kim anywhere, so I help myself to one of the little sandwiches and find a seat on the small built-in bench I made for the new sitting area, right next to the bookshelves. I take out my phone, scrolling back through the community's IG page for a post I saw the other day about the annual *Nutcracker* show.

That's when Maddie and Jake find me with their own food and drinks. I try to make myself sound as casual as possible when I ask, "So, you like going to your dad's house?" From their surprised arched eyebrows, I suppose that wasn't as nonchalant as I hoped, and I go for coolly aloof with a shrug and careless toss of my hand. "I was just talking with your mom about how we should all hang out, but you two are going to his house tomorrow."

Jake sneers while Maddie seems a little more optimistic about it. As if she wants to go to her dad's place. "Yeah, but we're supposed to go with him twice a month, so it's not like it's that much time to begin with. It's not bad. It's okay."

Jake slants his gaze to his sister and shakes his head, almost as if he feels bad for her naiveté.

I hold out my cell phone so they can both see it. "I was thinking about getting tickets to the show tomorrow. The matinee. So you'd still be able to go to his house after."

Maddie gasps in delight. "*The Nutcracker?*"

"Yeah, I was thinking all of us could go."

Jake shakes his head. "No way, man. I'm not gonna watch a ballet."

"It's not so bad," I say, elbowing him. "Besides, it'll give us a chance to hang out. We can go to the Christmas market after. Me and you can grab a bite to eat."

"Just me and you?" he asks, and I nod.

"Yeah. I'm a sucker for Christmas fun."

"Me too!" Maddie jumps in her seat. "Oh my god, yes! Let's do it!"

"Well, first we have to talk to your mom about it," I say, but Maddie's up and halfway across the room before I even finish speaking.

Jake sniffs a dubious laugh. "You really want to go watch people dance?"

"Not necessarily, but that's a part of relationships. Sometimes you need to spend time doing things you may not enjoy but they do, because it's important to them. Right? I don't know a whole lot about soccer, but I would be happy to go to a game with you, learn all about it because you like it. And I like you. I like spending time with you. Same with your sister and your mom. When we love people, we love everything about them. Not only the things we enjoy, but everything."

He considers this, his gaze on his empty drink cup for a long time before he finally lifts his eyes. He nods and smiles. "Yeah, okay. Makes sense."

I slap his back a few times before Maddie returns with Taryn in tow, glaring at me. "What is this I hear about a show tomorrow?"

"Threw the idea out to the kids, and they were into it. There's a matinee, and then we can walk around the market for a bit after. They'll still be able to go to their dad's."

"Please, Mom," Maddie pleads, tugging on her arm.

Taryn turns to Jake, who shrugs. "I'm in."

"Really?"

He nods all magnanimously. "Yeah. Sometimes you have to do things you don't enjoy for people you love."

I smash my fist against my mouth to cover my laugh as Taryn's eyes bug out. Then, because she knows she was set up, she points her finger at me. "You did this."

I ignore her ire and smile. "I didn't get a chance to tell you, you look really pretty in that dress."

Finally, she's wearing a dress, and I can't even take advantage.

But with the kids on my side, she has no other argument against me and sighs. "Fine."

Winner, winner, chicken dinner.

Chapter 24
Taryn

This isn't a date.

Number one, because I said so.

And number two, because I'm wearing my frumpiest sweater.

So, it's definitely not a date.

But Dante is refusing to accept that it is not.

He kept putting his hand on my lower back as we walked from the parking lot to the auditorium and then while we waited in line to show our tickets, and now he sits on the other side of Maddie, with his arm on the back of her chair, his knuckles brushing my shoulder.

During intermission, he took Jake with him to buy a round of waters and snacks for us, even though I told him I didn't want any, and then he refused to accept money for my kids' food. Like a gentleman.

What an asshole.

Maddie's attention has been glued to the stage for the last hour, but every once in a while, Dante ducks down, whispering something in her ear that earns a snicker or whispered response. Because they're good buddies.

And Jake? I can't even believe he's here. Even though he clearly hates it and is slouched so far down in his chair, I can barely see his head, he's spending the day with us because of Dante. Because Jake has begun to look up to the man.

I am outnumbered.

And out of excuses.

It was easy to cling to my anger and jealousy yesterday, when I saw Dante and his shrew of an ex hanging all over him, but today, there is nothing to keep me anchored to earth. Nothing to keep my heart tethered.

That dumb organ is off floating on cloud nine.

To say nothing of my sex drive.

I hoped by wearing the thick cream sweater and wide-leg pants, I'd be able to prevent Dante's constant horndog eyes. But any time I catch his gaze, I can practically see the movie in his head. The visions flickering of me on my knees in the kitchen. Bent over in the shed. Splayed out between his legs in my bed.

He's replaying it all in his mind.

So am I.

I can't help it.

Especially when he wraps a lock of my hair around his index finger, tugging gently.

Makes me think of our first night together.

Strip.

Get on top of me.

Feed me your tits.

I don't realize the ballet is over until everyone around me stands in an ovation. I jump up to follow suit, although I haven't actually watched anything since the dancers in the candy-cane-striped costumes left the stage.

Dante tosses a knowing grin at me, and I barely restrain myself from flipping him the bird.

The audacity of being hot *and* charming.

After the show, he ushers us all out of the theater like a mother duck and her chicks to the Christmas market downtown. It's a cold but clear day, the blue sky just starting to bleed into orange as the sun sets. The market is only a few blocks and Dante entertains us on the way by talking about which bits of the ballet he enjoyed most and that he could "totally hit that triple axel jump that guy did."

Jake dares him to, and he takes a running leap into the air only to do half a spin, but he lands with a flourish that sends Maddie into a fit of giggles. I dip my chin down, tucking my mouth behind the collar of my coat, so he can't see me smiling when he comes to my side, asking, "Did you see that?"

"*So* impressive."

"Yeah. I thought you'd like that." He curls his hand around the side of his mouth, shouting to Jake, who's performing his own jump spin. "Hey, you gotta get better height. Come on!" Then he shoots me a wink before sprinting ahead to complete a 180 this time.

Sighing up at the sky, I let a laugh loose. Whoever is up there really did break the mold with Dante Moretti.

And I would never want him any other way.

The market is set up every weekend in December on Aster Street with wreaths on lampposts, lights strung across storefronts, and booths set up in the cordoned-off street, selling wares from the local vendors. We stop to say hello to Ian at his shop, where Dante spends a few minutes looking over my brother's art pieces framed and hung up on the walls as they chat about tattoos. Dante has two. One on his forearm, with a cross and rays of sun behind it, and another above his collarbone with Roman numerals for his birth year.

As if I need a reminder that he is so much younger than me.

"Nice seeing you again," Dante says, clasping hands with my brother, who flicks his gaze to me in silent communication.

One that means he *knows* something is going on between us.

Because, first, I invited Dante over for Thanksgiving, and now, we're out with the kids. On something that probably appears very much like a date to an outsider.

Even though it is *not* a date.

We are not dating.

We're hooking up. That's it.

"You can fill us in when we get coffee," my brother says when I offer him a quick hug goodbye.

"No, I won't be doing that. 'Kay, thanks. Byyeeeee."

We move on toward the hot chocolate stand as Jake whines that he's hungry. What's new? Dante throws his arm around my son's shoulders. "Let's go find something. We'll give the girls some time alone."

Jake nods, and Dante swings his gaze to me, making sure it's okay. "We'll meet back up here in thirty minutes?" I ask, and when the boys agree, they take off to the other end of the block where a band is playing and someone is grilling something. I turn to Maddie. "What are you hungry for?"

She points back to a small food truck. "Crepes."

"Yes. Good call."

We order a ham and Gruyère along with one that has cinnamon apple compote and caramel drizzle and share them at a small table, where I ask casually, "So, what do you think of Dante?"

"Love him," she says without a second's hesitation. "He's so funny and really nice. Like, would trust him to stand guard outside of the porta-potty at a concert nice, you know?"

I bite back a laugh. I took my daughter to one Olivia

Rodrigo concert last summer, and you'd think she'd been to Woodstock with all her new, worldly knowledge. But I have to agree with her. Dante is nice. Too nice.

For me, at least.

I'm mean and prickly and don't deserve him standing guard in some theoretical scenario where I have to pee in a broken porta-potty, and he's outside of it holding my purse and keeping the door closed.

Because he would do all that and more.

He's the type of guy who puts you on his shoulders without asking. Who makes friendship bracelets and acts as DD. He's the one guy to trust at a bar to get you home safe. The late-night call you make when you need help.

He is everything "nice" guys pretend to be and looks like what every man behind a social media avatar image wishes he could.

"Do you like him?" Maddie asks, and I give her a slight nod. She tips her head to the side. "*Like* him, like him?"

I narrow my eyes. She's too smart. "Why would you ask that?"

"I don't know." She carefully scrapes up the last of the caramel from the plate with the final bite of the sweet crepe. "He's around all the time, and I think he likes you. *Like* likes you, I mean."

"Oh. Hmm."

She watches me as she chews, and I suppose she's getting to the age where we can start having conversations on the same level. The kinds of conversations I used to have with my mother. About what it means to be a woman and share in the communal experience of it sucking a lot of the time.

My time with Dante doesn't suck.

"Yeah, I like him," I tell her honestly. "But we're just friends. We're going to stay friends."

She toggles her head side to side. "Sometimes friends turn into lovers."

"How do you know that?"

"I read romance books," she says, as if it should be obvious. Neither one of my kids reads *a lot*, but Maddie enjoys a good shopping spree for paperbacks that will stay in the same tower next to her bed for the whole year until she spends two weeks over summer break obsessively reading. Only to start the routine over again.

"Is there sex in those books?"

"Not in all of them, and the ones that do have it don't have a lot."

I gather up our garbage to throw away. "I don't know what a lot is, but you know that's fiction, right? If you have questions about sex, you need to ask me."

"I know." She follows me up from the table with a smile. My mother let all of us kids read whatever whenever we wanted, and I don't police what my kids read either. Maddie's thirteen, and when I was thirteen, I read *Flowers in the Attic* on my own and *Flowers for Algernon* for school, arguably both just as traumatic. So, if she wants to read romance with sex, I'm going to let her. As long as she continues to communicate with me.

"Ooh, can we go look at that jewelry?"

I trail her to the booth with the handcrafted pendants and necklaces, where we bump into Marianne and Clara.

My best friend frowns. "You didn't tell me you were coming out."

Marianne and I regularly update each other with our schedules. Daily check-ins and mental health updates. *On the struggle bus today. Gotta stay late at work. Or I'm going to murder my ex-husband. Prepare bail money.*

After all these years, we can pretty much guess what's

going on with each other, so for me not to tell her I was going to be here is a red flag.

Maddie fills in the missing information. "Dante got us tickets to *The Nutcracker*."

"Did he?" Clara crows with a knowing grin in my direction. "How nice."

Marianne tips her head toward me. "So that's a thing, huh?"

"Nope."

"Definitely yes."

I shake my head.

She nods.

Clara claps like Snow White when she's listening to the dwarfs sing. Utterly enchanted.

Maddie glances between us before slinking away to check out the rings.

As soon as she's out of earshot, Clara slaps my arm. "I knew it!"

"You did not."

"I knew you'd be good for each other."

"We are not good for each other."

Clara heaves a sigh. "Why are you so obstinate? Can't you see how well you complement each other?"

"So?"

Marianne buts in then. "I do feel like you're fighting this extra hard."

"Because nothing's going on." When they both glare at me, I lose my temper. "It's just sex!"

A few people shoot their attention to me at my outburst, and I lower my voice. "It's just sex."

"And yet you're here on a date," Marianne says, and I knock her elbow.

"Why are you pushing me on this?"

"Because you're self-sabotaging."

I wrench back, jaw hanging open, huffing perturbed puffs of air. And yet no words exit my mouth.

"What's holding you back?" my best friend asks, her head angled in that way she does whenever she's breaking down a problem.

"He's twelve years younger than me."

Marianne blinks wide eyes at me while pointing to her wife. They have the exact age difference that Dante and I have, and it's worked out pretty well for them.

"You don't think he's mature enough?" Clara guesses, and I shake my head. I'm the older one, but he's the one who has a better handle on himself. Sure, I have a house and kids and all the things an adult is supposed to have, but sometimes I feel like I'm still figuring it all out. After my divorce, I had to start my life over from scratch, and most days I don't know what the hell I'm doing, overwhelmed and stressed out because of all the plates I'm spinning.

It's Dante who dragged me out of my corner kicking and screaming, forcing me to have fun and relax, forget about what I *need* to do and focus on what I *want* to do.

Fuck the plates. Fuck juggling balls. Fuck the past.

He lives in the present and has brought me along for the ride.

"For all of his big golden retriever energy, Dante is one of the most mature and level-headed people I know," I tell them. "Which is why I think he needs to find someone else who's not jaded and still trying to overcome drama and trauma and—"

"These all sound like excuses to me," Marianne says to Clara. "What do you think?"

"Excuses," she confirms, and I really don't have time for this impromptu therapy session.

I motion behind me. "Whatever. We have to go and meet up with Dante and Jake. Mads, come on, hon."

She holds up a pair of earrings. "Can I get these?"

"Yeah. Your aunts said you can get whatever you want as your Christmas present."

Maddie hops up and down excitedly. "Really?"

They roll with it. "Yeah, of course!"

Clara pulls out her wallet, like she's going to blow on dice. "Earn those airline points. Mama wants a trip to Aruba next year!"

Marianne is practically a sister to me, her parents letting me sleep over so many nights, they bought me all my own toiletries. Her father, Larry, became a stand-in dad, helping me with homework and cheering me on at soccer games. Her mother, Vanessa, held my hand at my own mother's funeral and brought me food and groceries after both of my kids were born, then slipped me a business card for a divorce lawyer when the time came. Without the Wilkensons, I don't know how I would have survived. Sure, I had my brothers, but as the only girl in the family, my place and experience were very different, and if there are such things as soul mates, I know Marianne is mine.

With her hand on my daughter's shoulder, she turns to me, mouthing, *I love you.*

Love you too, I mouth back.

After all these years and everything that's happened, I have never been able to scare her away, and I know deep down I won't be able to scare Dante away either.

With Maddie's new purchases in hand, we say goodbye to Marianne and Clara and head back to meet Dante and Jake. They return, all smiles, each holding a container of candied pecans. Curious, I ask, "What did you guys get up to?"

Jake shrugs. "Nothing."

Dante tosses a pecan up in the air and catches it in his mouth. "Bro stuff."

Jake imitates Dante, tossing and catching the pecan before saying, "Eating and talking."

Dante nods to Jake, a signal to get ready, then tosses a nut to him to catch in his mouth. When he does, they high-five, and I suppose boys will never truly grow out of being boys.

Then Dante offers me a pecan, but when I reach for it, he snatches it back, holding one in his hand, like I'm supposed to let him throw it at me. There is no way I'm letting him.

Until he waggles his eyebrows all cute, and I sigh, tilting my head back. He lets it fly, and I catch it, barely. The thing bounces off the corner of my lip and into my mouth, but Dante and my kids cheer anyway.

He grins, and I hear his voice in my head from a few weeks ago. *Don't try to scare me away. You can't.*

Chapter 25
Dante

It never occurred to me until today that I might actually need to buy a car. I have use of one of the company's trucks, but my dad is a stickler that it's not "my" vehicle. It's Moretti's, and I have to track all my mileage. I personally get around on my motorcycle; though, if I'm going to be driving around with the kids more, I'll need to invest in something of my own. As much as I love watching Taryn drive—the tip of her tongue at the corner of her mouth as she waits to make a left turn, or how she sets her elbow on her door when she's impatient with the driver in front of her—I want to be able to chauffeur her around. Especially because she's dead set against my motorcycle. I think it would take an act of God to get her on the back of my bike again.

A pity.

Because there was nothing better than having her plastered to my back, her arms hugging the life out of me.

I'm in the middle of scrolling a list of the best family cars when I hear Taryn mutter a low curse. I glance up, noting a shiny BMW outside of her house. The sun has set, and it's too dark for me to make out the man leaning against it, but I can guess. And as hot as it is to watch Taryn parallel park so motherfucking perfectly, all of my attention is on Craig Barrett.

All the good vibes from the day evaporate as she turns off the car. Jake lets out a loud breath before he opens his door. Maddie follows, but Taryn doesn't move from behind the wheel.

"All right?" I ask her, and she shakes her head.

"Fine."

It absolutely is not going to be fine. It's a problem. I can feel it, but before I can say anything else, she steps out of the car. "Hey, Craig."

"I've been waiting here for twenty minutes," he snaps, and I shut my door as quietly as possible, though he still notices me, and I can already tell this is going to be more than a problem. He's looking for a fight.

Taryn flops her arms at her sides like they're so heavy she can't hold them up anymore. "I'm sorry. We ran a little late."

"Twenty minutes is not a *little* late, Taryn."

I don't like the way he speaks to her like she's dumb, and I step around to her side. Of course, he takes note and scowls. Taryn sighs. "I left a voice mail that we were on the way."

"Bullshit. You never called me."

"Yes, I did, about twenty-five minutes ago, actually."

"No, you didn't."

I don't know how she dealt with this toddler for so long. He huffs out a laugh that is so grating I reflexively grind my molars. "Maybe you meant to, but—"

"Here. Look." Taryn pulls out her phone, scrolls through it, then holds up her screen. "You didn't pick up, so I left a voice mail."

He knocks her hand down, and I make to step forward, but Jake catches my arm. I hadn't realized he had come to stand next to me. Maddie's on Taryn's other side. Like we're forming a fucking army against Thanos.

"It's my weekend with them," he says, angry finger in the air.

Taryn spends a few seconds merely glaring at him, and I'm sure she's calculating her words. Making sure to stay calm. "You're right, it is your weekend with them, when you are supposed to get them at ten. But since you changed the plans last week yet again, your time is cut short by hours. So even if we *had not* made other plans, and I *had not* called to inform you that we were running late, why didn't you come pick them up this morning like you were supposed to?"

"Because I was busy. Not everyone has time to jaunt off for some bullshit."

"We went to see *The Nutcracker*," Maddie says, in a voice so small I recognize it in myself. Trying to stand up to a bully, but the bully is the person that you were taught to always respect. That you thought would love you, no matter what.

Craig scoffs. "*The Nutcracker?* That's why I've been waiting here all night?"

"All night?" Taryn cants her head to the side. "I thought you said it was twenty minutes. Or was it really two minutes?"

He ignores her questions, turning to Jake. "You had a good time at *The Nutcracker?*"

Jake shrugs, mumbling an affirmative, which only pisses this asshole off more. "You're kidding me with this, Taryn, forcing our son to go to a goddamn ballet!"

Out of the corner of my eye, I see Maddie flinch. She loves dancing and singing, and her father shitting on the thing she loves is only reinforcing what she probably fears most—that her father doesn't really love her.

But he doesn't stop. He goes on, shouting, "You're turning our son into a pussy!"

"Hey, whoa, no." I step forward with my hands up. "You can't be saying stuff like that."

"Who are you?"

"My name's Dante."

"Well, Dante—" he spits out my name "—this is none of your business. My family is none of your goddamn business."

I shake my head. "Actually, it is, when you're out in my neighborhood yelling at your children and ex-wife."

He laughs sarcastically, pointing at me as he asks Taryn, "*Really?* You're fucking a kid?"

"Why don't you go home?" she says, motioning to his car.

"I'm not going anywhere without my kids."

A big act for a guy who doesn't really seem to care about his weekend. If he did, he would've been here this morning, like Taryn said. Not outside shouting at us for being twenty minutes late.

"Go get your stuff," he tells the kids, but they don't move. Instead, they look to Taryn. I watch Craig's temper rise with a locked jaw and flared nostrils as he realizes his kids don't take what he says seriously. They're choosing to follow only what their mother says. And he lashes out. Because that's what insecure men do.

"Go get your fucking stuff now!"

Maddie jerks back at the outburst, but Taryn captures her wrist, soothing quietly, "It's okay." Turning to Jake, she hands her house keys over to him. "It's your dad's night. Go ahead."

Jake holds out his hand for Maddie to take as they walk inside, and my stomach churns. I know what it feels like to be intimidated by your parent, and I'm not sure exactly what to do, but I know having Craig out here yelling and stomping like some roided-up bull isn't it.

I try to keep my voice even as I tell him, "How about you go wait in your car? Nobody needs you yelling out here. You're embarrassing yourself."

Craig turns his anger on me, taking a step closer until we're chest to chest. "Who the fuck do you think you are?"

I stick my hands in my pockets so I don't do anything stupid, even though I would really fucking love to. "I'm just saying, your kids are watching. Don't make this worse than it already is."

Craig's jaw clenches, and for a moment, I think he might take a swing at me. But then he takes a step back, his eyes darting toward the house, where his kids are watching from the porch.

Without taking my eyes off him, I nod to Maddie and Jake. "It's okay. It's cool. Everybody's good."

As soon as the door shuts, Craig scoffs at Taryn, waving his arm in my direction. "You think you can replace me? With this...this kid?"

"I'm not a kid, but you seem to be doing a pretty good job of proving you are. Out here acting a fool in front of your children."

"Fuck off," he mutters in my direction before opening his mouth to go in on Taryn again, but she cuts him off.

"If you don't respect my time or the kids' time, you cannot expect to be respected in return. As I've told you before, they're old enough now to understand what's going on, and you need to be prepared to face the consequences of your behavior."

"Don't condescend to me."

She lifts her shoulders in a careless gesture. "I'm telling you the truth. I'm warning you that you will lose your children, and it won't be because of me. It will be because of you and your actions. And I'm not going to let my children go home with you if you don't calm down. You are not in the right state of mind to be their parent, let alone drive."

He opens his mouth to respond but thinks better of it. His jaw snaps shut, gaze flicking between Taryn and me. Eventually, he grates out, "My children don't need a replacement daddy."

I rub my jaw, wishing I could punch his, though I am going to do the thing he should have and walk away. I take three steps back, putting physical distance between myself and Taryn. At this point, I believe any man would be a better father to his kids than he is, and I would love to let him know, but I keep quiet.

The kids shuffle back outside with backpacks over their shoulders, and I offer them a small wave and smile, sending all my support their way, hoping they can feel it. While Craig fumes, Jake and Maddie hug their mother, each of them telling her they love her, and in return, she kisses their cheeks, whispering words only they can hear. Then she nudges them to Craig's car. "I'll see you tomorrow night, okay?"

Craig storms to the driver's side without another word after the kids are in his car, and I move right behind Taryn, close enough that she can lean her weight into me. After they drive off, I wrap my arm around the front of her shoulders, pressing my face against the side of her head. "You okay?"

Her shoulders and chest rise on a breath. "Yeah, I'll be okay."

Except she's not okay. Her voice is small and shaky, and I can feel her wilting in my hold. "Let's get you inside. It's cold out."

She lets me lead her to the living room, where I hang up her coat and purse and urge her to sit on the couch then lock up the front door before taking Frankie out back, where I scream silently, adding a few shadow punches for good measure. The dog comes to sit at my feet, eternally happy, and I wish we could all be so lucky to be as oblivious as him. Inside, I toss down a bunch of treats so he'll leave Taryn and me alone then walk back into the living room, where I find her curled up on herself. I feel downright useless. "I'm sorry you have to deal with that."

"I'm used to it."

"Yeah, but you shouldn't have to be."

She wiggles her nose, blinking rapidly, and I start toward her, but she holds her hand up, not wanting to be touched right now, so I stay in place. Standing in front of her, desperate to do something yet unable to help.

"Talk to me," I say quietly, and she sniffs, turning her face away from me, clearing her throat.

"I..." She shakes her head as if to clear it. "I hate that he's in my life forever. That my kids have to witness that. I always promised myself I wouldn't put my kids through what I went through, and..."

I sit on the edge of the chair across from her. "You are an amazing mom, and you shouldn't feel guilty about anything."

Her throat bobs on a swallow, and I can tell she's really trying not to cry. I wish she would. I wish she'd give me her tears.

But she doesn't. Instead, she lets me in on her innermost thoughts, "I want to be a good example for Maddie. I want her to see what a strong woman looks like."

"You are a force to be reckoned with. You might not feel like it right now, but I can promise you that Maddie knows you fight for her." I am sure of that because I know what it feels like when your mother doesn't.

"I want Jake to know what it is to be a good man." After a moment, she meets my gaze. Her eyes are clear, and her voice is even. "Like you."

Her words hit me square in the chest, and I press one hand to my heart, the other on my knee when I bend over to catch my breath, all the air knocked from my lungs.

"And I feel like I'm fucking it all up," she says, another wallop. This time to the gut. Because she's vocalized that sentiment before, but she's not fucking it up. She's doing everything she can, all while convincing herself that it's not enough.

That *she* isn't enough.

"How can I help you?" I ask, standing up, and she licks her lips, sawing her teeth into her bottom one in thought.

"Nothing. There's nothing you can do. There's nothing I can do either. I can't protect my own children because a piece of paper says I have to send them with him. I can't protect Maddie from hurting. I can't keep Jake from potential trauma. I am completely powerless."

"You're not. You're resilient and caring and the best mom for your kids, and you should be proud that you're here. I'm sure it feels like shit sometimes, but you have proven to everyone how strong you are. You are powerful, Taryn." I take two steps toward her, hoping she'll finally allow me to comfort her. "What can I do? Make you coffee? Get you candy? Put on *I Love Lucy?*"

She sniffles, picking at the blanket next to her. "I don't know."

It kills me that she feels this way. Her heartache is physical. A visceral thing. Every atom in my body screams to help. To take all of her pain away. She could ask me for anything right now, and I'd do it. Go drive to Barrett's house and dig his eyes out with a spoon? Absolutely. Build her a castle with a moat where no one would ever be able to get to her? Immediately. Hand over my own heart to her? Yes, please.

"Tell me what to do, and I'll do it."

"I told you, there's nothing you can do. I feel like I failed as a mom, and I need to sit in that for a while."

But I can't simply sit here while she's in distress, so I find her candy stash and then start a pot of coffee. According to her, it's never too late for caffeine or sugar, and it's one of the reasons I love her. When I have a mug and some chocolates in hand, I head back to her, depositing them on the side table.

"You didn't—"

"I know." I cut her off. "I didn't have to, but I always will. If there is only one thing you understand about us, I will always *do* for you, Taryn."

After she's had a few sips of coffee and eaten one of the chocolates, I take a seat in the chair, mindlessly scrolling on my phone. If she needs to "sit in that for a while," I will too.

After about fifteen minutes, she squeaks out a noise, and I lift my attention to her, where she's tapping out something on her cell phone. Without my having to ask, she informs me, "Jake texted. They got to his house, and he said Craig ordered them a pizza, but he pretty much hasn't said anything else to them."

"How's Maddie?"

"According to Jake, she won't leave his side and it's, quote 'bugging the shit out of me.'"

I laugh. "Good."

Tension visibly seeps out of her as she messages for another minute with her son, and when she finally raises her eyes to me, I smile. "Feeling better?"

She shrugs.

"What else can I do?"

Another shrug.

"I mean right now, duchess. Let me make you feel better right now. Whatever you want. Whatever you need. You have all the power here, so tell me what you want, and I'll do it."

I don't think she understands at first, but I can see the change in her posture and the flicker of heat in her gaze when it clicks.

"You're the boss," I say. "And I'll always take care of you. So tell me. What do you want?"

Taryn has been hurt by the men who were supposed to protect her, so it would make sense that she would want to be protected and cared for by me, but also given the opportunity to take that power back. Make up for all those times she was shouted down or ignored, deserted or made to feel helpless.

I want to give her the chance to take it back.

So I wait.

A minute passes as she stares at me, slowly unwinding from her curled-up position on the couch to sit with her feet on the floor, knees straight, and head held high. Like royalty.

Like the woman I fell in love with.

"Crawl," she commands quietly, and I put my hand to my ear.

"Didn't catch that, babe. Gotta speak louder."

She fights a smile and raises her voice. "Crawl to me."

I nod and sink to my hands and knees on the floor. My dick, obviously, is already hard because it'll take my last breath for me not to want her. And even then, I'm not so sure St. Peter wouldn't think I was a pervert, showing up to the pearly gates with a hard-on.

Now, though, I keep my eyes locked on her and crawl across the floor. She watches me, her breath hitching slightly as I reach the couch and place my palms on her knees. Her eyes are dark, pupils blown wide, the pulse at the base of her neck fluttering rapidly.

"You want me to kiss you, duchess?" My voice is like a rip of paper through the silent living room.

She nods, her tongue darting out to wet her lips, and I lean in, pressing my mouth to hers. She tastes like the chocolate and coffee, my bittersweet girl, and I sink my hands into her hair, holding her as I ravish her mouth with my tongue, licking up every morsel of that innate flavor of Taryn.

When we finally pull apart, we're both breathing heavy, and I rest my forehead against hers, waiting for her next command. I'm hers, completely, and I'll do whatever she asks.

"Kiss my feet," she whispers, and I grin against her mouth.

"Yes, ma'am." I drop one last kiss to her lips before moving down her body. I slip off her socks, smoothing my thumbs over the arches, then raise my eyes to hers, once more holding her gaze as I worship her.

"Good boy," she croons, and *holy fuck*, it's the hottest thing I've ever heard in my entire miserable life. Nothing, and I mean *nothing*, feels as good as pleasing this woman.

I lift her left foot, pressing my lips to the top, then her toes, and down to the arch. She's ticklish and squirms, a soft laugh escaping her. I smile, placing her left foot down to take her right one in my hands, following the same path, top, toes, arch. The fit of her pants allows me to push the hem up to her knees, and I skate my lips over her calf and down her shin before sitting back on my heels, waiting for my next command.

She doesn't let me down.

"Make love to me, Dante."

Without a second's hesitation, I stand and scoop her up into my arms. She wraps her legs around my waist, her arms around my neck, and I carry her to her bedroom, where I lay her down on the bed, my body covering hers. I kiss her again, slow and deep, pouring all my feelings into it. All my hope, my lust, my pride. Goddamn. So much pride.

I am proud of who she is, of what she's overcome, and how she so willingly gives herself to me even when it's hard.

I break away only to remove her clothes until she's laid bare before me, and I take a moment simply to *look* at her. Appreciate the beauty she no longer hides from me. The line of her throat, the delicate slope of her collarbone and arms, the heaviness of her breasts, the roundness of her stomach, and the softness of her thighs, with the dark thatch of hair between them.

Perfection.

More than how physically attracted I am to her, it's her strength, her resilience, her kindness that draw me in. She's a goddess made human, and I'm honored that she's chosen to be with me.

I swiftly shed my own clothes, tossing them to the side to crawl back onto the bed. I take my time, exploring every inch of her as if I don't already know it. I reacquaint myself with the taste of her throat, the sensitivity of her nipples, the quiver of her belly.

I spread her legs, settling between them to dip my tongue into her most intimate place and kiss her clit. I use my tongue and fingers to bring her to the edge, then back off, only to do it again. Unlike the first time I edged her, she doesn't plead with me to make it stop and let her come already, but she still pants and writhes the same way. She's all swaying hips and fisting hands, holding anything she can, the sheets, my hair, her tits.

When I feel it getting to be too much, her body tensing so hard she's squeezing my head between her thighs, I give her what she requires and suck on that swollen pearl of her sex, curling my fingers inside her, stroking until she comes undone. It's beautiful how she breathes my name in a hoarse voice, her body convulsing, her orgasm washing over her in waves.

But I don't give her time to recover. I'm much too greedy for that. Instead, I wipe the back of my hand over my mouth then use it to hold her leg up and slide inside the sweetest place I've ever known to be home. Her neck arches as I fill her completely, and I know it won't be long until she's coming again.

"Look at me, duchess."

She does, eyes heavy lidded and glazed with lust.

We stay connected like this, physically and emotionally. I can feel her heart beat, see the things I wish she'd say out loud in her eyes. This isn't just sex; it's making *love*.

There is no denying what we have anymore.

And with every stroke, I pray that she'll open herself up to me. Allow herself to be loved. Love me in return.

My own orgasm builds, tingling in my limbs, a delicious burn in my lower back and balls. Because I know she likes it, I spit on my fingers then reach between us to find her clit. In no time at all, she comes again, her body clenching around mine, her nails digging into my back. I follow her over the peak and collapse on top of her, muscles spent, my heart in my throat.

The only thing that stops me from declaring myself is the shadow of the confrontation with her ex-husband still hanging over our heads. The first time I tell Taryn I love her, I want her to know it's the truth and not something forced or fake to make her feel better.

I roll onto my side, and we lie together for a long time, her head on my bicep, my fingers stroking her side. We don't speak because we don't need to, but I know I'll do whatever it takes to make sure Taryn knows that she's loved, that she's cherished, that she's mine.

Forever.

Chapter 26
Taryn

I wake up to my phone buzzing on the nightstand. Dante's arm is draped over me, his breath steady and rhythmic. After everything that happened yesterday with the kids and Craig and then the earth-shattering sex, it was a long time before I was able to find my balance again, so Dante and I stayed up until the middle of the night watching *I Love Lucy* in bed.

Then we spent the morning talking and laughing and playing with Frankie and Tortellini. We made pancakes and did laundry together before falling back into my bed with clean sheets to take a nap. A glance at my phone screen tells me we've only been sleeping for about thirty minutes.

I sit up to answer Maddie's call. "Hey, honey. Everything okay?"

Her voice is low and rushed on the other end. "No. Can you come pick us up?"

I tense. "What's wrong?"

"Dad and Jake are fighting. Jake said... He said Dad was

shitty, and now Dad's mad. He said if Jake doesn't need him for anything, he can leave, and good luck paying for college."

"Sit tight. I'm on my way." I don't think. I move on instinct. To go get my kids.

Dante stirs, propping himself up on his elbow. "What's going on?"

I hastily shove my feet into shoes. "Craig and Jake had an argument. I need pick up the kids."

The sheet pools around his waist when he sits up, his chest bare because he can't ever sleep with clothes on. "Want me to come with you?"

"No."

He stands in only his underwear, reaching for his pants on the floor. "I think maybe I should, just in case."

"No, it'll only make everything worse. I can handle myself."

He watches as I run my fingers through my hair and throw on a hoodie over my shirt, and I know he doesn't like that I'm going alone, but having Dante there with Craig might escalate the situation. I can't risk it.

Eventually, he nods in understanding and kisses my cheek. "Call me if you need anything."

The fifteen-minute drive to Craig's house is a blur of anger and anxiety, and when I pull up to the curb, I immediately spy Jake sitting on the front steps. It's freezing out, and he's only in a hoodie and sweats.

I step out of my car, slamming the door behind me. Jake peers up at me, his eyes red-rimmed. "Mom—"

"Where's your father?"

"Inside."

"Go in the car and get warm. I left the keys in there."

I stride past him, pushing open the front door and storming to the back to find my motherfucker of an ex-husband. He's in the kitchen and spins to face me with a beer in his hand, expression stony.

"What the hell happened?" I demand, but he doesn't answer right away. Merely takes a leisurely sip of his beer then moves to lean against the counter. The kitchen—my old kitchen —is huge. The whole house—my old house—is huge because he can afford it. When we divorced, he bought me out, though he fought me tooth and nail on everything. Even wanted to split the garden tools, the rakes and shovels.

Though none of his money can buy him any goddamn sense, compassion, or parenting skills. He sets his beer down and crosses his arms, all smug. "Well, your son thinks I'm a shitty dad, so maybe you should ask him."

"I'm asking you, Craig. What did you say to him?"

He clucks his tongue. "I told him the truth. If he thinks I'm so shitty, then he doesn't need me for anything. Good luck paying for college without my money."

My vision blurs with rage. "You selfish bastard. You think money makes you a father? You think throwing cash at them makes up for all the times you've let them down?"

Craig slams his hand on the counter. "I provide for them! That's more than you can say."

"You provide the bare minimum," I hiss, my finger up and pointed in his direction. "You're always late for Maddie's events, if you even decide to show up. You never help with homework, you don't do their laundry, you don't cook their meals. I mean, my god! You get them for two weekends a month! How much do you think you're providing for them in that time?"

"I am their father!" he shouts, as if that makes it so, and I take a step closer to him, all of the pent-up rage I've felt over the last fifteen years boiling over.

"Being a father is more than monthly checks. If you haven't

figured that out by now, then you have your answer as to why *my* son would call you a shitty dad, because that is what you are."

His smile is pure self-importance. "You wouldn't even begin to know what a good dad is, seeing as yours walked out on you."

I refuse to let him see how much that hurts and instead throw it back on him. "Unfortunately for you, yours stuck around to spoil you and give you everything so you never had to work a day in your life. Just ran to Daddy with every problem or whenever you needed money. It's so easy for you to play the victim when you're really the villain."

He steps closer to me, and I'm not afraid of him hitting me. In fact, I keep my hands behind my back, because I fear what I might do without thinking, and he would *love* to call the cops on me. "You've been poisoning the kids against me from day one," he grits out, proving my point. "This is all your fault."

"Sure. Go ahead and believe that, but it's not me they are trying to get away from right now. It's you. And it's not you they call when they need help. It's me."

"You're such a—"

"Mom?"

Craig and I both swing around at the sound of Maddie's voice. Madeline is not a little girl, but the way her shoulders are drooped and her eyes are full of tears, she looks so young now.

"It's okay," I tell her, stepping toward her. "Everything is fine. We're going to go home now."

Craig makes a sound as if to speak, but when I shoot a glare at him, he closes his mouth. Typical. When the time comes for him to prove he can be a good father, he can't. He doesn't know what to say or how to act.

I provide an example of what he should do and caress Maddie's head. "I'm sorry, sweetie. Whatever you heard, I'm sorry. You shouldn't hear us yelling at each other, but everything is all right. Go get your stuff. Your brother is already in the car. I'll be out in a minute."

She nods and turns away. I wait until I hear the front door open and close to face Craig once more. "I'm going to be contacting my lawyer. Don't expect to see the kids again unless you're ready to act like the man they need in their lives."

I'm impressed that my voice is so steady. Resolute. When I'm shredded inside. For my children. For myself. For what could have been. For what I haven't been able to protect them from.

But I'm done. I can't continue to put them or myself through this anymore.

Craig doesn't respond, and I stalk out of the house, leaving him standing alone in the house we used to share. Jake and Maddie are both in the car, buckled up. He's in the passenger seat, features unreadable, while she's in the back, crying quietly.

I don't know what else to say to them besides, "I love you both so much, and I'm really sorry."

They don't reply, not that I expect them to, and I swallow down the lump of anxiety in my throat to focus on driving us home, where we all crash on the couch with Frankie. We watch reruns of *New Girl*, and it isn't until about forty minutes later that Jake finally says, "He brought up Dante, asking about who he is and what I think about him. He was acting like... Like suddenly he had a say in things and had to protect us against this stranger, so I told him Dante has been around more in the last month than he's been around in the last year. That pissed him off, and I said it wasn't my fault he's a shitty dad. That's when he said if he's so shitty, I don't need him for anything. That I could leave and figure out another way of paying for college because he wouldn't be."

I put my arm around him, kissing his head, holding him to me like I used to do when he was younger. "You have every right to stand up for yourself and shouldn't feel bad about speaking your mind." I rub his back. "You did good." Then I kiss him again before turning to Maddie to drop a kiss on her head too. "Time for dinner?"

Maddie smiles timidly. Jake lifts a tired shoulder, but he doesn't say no, so I get up, making sure to tuck the blanket back around them and the dog then shuffle to the kitchen. I'd planned on going to the grocery store this afternoon, but since I never got to do that, I reach for a box of spaghetti and jarred sauce.

We eat huddled together on the couch, balancing our plates in our hands. Whatever was broken today won't be healed anytime soon, but this is a start, our time to relax and be near one another.

As I hold out my hand to gather their dishes to take to the kitchen, Maddie looks up at me, her eyes serious. "Mom, I don't want to go back to Dad's again."

I pause. "Okay, honey. You won't have to."

Her eyes expand to three times their normal size, and my heart breaks all over again. "Promise?"

My nose stings with unshed tears I refuse to let my children witness. "I promise. I don't know how we'll make it work yet, but I'll talk to my lawyer. We'll go for full custody, if that's what you want."

Maddie doesn't answer, wiping her eyes with her hands, so I look to Jake, who shakes his head. "I don't want to see him again if I don't have to."

"Okay, then we'll figure it out."

He sniffs, his mouth working side to side. "What if... What if he fights it?"

"I honestly don't know. He probably will, but we'll figure it out. We always do."

Forgetting about cleaning up for now, I snuggle with my kids. Maddie rests her head on my shoulder, and I pat Jake's knee. Thankfully, everything begins to feel a little more normal when they argue over what to watch, and I take the opportunity to text Ian, Griffin, Marianne, and Clara on one thread because it's better to rip off the Band-Aid at once. I give them a short-hand version of the events from today and let them know that I'll be asking for full custody, and that if they ever see Craig to not engage.

To which they respond:

IAN

Oh, I'll fucking engage.

GRIFFIN

With my motherfucking fist.

CLARA

From the man who took an oath to the Constitution!

CLARA

But, yes, I would pay to see it.

MARIANNE

Tar, We're all behind you 10000000%

I suppose it's the most I can ask for. Unwavering support in the face of an uphill battle.

Eventually, the kids wander off, Jake to play video games, and Maddie to watch yet another Cynthia Erivo interview. I curl up with Frankie until Dante texts that he wants to come over and make sure I'm okay. I don't really have the energy one way or the other, although I know if I don't let him see proof in person that I am indeed okay, he'll keep hounding me. Because that boy is nothing if not dogged.

I probably should have texted him earlier; I know how he worries. But I am completely wrung out, emotionally drained, and I don't want to have to deal with him and all my complicated feelings about him while also trying to keep my family together. So hopefully he'll settle for a few minutes and then let me go to sleep.

If only I weren't such a bitch.

Maybe then I wouldn't know what it feels like to break his heart.

Chapter 27
Dante

Taryn flew off earlier in such a rush, stress written all over her face, that I've been nonstop chewing my nails. After what happened last night with Craig, I don't trust that motherfucker as far as I can throw that bald-headed broad-backed son of a bitch. And I'd been waiting to check up on her and the kids. So as soon as she gives me the go-ahead, I practically sprint downstairs and across her backyard. Through the kitchen window, I view her standing at the sink, and I raise my hand for her attention so she'll unlock the back door for me.

"Where are the kids?" I ask once it's open, and she steps back, allowing me inside.

"Upstairs."

Since they're out of sight, I duck down, placing a quick kiss on her lips. "How are you?"

"Fine."

Except she's not fine. She slumps away from me to go back to the sink, where she studiously cleans a pot. Her eyes are bloodshot, and she keeps wiggling her mouth back and forth like she might cry.

"What happened?"

She shuts off the water, picking up a striped kitchen towel to dry the pot. "I don't really want to talk about it."

I coast my attention around the small room, from the *I Love Lucy* salt and pepper shakers to the tiny succulent on the windowsill. There is a pile of Frankie's stuff in the corner, bags of food and treats, his leash hanging from a hook, and dark-stained cabinets that I know if I opened would have a few boxes of cereal, a bunch of ramen, and grape jelly that's four years old and unopened. I have plans for this kitchen. Beginning with updated cabinetry and ending with adding my favorite protein bars to the shelves.

When I spot the empty jar of marinara sauce on the counter, I try a different tactic. I take the dry pot from her to put it away. "You have spaghetti for dinner?"

"Mm-hmm."

"With sauce from a jar?"

She sighs, finally meeting my eyes. "Yes."

I grin, hoping to disperse the dark cloud over her head. "No good, duchess. One of these days, I'm gonna make you some real sauce. No more of this stuff from a jar."

She ignores the suggestion, opening the dishwasher to load up the plates and utensils.

I try again. "I was actually thinking that you should come to Christmas Eve with me."

She opens the cabinet underneath the sink for the detergent, and I'm about to tell her to wait so I can redo how she loaded everything. She could fit another few items in here if she stacked everything differently, but I don't think now is the time to bring it up. Instead, I let her pour in the blue liquid and press the button to run it before she faces me with a scowl. "What are you talking about?"

"I want you to come to my parents' house for Christmas Eve. We do Seven Fishes."

"I..." She scrubs her hand over her face. "I don't know what that means."

I feel her tension rising because I am as attuned to her as I am to myself. "It's an Italian thing. We eat seven fish, but I'll make sure there's food for you. Braciole or something."

"Braciole?"

Taryn doesn't like fish, and normally we wouldn't have meat on Christmas Eve, but it's not a big deal. Nobody even knows why we eat seven fish, so I don't care about breaking a made-up rule in the first place. "Beef braciole. It's, like, flattened—"

"No, no, no," she mutters, waving her hand. "No, I'm not going to go to your Christmas fish meal."

"I told you, you don't have to eat fish. It's—"

"I don't care about the fish, Dante. I'm not going to your family's house."

That sets me back on my heels, but I expected a little bit of pushback. She's tried to keep this as emotion-free as possible, but it's too late. I am in love with her, and I'm pretty sure she loves me too. I am willing to wait and be patient for her to realize it, but I want her to get to know me better. Might speed the process up.

Especially after all the conversations we've had about my family. I would like her to be at my side for the next big family event. If only so she might lend me some of her strength.

"It doesn't have to be a big deal," I tell her. "My whole extended family comes, so it's not like anybody would care who you are. You'd just be another person for my mother to feed, which she loves so..."

Taryn shakes her head. "No."

"Why not?" I ask, a spark of irritation at the complete shutdown. Not even considering it.

"Because I said so."

Planting my feet and crossing my arms so she knows I'm not going anywhere, I take a deep breath and remind myself that her reaction isn't about me. It's about whatever happened today. "Okay, so we'll talk about that later."

She rolls her eyes with a grumble as she pivots away from me to stare out the window at the dark sky. Not a star in sight.

"What's going on? You gonna tell me what happened?"

Almost a full minute passes, the mechanical clock on the wall ticking the seconds. Eventually, she says, "I'm going to go for full custody of the kids."

I close the space between us, placing my hand on her back. I'm not sad about it, but that's a big decision. One I know she hasn't made lightly. "How come?"

"He got into an argument with Jake. All but threw him out of the house, threatened him with not paying for his college, which he promised me he would when we signed the divorce papers." She curls her fingers into fists on the countertop. "The kids don't want to see him anymore, and I'm not going to force them because of a stupid piece of paper."

"Are the kids all right? How's Jake?"

"Pissed off. Maddie's been crying a lot. You know... They're finally facing the fact that their father is a piece of shit, and I'm not going to let him hurt them anymore."

"Yeah, that's a really tough situation, but I'm here for you. Whatever you and the kids need, I'll support you."

She laughs a bitter sound, breathing out a sarcastic, "Okay."

I wrench back. I've always put up with Taryn's prickly nature, have even been enticed by it, but I don't like this sudden condescension. I'm not the one she's mad at, but she's taking it out on me. "Listen, I know you're upset, and I'm here for you, but I'm not going to be your punching bag."

She scoffs, angling her head to me, but where I expect to see ire, all I can read in those chocolate-brown irises is sadness. Even as she narrows her brows at me. "You're the one who came here wanting to have this conversation. If you can't handle my dramatics, then leave."

Clearly, she's speaking from her past. Bullshit that Craig fed her. It's so simple to understand, and yet she's living in this cycle, when all I want to do is pull her out of it. "You're not being dramatic. You're emotional. You should be. I want you to be. But don't mistake my kindness for weakness. Don't take your anger out on me. I'm not the one you're mad at."

She rolls her eyes. "Can you stop for once? All of your, like —" she shakes her hands out, scornful "—happy-go-lucky bullshit. I'm dealing with real stuff here, and you want to talk as if it can be solved with some cute therapy words."

I keep my voice quiet even though my skin is hot and my pulse is racing. I'm fighting the reflexive impulse to raise my voice to match hers. "I don't think that at all. I'm here for you, that's all I said. I want to help you and the kids out however I can. I..." I blow out a breath and decide it's now or never. "I know you might not be ready to make any decisions about us right now, but I want you to know—I need you to know—that I'm in this."

"*In this?*" she repeats, full of derision. "What? You want to be Maddie and Jake's stepdad?"

Yeah. That is exactly what I want. When the time comes, I will be ready to step into that role.

But Taryn doesn't think so. Or, maybe, doesn't want to believe me.

"You have no idea what it's like to be a parent. Spending a

few hours with me and the kids isn't the same thing as parenting."

"I know it's not, but I know I can do it. I want to do it. With you. I want you and the kids forever."

She straightens to face me fully, her jaw tight as she shakes her head, but I'm not sure if it's in disbelief or refusal. It probably isn't the best time to discuss my feelings for her, but I'm tired of hiding it. Especially when she's hurting so much. She needs to know that she isn't alone.

"You'll regret it," she says, and it's my turn to huff in agitation.

"Don't talk about things you don't know. You're pushing me away, and I don't understand why."

"Because it's not real. You don't really want this. You don't even know what *this* is."

"I do!" I wrap my hands around her shoulders. "I know exactly what this is, what you are, what it takes to be with you, and I want it. All of it, kids included."

She tries to shake me off her, but I don't let go, tightening my grip and pressing my forehead to hers. That's when she sniffles. "You're too young to know what you want."

I grit my teeth, fighting a shout. This goddamn woman! I love her so fucking much, and she's too goddamn stubborn to see it. "And you're too fucking scared to admit you want me too," I whisper before stepping back and dropping my hands. Her face is flushed, eyes glassy, but I don't let that stop me. I can't stand here and listen to her try to tear what we have apart simply because she's in the mood to break things. "Talk to me when you're ready to admit the truth."

I spin on my heel and stomp out the back door, careless about slamming it on my way. The cold air hits me like a slap in the face, cooling the anger riding my bones. But it's not enough. I need to rid myself of the tension coiled in my gut and head upstairs for my leather jacket and helmet before striding right to my bike. I rev the engine, the vibration familiar and calming as I take off.

The streets are dark, the temperature frigid. It's not a great night for a ride, but after pouring my heart out to the woman I love only to have it rebuffed, sulking in my PJs doesn't have the same kind of oomph. Nothing short of a laser meant to obliterate broken pieces of a human heart would do, but this is a close second.

Once I'm out of town, I open up the speed and let my mind wander back to our argument. I stupidly assumed after all our conversations, all the secrets we've shared with each other, we were past this bullshit. Past her pushing me away. Past her thinking I'm too young, too immature, too whatever the fuck else.

I thought she trusted me, trusted *us*. But maybe she doesn't, maybe she never will. And that thought fucking stings.

Yet I'm willing to take another lashing to make her comprehend the possibilities. I doubt she'll let me in today or even tomorrow, but I can have hope that someday soon she will. I circle my bike back toward home, knowing we've got shit to sort out. Because I meant what I said. I want her, want the kids, want this life we're building. And I'll be damned if I let her fears get in the way of that.

So, yeah, I'll go back. I'll talk to her, and we'll figure this out, one way or another. Because that's what you do when you love someone. You fight for them. And I love Taryn enough to fight.

Chapter 28
Taryn

After Dante storms out, I exhale a ragged breath that gets caught in my throat, and suddenly I can't see, my eyes so blurry I need to cling to the counter to lead me over to the corner where I have a box of tissues. Of course, no one in this house refills or throws anything out, and it's empty.

The straw that breaks the camel's back.

I release a shuddering sob, covering my mouth with my hand so the kids don't hear, but my sweatshirt sleeve is almost immediately soaked with my tears. I need to find more tissues.

After flicking on the light, I carefully make my way to the basement, sniffing and coughing, throat burning, face tight, and I hang a right to the corner that has the washer, dryer, and storage for things Ian insists he buy me from Costco—one hundred rolls of toilet paper and a million boxes of tissues. For once, it comes in handy, and I grab a box, ripping it open carelessly as I trudge out into the main space of the basement.

It's unfinished and mainly a place to keep anything I don't know where to put, but since all of my pottery has moved out to my shed, I'm able to appreciate this as usable space. Like Dante said.

One day, he randomly mentioned that he could finish it, giving the kids and me a little more room. In a house this pea-sized, sometimes it feels like we're right on top of one another, especially with only one bathroom and only one communal living space.

I blow my nose a few times and wipe my face dry before tilting my head back, filling my lungs with air, willing myself to settle down. I shouldn't have acted that way with Dante, but I felt like a cornered cat. I couldn't listen to him and his fantasies about being a family when I'm in the middle of fighting for mine.

Yet he kept pushing and pushing, and I lashed out.

After the chats we've had about how his father treats him, I went and treated him the exact same way. As if he doesn't know his own mind, as if he wouldn't be able to be a good parent.

That's not true. He is smart and capable, and anyone would be elated to have him offering himself up on a platter. Except for me. Because I self-sabotage. I am afraid of getting hurt, and it's easier to break things first than to have to experience the pain when they cut me later.

But Dante is the last person I want to hurt.

I pivot, intent on going back upstairs, and freeze when I finally notice the new piece of furniture in the corner. A curio with glass panels and dark-stained wood, filled with all my *I Love Lucy* knickknacks. All the pieces my mother amassed during her life: the Barbie and porcelain trinkets, a collector's plate, a rare first edition of Lucille Ball's memoir. There are pins, a lunch box, and small tins that can't hold more than a few quarters but are set up to show the many faces of Lucy.

It's a display of all the things I shared with my mother, the only items I have left of her.

Dante built this for me.

For my mother.

And I pushed him away.

A sob escapes my throat, raw and painful, and I fall to the floor. I'm a fucking idiot.

Dante *loves* me, and I acted as if it wasn't enough.

When it is everything.

I cry for myself, the grief of my mother, the resentment of my father, the rage for my ex, and the overwhelming love I hold for the man who has built me a curio, shed, and safe place to land.

I don't know how long I sit, crying into my hands, but it's long enough for my face to ache and my back to hurt from the position I'm in. But as I finally hoist myself to standing, my cell phone buzzes in my pocket with a phone call from my brother.

Instantly, I know something is wrong.

Griffin would sooner do another tour with the service than have to make a phone call. A pit forms in my stomach, heavy and foreboding, and there is a moment while staring at my screen that I wonder if I can simply ignore it. If I don't pick up, will the bad news on the other end simply cease to exist? If I never hear the words, does that mean it never happened?

I recall the phone call from Ian, informing me of Mom's passing. My life changed in those seconds, and I know whatever it is Griffin tells me will change it once again.

I cannot stand another heartbreak. How many can a person withstand before they crumble?

I don't know, but I compose myself to answer and hope I will survive it. "Hi, Griffin."

There is no preamble. "Dante's been in an accident. It's bad, Tar. Really bad."

My heart stops, and I slap my hand on the wall to steady myself as my brother continues. "I thought you'd want to know. I was called to the scene. He was hit by a car."

"Oh god," I cry, knees threatening to give out.

"The ambulance left for the hospital a few minutes ago."

My breath hiccups as I force the words out. "I want to go. I have to go."

"I'll meet you there."

I stuff my phone back into my pocket and trip up the steps, furiously wiping at my face. If I'm going to go, I need to have some semblance of awareness. I race up to the second floor, yelling my kids' names. They both rush into the hall before I've even made it to the top step.

"Mom? What's wrong?" Jake asks, holding out his hands for me as if I might fall. My boy, now a young man.

"It's Dante," I say, trying to keep my voice steady. "He's been in an accident. I need to go to the hospital."

"Is he okay?" Maddie asks, and I shake my head, tears filling my eyes again.

"I don't know." A wave of nausea passes over me, and it takes a few moments for me to feel like I'm not fighting the ocean current. "I don't know," I repeat again, unable to make the promise this time, that everything will be okay.

Because I don't know.

And I'm afraid it won't be.

Maddie lunges at me, throwing her arms around my middle. Jake loops his arms around the both of us, and then we're all crying. They've both grown so attached to Dante, losing him would not only be a blow to me but to the kids as well.

As much as I tried to deny it, the four of us have formed a special bond over the last few weeks. One of laughter and safety. Hours spent watching Frankie chase Tortellini on his skateboard. Sharing dinners and watching Dante gossip with Maddie and play soccer with Jake. The nights he spent in my bed.

All of it has imprinted on my skin, soothed my soul, and strengthened me to keep going. I kiss both of my children on the head. "Take care of each other. I'll let you both know as soon as I hear something."

The drive to the hospital is a blur. I don't remember parking or rushing into the ER, but suddenly, I'm standing in the waiting room, my heart pounding in my chest, white noise in my head. There are a handful of people here, including a couple in the corner who catch my attention. The man has a full head of dark hair and a familiar-looking profile. The woman clasps a rosary, her lips moving silently in prayer. They must be Dante's parents.

I hesitate, unsure of what to say—if I even *should* say something—so I stay rooted in my spot, nervously plucking at the zipper of my coat until I hear my name. I whirl around and run to my brother. He hauls me into a hug, one hand on my head, the other around my back. "I'm sorry, Taryn. I didn't know what I should do, if I should call..."

"No, you did the right thing," I say against his coat. When he relaxes his grip on me, I step back but hold on to his arms to keep myself steady. "What happened? How bad is it?"

"I don't know for sure." He winces. "My crew was called to the scene, and from what the driver said, it seems like he came out of nowhere, like Dante didn't see the car around the curve. He was unconscious, and... It wasn't good. Most likely a few broken bones and probably some internal bleeding, but I don't know the details, only what I could gather from the EMTs."

My eyes sting with tears, but I blink them back, needing to stay in the moment, cognizant enough to understand the information.

"It'll probably be a while," Griffin says, and I nod.

"I'm not family. They won't let me see him."

He glances to the hospital wing doors as if he might be able to throw his weight around and get me into Dante's room.

"I'm staying," I tell Griffin resolutely. "I'm staying here until I know what's going on."

He squeezes my hand. "I'll make sure the kids are taken care of. Don't worry about them. Just take care of yourself, all right? You're no use to anyone if you're not functioning."

The last person I'm worried about is myself. In fact, it feels like penance. I don't deserve to feel comfort right now. Not until I see Dante and win his forgiveness.

Griffin curls his arm around my neck, tugging me to him again, his lips against my hair. "Keep your head, yeah?" When I nod, he offers me a soft chuck under my chin. "Let me know if you need anything."

I open my mouth to answer, but instead of my gratitude, it's a shuddered breath. Griffin merely kisses my forehead, understanding and compassion in his dark eyes. The same ones as mine. The same as Ian's and Roman's. As our mother.

Once he's gone, I take a seat close to the doors and settle in to wait.

Twenty minutes.

Thirty minutes.

Almost an hour into me reliving my fight with Dante, I receive a text message. The buzzing jolts me into reality, and I shift in my seat to retrieve my phone from my coat pocket.

For another surprise.

ROMAN

Ian told me Craig tried to act tough with you and the kids.

ROMAN

You want me to kill him?

I bark out a laugh, the sound echoing in the sterile waiting room. After everything that happened tonight, to receive that message is the cherry on top of this unexpected shitshow sundae.

I text back, my fingers shaking.

No, thanks. I have it handled.

ROMAN

Then add this one to my tab.

ROMAN

My IOUs are long, but you can call them in whenever you like.

Yet again, my vision blurs the words on the screen, and I'm not sure how I have any moisture left in my body. I use a couple of tissues and lean over to toss them in the can underneath the table covered with magazines and pamphlets before meeting the concerned gaze of the woman from the corner.

She's still holding her rosary, but she's now sitting uncomfortably close to me.

Her smile is tremulous when she speaks. "I think you might know my son."

I press my hand to my chest, my heart beating hard against my palm. "I think you might be the mother of my...friend."

She nods. "I'm Angela. Angela Moretti."

"Taryn Stone," I say, angling myself in my chair, our knees touching, each of our hands curled around the wooden armrests.

"I'm guessing you're the woman he's renting his apartment from?"

My throat swells, and I croak out a quiet, "Yeah."

Her answering smile is tepid. Sad. She pats her upper lip with a tissue and sniffs then clears her throat. "I'm happy to meet you."

Everything hurts. My jaw, from holding tension. My back, from sitting so ramrod straight. My feet, from digging my toes into my shoes. My heart...

My heart feels like it's been put in a shredder, but as a mother, I can imagine her pain, and everything hurts all over again.

"I'm sorry it's under these conditions," I say when I'm sure my voice won't break.

She clears her throat a few times. "I'm glad you're here. Dante's been...different lately. Happier, I think...because of you."

I drop my gaze to my hands, not sure how to respond. The first time I admit the depth of my feelings for Dante can't be to his mom. It has to be to him. When he opens his eyes. When I know he'll be okay and smile at me.

"I know I haven't been the best mother," Angela confesses, and I shake my head. We all feel like we can do better, but Dante has never said a bad word about her. "With three boys, I did the best I could, but my Dante... I know he sometimes got lost in the shuffle." Her mouth turns down in a frown, chin wobbling like she might cry, but she takes a breath and settles herself before continuing, "He seems like he's found what he's been looking for."

She lifts her watery eyes to mine, the meaning of her words clear.

He's been looking for me.

Her lost boy has been found.

A man no longer searching for what he wants. Because he *knows* what he wants.

And I have the awesome privilege of keeping him. Supporting him. Lifting him up. Standing by his side as he has stood by mine.

I won't let him go.

All I need is for him to wake up.

I lock my fingers together, squeezing them, attention on the linoleum, unable to meet his mother's gaze. "He's a good man. He's been there for me and my kids in ways I can't even describe."

"He cares about you," she says without hesitation.

That is easy enough to admit, and when I finally lift my eyes to her face, she's smiling in a way that is so similar to her son, it is another physical blow. I have to witness that smile again.

I need to.

"I care about him too." Tears threaten to spill over, but I blink them back. I won't break down in front of her, not when I know what she must be feeling. I need to be strong for her. For Dante.

"I'm glad you're here, Taryn. He needs you right now. He needs all the love he can get." She places her hand over mine, still knotted together, but the gentle pressure has me relaxing until I turn my palm up, folding my fingers over hers.

We sit in silence for a minute, a comfortable affection passing between us. Then Angela speaks again, her voice filled with worry. "I never liked him riding that motorcycle. I always feared something like this would happen."

I agree with a frustrated huff. "I know. I've ridden with him before, and it's terrifying. But he loves it. I wish he didn't."

Angela sighs with her whole body. "He's my baby, no matter how old he gets."

I squeeze her hand in mine, wiggling it so she'll focus on me. "The worry never ends."

"We're mothers. It's what we do."

We share a smile.

Despite the circumstances, I feel a sense of comfort in Angela's presence, and I can see where Dante gets his warmth and kindness from.

I haven't had the embrace of my mother in a long time, but I can guess I would enjoy his mother's hug. I only hope that we will come out on the other end and have reason to celebrate.

Until then, I close my eyes and pray to my mom to send me her strength. Because while I wish she and Dante had met on this plane of existence, I'm not ready for them to meet on the other.

Chapter 29
Taryn

I blink my eyes open, the harsh fluorescent lights of the waiting room casting a cold glare. A dull ache radiates through my back and neck from falling asleep in the chair, and I carefully roll my neck side to side, noticing Dante's parents both asleep across from me. After Angela and I talked, we sat together for a long time until we received the first update from the doctors in the middle of the night. They stopped the internal bleeding and put his leg back together with pins. He also has a few broken ribs and most likely a pretty severe concussion, but he would make it.

It was the first time I was able to take a deep breath since Griffin called me.

Sleep was still fitful, and it feels like I just fell asleep even though the clock on the wall reads 6:23.

My joints crack as I stand and push my hair back from my face. I need to use the bathroom and take a few unsteady steps in that direction until my muscles and bones all remember how to work again.

My heart too.

It beats wildly, like it's figuring out its twin is somewhere in a room behind those heavy metal doors that have remained closed for the last few hours. I navigate the sterile hallways, lifting my hand in acknowledgment of the nurses before slipping into the bathroom where I use the toilet and splash water on my face.

I look hungover.

Feel worse than that.

But none of it compares to the relief that courses through me when I remember the doctor's words. *It will be a long recovery, but he's a strong young man. He'll be as good as new in a few months.*

I believe the doctor, but I also can't wait to see Dante. To prove it.

After making myself look as presentable as possible, I find a few vending machines at the other end of the hall and purchase a cup of coffee that might as well be dirt on my tongue, but it's warm and is the first sustenance I've had since dinner yesterday.

So much has happened in the last forty-eight hours, it's almost impossible to wrap my head around it. How fast life can change.

I text my kids and my brothers, as well as Marianne and Clara, who stayed over at my house last night after Griffin explained what happened. I let them all know I'm not leaving the hospital anytime soon. As expected, my brothers and best friends tell me not to worry about a thing. Then I call my assistant manager at The Nest to inform him that he'll need to take over my duties for the next day or so, at the very least.

I return to the waiting room, where Dante's parents are speaking to a nurse. My heart drops, an anxious gasp escaping my throat before I can stop it, stealing their attention.

Angela holds her hand out to me, and I immediately close

the distance between us to take it as she smiles brightly. "He's awake."

I sag. "Oh, thank god."

"He's still pretty out of it," the nurse explains, "but if you'd like to come back one at a time, that'll be fine."

I look to Angela, expecting her to be the one to go first, but she nudges me. "Go ahead, sweetheart."

"Really?"

Dante's father echoes my sentiment. "Really, Angela?"

She whips her head to her husband. "Yes, Robert. I know my son will want hers to be the first face he sees. That's what you want when you love someone—what's best for them. But I'm sure that's news to you."

He scoffs and rolls his eyes before flicking his hand like he doesn't care anyway. If this were any other time, I might high-five Angela for that one, but instead, I face the nurse. "I'm ready."

Angela takes my coffee, but I warn her. "It's not very good."

"Like I know the difference at this point."

And I laugh for what feels like the first time in one hundred years.

I follow the nurse through the doors and down the hall to a room with its door half open, the beep of monitors reaching my ears before I even step inside.

But when I do, I don't see or hear anything except for Dante.

His head is faced away from me, but when I step up next to his bed, gripping the sides of the railing, he slowly turns, eyelids fluttering. Seconds pass until those dark eyes of his focus and another few until he speaks my favorite word in a shadow of a rasp. "Duchess."

I fold in half, my forehead on the backs of my hands and sob. Great heaving sobs that send tremors down my spine and clog my lungs. Relief and gratefulness fill my veins, the cloud of terror and worry still hanging over my head. All I wanted was to see him again, but now that I have, it pains me to see him lying here, only half conscious and strapped up to more wires than I can count.

Something tugs on my scalp, a few strands of my hair being pulled, and I force myself to lift my head. Dante watches me under heavy lids, his lips parted like he wants to speak, but all he can get out is a grated, "Taryn."

"I'm sorry." I lean over to kiss his temple. "I'm so sorry."

Even in his state, *he* comforts *me*, his hand moving like it's not really attached to his body as he pats my arm. "It's okay."

"It's not okay." I back up, shaking my head, anger replacing everything else. "You're here because of me! Because I pushed you away."

Again, he starts to talk, but I cut him off.

"I was so scared I would never see you again. That I could never tell you I love you."

His eyebrows slowly rise, and if I weren't already out of breath from crying, I might have laughed at the slight spark of amusement on his features. The edge of playfulness in his slow whisper. "You...love...me?"

"Of course I love you!" I whack at the air since I can't whack him. "You have been so annoyingly perfect, how can I not? You built me a shed to make my pottery and..." I sniffle, dabbing at the corners of my eyes with my knuckles. "I saw the curio you made. When did you do that?"

He closes his eyes and swallows, sluggishly lifting his shoulder. "I want...to put it...in the living room."

"Yes, of course."

"Fix your...kitchen too," he says, his eyelids heavy with exhaustion.

"You won't be fixing anything for a long time."

He lifts his arm about three inches up from the bed like he's a tough guy. "This? It's nothin'."

I snort a laugh. "I love you."

"Say...again?" He squints at me. "Couldn't hear."

I gently brush my hand over his forehead and hair, tracing the tip of my nose down his, breathing my words into his mouth. "I love you."

He groans in satisfaction.

I step back. "And you almost died."

He groans in displeasure.

"No more motorcycles. Swear it, Dante. I can't take it. I can't go through this again. Neither can you."

He points his index finger at me, mouth curving in an approximation of a smile. "You love...me."

"Yes. That's why you need to get rid of the motorcycle. No more. Promise me. I can't lose you. The kids can't lose you."

He frowns. "The kids."

"Yes, they were really upset when I told them you were here. That you had an accident."

"I'm sorry," he says, and I can tell he's fading fast, sleep pulling him back under.

"Don't scare us again like that. We need you. Please, Dante. Don't leave us." I sit on the edge of the bed, a few inches of space, and he reaches for my hand, directing it to his head. When I understand what he wants, I pet him, and he nuzzles into my palm on his cheek. "I love you."

He smiles sleepily, eyes closed. "I want...you. The kids. I love you...all."

"I know." I trace his cheekbone, the shell of his ear. "I can never pay you back for everything you've done for us, that I know you'll do for us, but I'll try."

He shakes his head, barely a movement. "Love is free."

"Love is free," I repeat back in a whisper, my nose stinging. "Sleep now."

His eyelids crack open as his fingertips inch toward my thigh. "Stay."

"I'll stay right here. I won't move. I promise. Now, be a good boy and sleep."

Even in this state, he can't stop his flirtatious innuendos, the tip of his tongue barely poking out of the corner of his mouth, and I laugh because it can be translated in a few ways. All of them lewd.

But then he relaxes, and I stay exactly where I am, skating my hand down his shoulder and arm, passing over the place where the IV is stuck into him, to his long fingers, and eventually to his torso. I'm afraid to press anywhere that he might have broken bones, so I settle my palm on the middle of his chest, barely enough to feel the slow yet steady rise and fall of every breath. Then I lay two fingers at the base of his throat, finding his pulse.

The proof of his life.

His love.

Mine.

It is a long time before I'm willing to shift even a centimeter, but I turn to relieve the kink in my neck and inspect the room. The curtains across the window are open a few inches, and early morning light spills through the slim break, a stream of hazy sunshine that highlights the whiteboard on the wall, noting Dante's information along with his nurse's name: Violet.

My breath catches, skin peppering with goose bumps, and I tilt my head up to the ceiling as I close my eyes, smiling to myself. "Thanks, Mom."

Chapter 30
Dante

I spent a week in the hospital, and I've never been so grouchy in my life. It was as if Taryn and I traded places. She was smiling and bringing in cookies for the medical staff. Meanwhile, I cursed them for making me stay. I just wanted to go home. To Taryn's.

Between all the visitors and my mood, I'm sure they were finally glad to be rid of me by the time the doctor signed my discharge papers. Then I got to settle in Taryn's bedroom to convalesce. It was embarrassing to be waited on hand and foot, asking for help to go to the bathroom and wash, but Taryn never let me be alone for one second. If she wasn't hovering over me, it was Marianne or Clara, or one of her brothers, or Jake and Maddie. Even my mother showed up.

Apparently, she and Taryn had become friends, trauma-bonded forever. They made plans for us to attend Christmas Eve at my parents' house in two weeks. Like I wanted, but it was weird not to be involved in any discussions about anything. While I was recovering, *a lot* had happened.

Besides my woman becoming friends with my mother,

Taryn had also gotten the paperwork going for full custody. Craig tried to apologize, but she was standing her ground, and I couldn't have been prouder. Especially after Maddie and Jake both told me how they felt about him and the situation. That Jake got into the argument with his father defending me.

Even with a bunch of broken bones, I threw my arms around that boy, hugging him so tight he complained. But then I told him I loved him, and when he said it back, I actually cried. I know loving Taryn and those two kids is what I was put on this earth for, and I will do my damnedest to show it to them every day.

Which is why I worked hard to convince Taryn to let me have the run of the house after a week of being cordoned off upstairs. It's nice to look at a different four walls, have the chance to get my muscles moving with the help of crutches as I completed a few daily laps around the first floor. I started physical therapy, and I was ordered to keep moving to make sure I didn't atrophy in the twelve weeks I'd have my cast on. So, I follow directions, but my breathing is still off. I was given a plastic thing to breathe into with a ball that rises and falls with my inhales and exhales, so I can exercise my lungs. And fuck, it's harder than I thought it would be.

But Taryn forces me to do it multiple times a day...though she always makes out with me after as my reward, so it's all right.

I guess.

Now, I'm in the living room while Taryn makes us popcorn for our *I Love Lucy* marathon, and I take advantage of the rare opportunity that she's out of sight to speak with Maddie and Jake. I set my arm on the back of the couch behind Maddie, who lounges next to me, and glance to Jake in the chair in the corner. "I wanted to talk to you two while your mom is out of the room."

"Okay," Maddie says, already giggling. The girl loves her gossip.

Jake, on the other hand, narrows his gaze, cautious. "What's up?"

"I love your mom," I say, straightforward. No use beating around the bush. "And I want to date her."

Maddie tilts her head, nose scrunching. "I thought you were already dating."

"Yeah, I guess we are, but..." I scratch at the week's worth of stubble on my jaw. "I want to make it official. With your blessing."

"Our blessing?" Jake's expression softens, almost confused.

"Yeah. I'm not gonna do anything that will hurt either of you. I don't plan on hurting your mom either, but I want everyone to be on the same page. No secrets, all right? I know things are up in the air with..." I hesitate to bring up their father when we're having a nice night together, so I avoid it. "Things are stressful right now, so I want to make this as easy and clear as possible."

I slant my gaze to Maddie and then Jake, making sure to meet their eyes in turn. "I want to be in your lives for a long time. For as long as you'll let me. I want you to know my intentions from the start. I love your mom, and I love you both."

Maddie squeals and throws her arms around my neck, immediately pulling back when I suck in a sharp, painful breath. "Oh my gosh! I'm sorry! I'm so sorry!"

"It's okay." I rub my palm over the top of her head as she settles back beside me. "No harm done."

"I'm just really excited," she says with a grin. "I love you, and I love Mom, and I love you and Mom together. She smiles a lot more when you're around, and you're, like, so cool and fun and really nice to us."

I tug on a strand of her long hair. "So, that's a yes vote?"

"Yes!"

I turn my attention to Jake, who sits forward on the recliner like he's in a business meeting, hands folded. "If I say yes, what exactly does that mean?"

I shrug. "It means we'll do stuff together more, the four of us. I'll be around more to help if you two need anything. I'll take your mom out, just me and her."

"Are you going to be moving in?"

"Honest answer? I don't want to rush into anything, but, yes, that would be my goal. To live here with the three of you. Make our own little unit. I know your mom needs time to process things, and if you can keep a secret—" I whip my head to Maddie, who covers her giggle with her hand "—I've been coming up with designs to eventually approach your mom about renovating my apartment into a third floor. You and Maddie would be able to have it to yourself. Bigger bedrooms and a whole bathroom up there."

Maddie leaps up and dances in a circle. Frankie follows, hopping on his hind legs. "Yeeeeeeessssssssss."

Jake wags his head side to side, considering my proposal like he's Brando in *The Godfather*. "You drive a hard bargain."

I toss a pillow at him, laughing, and Jake catches it, stuffing it behind his head when he sits back on the chair. "Yeah, of course, you can date Mom. Just don't be all gross in front of us."

"Got it. No being gross." I make an imaginary checkmark in the air. "What about butt pats?"

"Dante," Maddie whines, and I knock the back of my hand into her knee with a chuckle.

"Kissing only?"

She gags and flops to the side in time for Taryn to stride back into the living room with a big bowl of popcorn. She hands it to me, but before she can get away from me, I grasp her wrist to pull her down for a wet, smacking kiss. The kids both groan audibly, and I laugh against Taryn's mouth.

"I feel like I missed something," she says when I let her go, coasting her gaze around at us as she wipes at her mouth.

"Maddie and Jake have both given me permission to date you," I say, and Taryn arches one of her brows.

"That is awfully old-fashioned."

"That's me. An old-fashioned guy."

She snorts and pats her leg to get Frankie to follow her to the other recliner, where he jumps up into her lap. The boxer who thinks he's a lap dog. "I'll believe that when I see it."

I waggle my brows at her. "You wait and—"

"See?" Jake points an accusing finger at me. "That is exactly what I mean!"

I raise my hands in innocence. "I'm not even touching her. How can I be gross right now?"

"Bruh," he grunts, and I wave off his worry with a flick of my hand.

"No being gross. Promise."

He obviously doesn't believe me, but I'll do my best not to hit on his mother in front of him.

I last all of one episode before I text her.

> you look so hot right now

She picks her cell phone up when it buzzes, shooting a scowl my way after reading my text. Then her fingers fly across her screen.

DUCHESS

> Don't try to be cute. I haven't showered today, and I'm not wearing a bra.

> yes my favorite.

Just This Once

> your sweatshirt looks so old I think it would take one good rip for it to fall to pieces

DUCHESS

How dare you. This is Ocean City couture.

> I'll buy you a new one

> as many as you want

> just let me see your tits

DUCHESS

The kids are in the room!

> not now you weirdo

> send them to bed then show me your tits

DUCHESS

They're in 7th and 10th grade. I don't send them to bed. They go on their own.

> well chop chop

> what do we do to get this started?

DUCHESS

It's only seven.

> I'm dying here

> I've been such a good boy

> I think I deserve some pets

Taryn rolls her eyes so hard, I fear they might never go back in place, and then how would she watch Lucy get trapped by a gigantic loaf of bread in her kitchen? This is a funny show.

After a minute, she texts her one word reply to me.

DUCHESS

No.

come on

DUCHESS
No pets while you're recovering.

I'm fine

healthy as a horse

DUCHESS
So that wasn't you this morning complaining
how everything hurt.

It's my turn to roll my eyes.

I need you to kiss it better

DUCHESS
No. Not until you're healed.

I huff.

spoilsport

see how old-fashioned I am?

That makes her mouth twitch. More motivation.

even with a bum leg I can make you see God

DUCHESS
Please. You can't go up the steps without
getting winded.

my tongue works fine

I'll lick your pussy until you scream my name

DUCHESS

I'm about to start screaming if you don't stop texting me during one of my favorite episodes.

tell me you love me

DUCHESS

I love you.

I screenshot that and save it to my photos. Then I look up to find her staring at me, that mean arch to her brow, mouth pinched like she might put me in my place with only a few words. It's my favorite.

The same order to her features from the night I first spotted her.

I love you, I mouth, earning a twitch of her lips, a losing battle with her smile.

A fight I want to have every day.

Chapter 31
Dante

The Moretti house is a spectacle on Christmas Eve. Every surface is covered in decorations, every corner filled with twinkling lights. It's loud, crowded, and overwhelming, but it's what I'm used to. Taryn and the kids, not so much.

Taryn has mostly stuck to my side, still acting as if I can't do anything by myself, but she has been a buffer with my brothers and father. Especially since everyone is interested in who she is. Who the kids are.

Jake stands with a soda in his hand, awkward but resigned as one of my cousins has his ear about why football is so much better than soccer.

Maddie sits next to him, taking it all in. My aunts trying to argue quietly even though everyone can hear them. My brothers talking shit to my uncles. My mother bustling about with appetizers.

And the whole place smells of fish.

Dinner is clams and linguine, branzino including the head, smelts, lobster, angel hair pasta with anchovies, and crab cakes.

Since I requested something Taryn would like, my mother also made ravioli and meatballs. This is all not counting the shrimp cocktail, caprese salad, fifteen-thousand-pound cheese tray, or my mother's special holiday drink that's a mix of Sprite, cranberry juice, and champagne.

She gets lit up on it every year by dessert.

Which is why it doesn't surprise me that she throws her arms around Taryn when she corners us in the kitchen.

"I'm so happy you're here," she crows, patting Taryn's cheeks. "I love having met you, and I'm glad we're friends."

"Me too. I'm happy to be here," Taryn says, attempting to wiggle out from my mother's death grip, and I have to bite my cheek to keep from laughing.

"You've taken such good care of my baby."

Taryn's lips part to speak, but my dad barges in with his glass of wine, obviously having heard the conversation. "Yes, your baby."

Mom spins away from Taryn to focus on my father. "What?"

"She's taken such good care of *your baby*."

It's an insult to me, clearly, but also to my mother. As if she raised me that way. As if I can't take care of myself. Like he believes.

"Always needs someone cleaning up after his messes," he says into his wine, as if he can't even be bothered to spend a few seconds insulting me. I'm not even worth losing a sip of wine over.

But before I can argue, Taryn jumps to my defense, stepping toward him with her hand up, forcing his attention on her. "I know you didn't just imply *your son* can't take care of himself while he is recovering from a near-fatal accident. I must have heard you wrong because you wouldn't insult a man in need of assistance like that."

"You haven't known him as long as I have, young lady." He shakes his head, a haughty laugh right in the face of the woman I love, but again, before I can come to her defense, she sticks out her hand, pressing it to my chest, a silent message. *I got this.*

"My name is Taryn, not young lady, and I may not have known Dante as long as you have, but I obviously know him better. Which is a shame. Because he is *your* son. The son who could have opened up his own renovation business by now but has stayed loyal to you and this family. Even after you mutter disrespectful barbs—" she holds up her finger to silence him when he opens his mouth "—and don't try to tell me you don't do it, because I know from the few minutes of being around you the kind of man you are, making him smaller so you can feel bigger. What I want to know is what you're so intimidated by. His competence in his work? His tenacity and determination? His joy in life? Or maybe all of the above? Because as a mother, I can't for the life of me figure out why a father would be so intent on embarrassing his child."

Dad's jaw flaps a few times until he finally sputters out, "I was joking, of course—"

"Right. Of course," Taryn says with a sarcastic thumbs-up that has me smiling against my fist.

God, I love her for sticking up for me, but it's my turn now.

"She's right. I could have left a long time ago. I have business cards and private work offers piled up. I've stayed because Moretti Construction is important to me. But it's not everything." I snake my arm around Taryn's shoulders, pulling her back against my chest. "Not anymore."

He doesn't speak, but when he tries to turn on his heel, my mom is there, blocking his path. She eyes him with a scowl. "We almost lost him, Robert. If that doesn't wake you up to what we have, then there is nothing I can do for you anymore. I'm done being quiet. I'm not gonna put up with your bullshit and your cheating anymore. I'm done trying to keep the peace. You better start appreciating everything you have and respecting *everyone* in this family, or I'm out."

There is a short standoff, one where I cannot guess which way it will go, though nothing comes of it. My father takes the coward's way out and slinks away, wineglass in hand. When he's out of sight, Mom yanks Taryn back into her arms, physically towing her away from me to kiss her temple and sing her praises more. Then she does the same to me, whispering about how proud she is of me, and that she is behind me, no matter what I decide to do, except losing Taryn. She warns me to treat her right with a smack to my arm.

As if there is any other way.

She packs up cookies for us to take home and then walks us all to the door, where she hugs Maddie and Jake like they are her own grandkids, and when we're all seated in Taryn's car, Jake blows out a big breath. "The food was good, but the people..."

"I know." I chuckle and hold my fist out for a bump. "Thanks for coming and hanging out. It means a lot for you all to be there and meet my family."

By the time we get home, it's almost ten and Maddie decides she's going to go watch *Wicked* on her iPad, and I swear she could perform the whole movie word for word if asked. Jake heads upstairs too, so with only a few hours until Santa is supposed to come down the chimney, Taryn and I are alone in the living room with the artificial Christmas tree lit up in the corner with homemade ornaments from the kids over the years and a few gifts piled up underneath.

I pull her next to me on the couch before digging into my pocket. "I have something for you."

"If it's your dick, you can keep it."

I hold out a small box in the palm of my hand. "Not quite."

She looks from it to me then back to it. It's too big to be a ring box, but it is still unmistakably a jewelry box.

"Dante," she chides quietly, and I extend my hand toward her, silently urging her to take it. She does eventually, and she tears off my terrible wrapping to reveal the black box, which she opens. "Dante," she says again, this time almost in reverence.

She carefully lifts the necklace out of the package to study the engraved gold pendants. A larger one with a violet flower, and two smaller ones with the initials J and M on each. Her eyes widen, and she peers over at me, speechless.

"I know you're not big on jewelry. I've never seen you wear earrings or rings, but... If you don't like it, I won't be offended."

"No, I do. I do. I love it. It's perfect," she says and leans in, pressing a soft kiss to my lips. "Thank you." She passes her thumb over each engraving before she places it back in the box and sets it on the coffee table. "I have a present for you too."

I squeeze my eyes shut and cross my fingers, muttering, "Please be a boob sculpture. Please be a boob sculpture."

She socks me in the arm, and I laugh, tugging her close for a kiss. "So, it's not a boob sculpture?"

"No, you degenerate." She pushes off the couch and plucks a small gift from under the tree. "But I did make it."

Her present is wrapped to perfection, including shiny paper, a bow, and a real tag. Not a sticker from the dollar store. I almost don't want to ruin it, but the pull is too much, and I rip that sucker open then tear into the cardboard box.

"I made it extra wide," she says when I lift up the ceramic coffee mug with her signature sandstone look. This one goes from red to brown to black in an ombre effect. It's extra-large with a handle I can stick my fingers through. I remember randomly complaining one day at The Nest that so many coffee mugs are made for dainty hands. And this woman went and created my very own.

"I love it. But I want to keep it here."

She easily agrees, smiling into a kiss that quickly escalates, until we're both breathing hard and my hands are tangled in her hair. She eventually takes my gift and puts it on the table next to hers then stands up, a gleam in her eyes that makes my pulse thrum.

When she curls her fingers around the hem of her sweater and tugs it up over her head, my skin goes hot and tight. I'm so excited, I forget for a second about my leg that is held together by metal and my ribs that are still sore, because all I feel is anticipation. It takes me three tries to splutter out, "Babe, are you serious right now?"

She laughs, low and throaty, and I swear to god, my cock tries to punch its way out of my jeans. He's more impatient than me. Desperate for attention.

I lick my dry lips as Taryn pushes her pants down her hips and legs. Her bra and underwear are plain beige, but I've never seen anything prettier in my life. "Oh, please," I mumble, waving her closer. "I'm aching for you."

"You're aching because you have multiple broken bones," she says, sauntering close to me, but not close enough.

I shake my head. "I missed you so much. Too much. That's what hurts. I need you to make it better."

She juts her chin to where I'm mindlessly palming my long-suffering cock. "You need me to kiss it?"

"I'd rather kiss you." With one hand, I catch her fingers and pull her to me. She comes willingly, her laugh breathy and so goddamn sexy, I'm gonna lose my mind when I finally get my mouth on her.

But she goes and kills my plans with a staying hand on my chest. "I'm not allowing you to go down on me tonight." She places two fingers on my lips to silence my argument. Which was going to be that I could lie down and she could sit on my face. "You get too excited, and I move around too much. I don't want you to hurt yourself, and if you fight me on this, I'll put my clothes right back on. So, are you going to be good?"

I stay quiet, and her replying smile is what I imagine an evil nun in a 1962 Catholic school would look like.

"Good boy," she says against my ear, breath hot, lips catching on my earlobe. It's an electric shock, and my balls draw up tight.

"Ah, fuck," I grunt, and I rip open my button and zipper to shove my hand down my underwear. I wrap a fist around my erection and squeeze, knowing I won't last long. It's been weeks, and the most beautiful girl in the world is dragging the straps of her bra over her shoulders like my fantasy come to life.

She bends toward me as she pulls down the cups, and my mouth waters when I finally get a peek at the light-brown areolas and those hard nipples. Without my having to ask, she lifts them up, offering them to me, and I moan, sucking on one of the peaks, tongue rubbing back and forth. Maybe a little too hard from her gasp, but I've been deprived for so long. I can't help it.

It is a feast after a famine, and I bite and suck on her other breast in the same way. Like I'll never have another chance.

Even as I know I'll have lots of chances. Every day for the rest of my life, if she'll let me.

I stroke my cock from root to tip as I suckle hard enough to make her cry out, and I pull back. "You need to be quiet, duchess. The kids'll hear. What if they come down here?"

"Better hurry up, then," she whispers, and I comb my hand into her hair, yanking her mouth to mine. Our kiss is sloppy. All tongue. No coordination.

Desperate.

Frantic.

Wild.

I pull back, panting, and her lips chase mine for just a second before she leans away, eyes heavy-lidded and glazed. There's a thin string of spit connecting us, and I swipe it away with my thumb, only to suck it into my mouth.

Her cheeks flush. "You're disgusting."

"Yeah, and you love it." I hold up my index and middle fingers. "Make them wet."

She does, licking circles around them, making them glisten, and only when it's too much to watch anymore do I tell her to stop so I can slip them beneath her underwear, sliding over her pussy.

"And you love me," I say, finding her clit.

She shifts her weight to push her knees wider, allowing me more room. "And I love you."

She moans, head falling back as I slip my fingers inside her. She's tight and hot, and I can't help but imagine it's my cock instead. God, when that day finally comes, I'm gonna lock her in the bedroom and strip the bed, because it's gonna be a fucking mess.

Her eyelids flutter open, mouth parting as she sighs quietly when I find that sweet spot inside her. She braces herself, one hand on the couch, the other on my length, and I nod. "That's it, duchess. Make me come with you."

Her grip tightens, and I groan, resting my forehead against hers, working her faster. She whimpers, her inner walls clamping down on my fingers, and I know she's close. I press my thumb against her clit, rubbing tight circles until she shatters, her orgasm ripping through her, taking me with her. Like I knew I would, I come fast, following her over the edge, spilling into her hand, my cock pulsing in time with her clenching heat.

We stay like that for a moment, breathing each other in,

pressing soft kisses to each other's mouths and cheeks and jaws until we hear movement upstairs. A reminder that we are not alone and could find ourselves in a compromising position at any moment. She hops up to grab a tissue, cleaning her hand off, then slips her sweater and pants back on while I put myself back to rights. Then she flops down on the couch next to me, and I sling my arm around her shoulders, grinning to myself. "Best Christmas ever."

She carefully puts her head on my shoulder. "Yeah?"

I press my nose to her hair, inhaling deeply. "At least until next year."

"What's happening next year?"

"That's when you get the good jewelry."

She tips her head back, brows drawn in confusion. When the lightbulb goes off, her jaw drops. I close it with the tip of my finger. "Don't worry. As much as it'll kill me, I won't ask a minute before next Christmas Eve, so you have more than enough time to prepare. And find a new place for Tortellini to live."

Funnily enough, it's not the possible future question that has her pointing her finger at me. It's my tortoise. "He can stay in the basement. He is not coming into the living room and definitely not into our bedroom."

Our bedroom.

I like the sound of that.

I nip the tip of her finger then lean my head back, relaxing with my girl in my arms as the tree lights send rainbows of color across the walls. It's heaven. "Famous last words."

Epilogue

With how nice the early spring weather has been, Cuppa Jo has put a few tables and chairs outside, so my brothers and I have forgone our usual booth inside to park ourselves in the sunshine. Up and down Aster Street, people mill around, window-shopping and chatting.

It's been a few months since Dante and I officially became a couple, but only a few weeks since he broke off and started his own renovation business. All it took for the word to spread about him and his work was a few well-placed recommendations by Clara and Marianne, and his calendar became booked out through the summer. And wouldn't you know it, suddenly Robert Moretti started trying to become friends with the son he always mistreated. Too bad he couldn't appreciate what a good thing he had going. Now, he's got to find a project manager with the same people skills who will work for less money and more hours, like Dante did.

"How's everything going at The Nest?" Griffin asks, and I recross my legs, tilting my head back to feel more of the sun.

"Great. We're doing more business than ever."

"Proud of you," he says with a knock of his knuckles on the table.

I've been working on accepting compliments lately, so instead of ignoring it, I nod. "Thank you."

"I talked to Roman last night," Ian says, and both Griffin and I turn to him.

I huff. "We've been sitting here for ten minutes, and you didn't lead with that?"

"I figured you two wouldn't care all that much."

Griffin shakes his head. "Well, that makes us sound like assholes."

"You are assholes."

"As if you aren't," I say, balling up my napkin to throw at Ian.

"Yeah, yeah, we're all grouchy motherfuckers. But he was asking about our house."

"Our house?" Griffin and I parrot in surprise.

"Wanted to know whatever happened to it."

All three of us go quiet. We were raised in a little ranch house with a stone fireplace and marks on the kitchen doorframe that showed our heights every year. I don't remember a lot from that house, other than the shag carpet in the living room and Mom's smile as she had us line up every year on our birthdays. Mom had to sell it when Dad left for good. After that, we moved to an apartment that was too small for the five of us, but it was all she could afford on her teacher's salary.

"I'm not sure who lives there now," I say, and Griffin shrugs, pretending like the question doesn't affect him. But since he's been with Andi, he's become easier to read, and Griffin is not as hard-hearted as he hopes people believe.

Ian finishes his coffee and sets the cup down on the table, rolling it side to side on its edge. "Yeah, I'm not sure what made him so curious all of a sudden, but it sounds like he's doing well."

Griffin and I nod. Not that I've completely forgiven Roman for ghosting our entire family, but I've softened on him a bit in the last few months from his occasional texts. Ian's right. It does sound like he's doing well, and that's all I've ever wanted.

While he might be a fuckup, he's still my brother. My baby brother who got a shit end of the stick.

"So, I was thinking," Ian starts, only to be interrupted by Clara, who strolls up to our table with a big smile and even bigger sunglasses on her face.

"Well, well, well, look what we have here. My former best friend hanging out with her brothers."

I wrench back. "Former best friend?"

Marianne sighs when she catches up. A sound I know I've made every day since I met Dante. They're dramatic, Clara and Dante. The two of them missed their calling in the theater.

"Whenever I text you to hang out with us, you're busy with your man. Like he's got you chained up to your bed."

"For fuck's sake," Griffin mutters, dropping his chin while Ian slaps his palm over his eyes.

"Jesus. I didn't need that picture in my head."

"I am not chained to the bed. Obviously."

"So you'll hang out with your brothers but not us?"

"You literally saw her two weeks ago," Marianne says and holds out her hand for my coffee, which I share with her.

"Yeah, for like a minute. We haven't been able to go to Tabby Cat for wine and whine."

I toss my hand up. "Because we're working on the house."

Dante convinced me to renovate, making his former apartment a third floor with two bedrooms, another bathroom, and a big walk-in closet that would give us a lot of extra storage space. When we aren't at work or with the kids, all of our waking hours are spent ripping out old kitchen appliances and putting up walls. I have no idea what I'm doing, but watching Dante do his thing is a sight to behold. If Clara were attracted to men, she'd want to watch him drywall too.

"A likely excuse," she says and points at my cell phone on the table. "Put it in your calendar. Drinks on Friday."

Following her orders, I type in the new event on my calendar, knowing Dante will receive the alert since we shared our calendars, along with the kids. All four of us are connected.

I'm still waiting on my day in family court for full custody, but the kids have yet to go back to Craig's house. Although he hasn't pushed me or them about it. I honestly think he wants to give up the little custody that he has because he doesn't actually enjoy being a parent. It's a chore to him, and I would rather he—really, all of us—realize that and work through to more friendly terms when the kids can maybe come to a place where they might call him when they'd like to see him. Instead of everyone being forced into something they don't want to do.

With Dante's help and the support of my family, I am more than capable of providing for Maddie and Jake, and they are much happier for it.

"So what are you two up to besides being a pain in my ass?" I ask Clara, and she tips her head back down the street in the direction they came from.

"We were at Chapter and Verse, and Nicole's husband was there."

Ian actually spins around in his chair as she goes on.

"He's such a dick. It seemed like they were in the middle of an argument, and she was trying to make him leave. I mean, Marianne and I were standing right there. That's her place of work, and he was, like..."

"Talking down to her," Marianne fills in, and Griffin folds his arms over his chest.

"She doesn't deserve that."

"I always got a weird vibe from him," I say, and Marianne nods.

"Condescending nerd."

"The worst kind of nerd," I agree.

Ian doesn't add to the conversation, but he's turned back around in his seat so I can see the set of his jaw. The way he's brooding.

He doesn't abide anyone being mistreated, especially women, and I know he has a soft spot for the mousy bookseller next door to his tattoo shop.

Clara, oblivious to the tension, slaps Ian's shoulder. "Oh hey, by the way. We needed a few more volunteers to run the cleanup, so I added your name."

Ian's eyes widen in surprise. "You *what?*"

Clara grins, unfazed by his reaction. "You're super scary-looking. If anyone can make people pick up trash, it's you."

Ian rolls his eyes, but Clara continues, undeterred. "Nicole's the other group director, so you can play good cop, bad cop."

His reaction to that news is minuscule, but I notice it. The rigidity of his posture, the rise and fall of his Adam's apple when he swallows. I would bet my entire *I Love Lucy* collection that he's got a thing for her, but he would never act on it. Not while she's married.

My phone buzzes on the table, and I glance down to see a text from Dante. It's a picture of him and Frankie on the floor next to Tortellini munching on lettuce. It took an hour of Dante edging me in the bedroom for me to finally give up the ghost and allow him to set up Tortellini's terrarium in the living room.

DANTE

are you coming home soon?

DANTE

we all require pets

I can't help the giggle that escapes my lips, and everyone—my brothers and best friends—all shoot their attention to me as if they've never heard me laugh before.

Griffin raises his brows in silent question. *Since when do you giggle?*

I don't giggle. At least, I didn't before Dante. Now, laughter seems to come easy, bubbling up from a place inside me that I thought had dried up long ago.

"What's so funny?" Clara asks, trying to peek at my phone.

I angle the screen, showing her the picture, and she goes all gooey. "Aww, that's adorable. You two are sickeningly cute, you know that?"

I feel the heat rise in my cheeks, but I can't wipe the smile off my face. "I know."

Ian clears his throat, bringing the conversation back to the present. "So, about this cleanup..."

As they discuss the details, I find my mind drifting back to Dante, to the life we're building together.

Who would've thought *just this once* would turn into *for always?*

Definitely not me.

But Dante? He always knew.

Famous last words.

* * *

Bonus Epilogue
Dante

I wake up to the scent of coffee brewing in the kitchen, and after I make my way downstairs, I'm greeted by Taryn's soft cooing to Frankie.

"Come on, be a good boy. Swallow it down… I know, I know, you hate it, but it'll make you feel better. Come on, baby."

Frankie's an old man now, being held together by four different types of meds and a few surgeries. But he's the best boy. Still keeping Tortellini company, though he can't chase Torts around on his skateboard anymore.

I lean against the doorjamb of the kitchen, watching my wife hug and kiss our dog, smiling into his fur, praising him, and like always, I start coming up with ways she'll praise me.

"Morning, duchess."

I bend down to kiss the top of her head, then pour myself a cup of coffee.

"You're up early. I thought you'd sleep in."

I shrug. I don't sleep well without her. She spends exactly ten minutes cuddling with me at night before rolling to her side to sleep, but I'm so used to her next to me that it's like my body knows if she's not there. Although, I didn't go to bed until after two last night, so I hoped to have more than a few hours.

I'll need to convince her to go back to bed with me.

"So," I start, excited to hear her verdict. "Did you see it?"

"Yeah."

"What do you think?"

"It's gorgeous."

"Yeah?"

She stands, moving to my side, her hand on my chest. "I'm very proud of you."

"How proud?"

She rolls her eyes. "Not that proud."

I heave a sigh and wrap my hand around her neck. "You sure about that?"

I'd gotten into carpentry over the past few months. Something to do in my free time. Now that both of the kids are out of the house, we have a lot of it.

The day Maddie packed up the last of her things to move to Philly to live with her friend, I actually cried. It's one thing to cheer for them as they cross the stage on their graduations because they were coming home, but knowing they are out there, in the wide world? It's scary. Though I'm so incredibly proud of both of them. Jake had a full-ride to Wake Forest for soccer, and now he's living down there in North Carolina, working to become a physical therapist. Maddie is in Manyunk, the marketing manager for some community theater group. The pay is shit, but she's sworn up and down that she'll be fine. That she has enough money. That she's being safe.

Regardless, I've started Venmo-ing her money every Friday, with the promise that she always tells me her plans. Any bar she goes to or date she has.

Yes, I'm a tad overprotective, and we may have had an argument or two over it, but I love my kids and need to know they're safe. Especially my sweet twenty-three-year-old girl, who can sometimes be a little too naïve.

But to take my mind off of my anxiety about everything that could hurt or harm them, I've started learning how to make furniture. And I finished my first big piece last night.

A new table.

I take Taryn's hand, tugging her to the dining room, the hardwood floor chilly under my bare feet. In the last ten years, I did renovate the third floor, and completely gutted the second floor, expanding the bathroom and bedroom for Taryn and me, and of course, put in a brand new kitchen. Next, I'd like to refinish these floors. But probably not until the spring.

Without warning, I lift Taryn up onto the table, earning a quiet gasp and then a whack at my shoulder. "What are you doing?"

"Making sure it's sturdy." I push her legs open, making room for me between them, then kiss her. She tastes of coffee and that chocolate peanut butter Tastykake she likes. I place my hands on either side of her, leaning down, forcing her to her elbows. "For when the kids come home. Uno nights can get pretty rowdy."

"I feel like that was a dig at me."

I breathe a laugh against her throat. "Definitely not a dig, but you are the poorest loser out of everyone."

She attempts to kick at me, but I catch her thigh, pulling her even closer to me, kissing her jaw. She puts up a fight with barely a whine. Groans my name. Mumbling something about it being too early for this, but it is never too early to sink into my favorite place.

I slide my fingers up her thighs, working her sleep shorts and underwear back down and off her legs, before placing her heels on the table. I capture her lips in a kiss, my tongue mimicking the movements of my fingers, and she moans into my mouth, her hips bucking against my hand. It doesn't take long to bring her to the edge, but I pull away.

I silence her protest whimpers with a kiss, my hands pushing my boxer-briefs down to free myself. She immediately wraps her hand around me, her thumb brushing over the tip, squeezing with the perfect amount of pressure to bring me to my knees.

Which I do. I kiss my *I love yous* on her ankles and inner thighs and then finally where she's hot and needy. I spend a few minutes making her wet with my fingers and tongue, but I've hidden little bottles of almond oil all around the house for occasions such as this, and find the one in the sideboard drawer.

After squirting some on my fingers, I spread it around her entrance and add some of my spit for good measure, because my lady likes it. And then I'm home in one easy thrust.

We fit together like two pieces of a puzzle, moving slowly at first, my head bent down, her fingers tunneled in my hair. I wasn't lying when I said I wanted to test if the table was sturdy, and while it does creak, it holds steady.

So I pick up the pace, my hands gripping her hips, her nails digging into my shoulders. Both of us chasing our release, breathing heavy. Neither of us are the spring chickens we used to be a decade ago, and while I like to prove my masculine ability with some hammer and nails, I'm a bit quick off the trigger anymore.

Thankfully, Taryn takes it into her own hands, and sneaks her fingers between us, getting herself off, her body convulsing around me when she comes. "Oh, thank Christ," I mutter, giving into my own orgasm before dropping my forehead to her chest. "I love you so much."

"Love you too," she murmurs in my favorite blissed out voice.

"Come back to bed with me?"

"If you carry me."

I pull my underwear back up my legs and scoop her up. "Whatever you say, Duchess."

"Good boy."

What's next?

To stay up to date with all things Sophie Andrews, use the QR code on the next page to stay in touch!

Acknowledgments

Indie publishing is a wild ride. Thank you, reader, for taking the ride with me. This series wouldn't be as successful as it is without you.

Thank you to Lily Bear for the amazing covers. As always, Libby and Lisa have turned my brain vomit into a pretty decent novel, which is always a miracle.

Biggest thank you to all of my readers. Thank you for your DMs and for your early reviews and for making all of this worth it. Without you, I'd literally just being writing these books and reading them out loud to myself like I used to do when I was a kid. And while that's fun, it's so much more fun to know people love these silly little books. I am forever grateful for you.

If you'd like more information about me, you can find it at https://sophieandrewsauthor.com/

About the Author

Sophie Andrews is a contemporary romance author who writes steamy books that will leave you smiling. As a millennial, she's obsessed with boybands, late 90s rom-coms, and will always be team Pacey. When she's not writing, she's most likely trying to wrangle her children or drinking red wine. Or both at the same time.

Also by Sophie Andrews

Stone Family

Under One Roof

Just This Once

Right Next Door

For The Weekend

Single Dads' Club

The Rehearsal Fling

The Nanny Tenure

The Dating Pact

The Bartender's Baby

Tangled Series

Tangled Up

Tangled Want

Tangled Hearts

Tangled Beginning

Tangled Expectations

Tangled Chances

Tangled Ambition

Stand-Alones

How to Ruin a Wedding

Love at a Funeral and Other Awkward Conversations